he old man began to speak to Conan, and though his voice was thin, there was power in it.

"Beware the woman of sapphires and gold. For her love of power, she would seal your doom. Beware the woman of emeralds and ruby. For her love of you, she would watch you die. Beware the man who seeks a throne. Beware the man whose soul is clay. Beware the gratitude of kings."

He hobbled toward the door. "Mark my words, Conan of Cimmeria," he said over his shoulder. "My prophecies always tell true."

The Adventures of Conan,
published by Tor Books

CONAN THE DEFENDER

BY
ROBERT JORDAN

A TOM DOHERTY ASSOCIATES BOOK
NEW YORK

CONAN THE DEFENDER

Copyright © 1982 by Conan Properties, Inc.

First printing: December 1982
First mass market printing: December 1983

A Tor Book
Published by Tom Doherty Associates, Inc.
49 West 24th Street
New York, N.Y. 10010

Cover art by Ron Walotsky

ISBN: 0-812-51394-0

Printed in the United States of America

0 9 8 7

o

L. Sprague de Camp

whose mighty thews have borne
the muscular Cimmerian on high
for lo these many years.

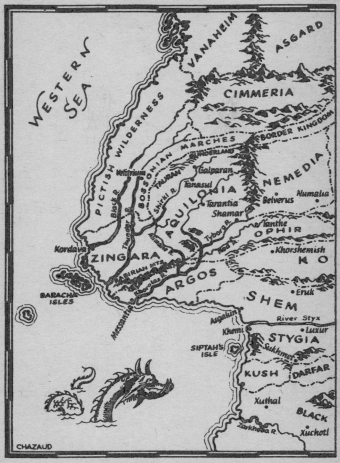

WESTERN SEA

VANAHEIM

ASGARD

CIMMERIA

PICTISH WILDERNESS

BOSSONIAN MARCHES

BORDER KINGDOM

SCHOHIRA

Velitrium

Black R.

Thunder R.

TAURAN

Shirki R.

Galparan

Tanasul

AQUILONIA

Tarantia

Shamar

Tybor R.

NEMEDIA

Belverus

Numalia

Kordava

ZINGARA

RABIRIAN MTS

Khoraja

ARGOS

Tanthe

OPHIR

KO

Khorshemish

BARACHA
ISLES

Messantia

SHEM

Eruk

Asgalun

River Styx

Khemi

Luxur

SIPTAH'S
ISLE

Sukhmet

STYGIA

KUSH

DARFAR

Xuthal

BLACK

Zarkheba R.

Xuchotl

CHAZAUD

Tundras

Haloga

HYPERBOREA

Deserts

Steppes

BRYTHUNIA

KEZANKIAN MTS.

TURAN

HYRKANIA

CORINTHIA

ZAMORA

Shadizar

Arenjun

KARPASH MTS.

TH

KHAURAN

Sultanapur

VILAYET
SEA

KHITAI

Isle of
Iron
Statues

IKHORAJA

Deserts

Akif

Aghrapur

Samara

Shangara

Zaporosca R.

Khawarism

Xapur

Zamboula

Kuthchemes

Ilbars R.

Preion

Nnmeto

KESHAN

Kassali

Kechia

PUNT

KINGDOMS

ZEMBABWEI

VENDHYA

IRANISTAN

CONAN

THE

DEFENDER

Sunlight streaming through marble-arched windows illumined the tapestry-hung room. The servants, tongueless so that they could not speak of whom they saw in their master's house, had withdrawn, leaving five people to sip their wine in silence.

Cantaro Albanus, the host, studied his guests, toying idly with the heavy gold chain that hung across his scarlet tunic. The lone woman pretended to study the intricate weaving of the tapestries; the men concentrated on their wine-cups.

Midmorning, Albanus reflected, was exactly the time for such meetings, though it rubbed raw the nerves of his fellows. Traditionally such were held in the dark of night by desperate men huddled in secret chambers sealed to exclude so much as a moonbeam. Yet who would believe, who could even suspect that a gathering of Nemedia's finest in the bright light of day, in the very heart of the capital, could be intent on treason?

His lean-cheeked face darkened at the thought, and his black eyes became obsidian. With his hawk nose and the slashes of silver at the temples of his dark hair, he looked as if he should have been a general. He had indeed been a soldier, once, for a brief year. When he was but seventeen his father had obtained him a commission in the Golden Leopards, the body-guard regiment of Nemedian Kings since time beyond memory. At his father's death he had re-signed. Not for him working his way up the ladder of rank, no matter how swiftly aided by high birth. Not for one who by blood and tem-perament should be King. For him nothing could be treason.

"Lord Albanus," Barca Vegentius said sud-denly, "we have heard much of the . . . special aid you bring to our . . . association. We have heard much, but thus far we have seen nothing." Large and square of face and body, the current Commander of the Golden Leopards pronounced his words carefully. He thought to hide his origins by hiding the accents of the slums of Belverus, and was unaware that everyone knew his deception.

"Such careful words to express your doubts, Vegentius," Demetrio Amarianus said. The slender youth touched a perfumed pomander to his nose, but it could not hide the sneer that twisted his almost womanly mouth. "But then you always use careful words, don't you? We all know you are here only to—"

"Enough!" Albanus snapped.

Both Demetrio and Vegentius, whose face had been growing more purple by the second, subsided like well-trained animals at the crack of the trainer's whip. These squabbles were constant, and he tolerated them no more than he was forced to. Today he would not tolerate them at all.

"All of you," Albanus went on, "want something. You, Vegentius, want the generalship you feel King Garian has denied you. You, Demetrio, want the return of the estates Garian's father took from your grandfather. And you, Sephana. You want revenge against Garian because he told you he liked his women younger."

"As pleasantly stated as is your custom, Albanus," the lone woman said bitterly. Lady Sephana Galerianus' heart-shaped face was set with violet eyes and framed by a raven mane that hung below her shoulders. Her red silk robe was cut to show both the inner and outer slopes of her generous breasts, and slashed to expose her legs to the hip when she walked.

"And what do I want?" the fourth man in the room asked, and everyone started as if they had forgotten he was there.

It was quite easy to forget Constanto Melius, for the middle-aged noble was vagueness personified. Thinning hair and the pouches beneath his constantly blinking eyes were his most prominent features, and his intelligence and abilities matched the rest of him.

"You want your advice listened to," Albanus replied. "And so it shall be, when I am on the throne."

It would be listened to for as long as it took to order the man banished, the hawk-faced lord thought. Garian had made the mistake of rebuffing the fool, then leaving him free in the capital to foment trouble. Albanus would not make the same mistake.

"We seem to have passed by what Vegentius said," Sephana said abruptly, "but I, too, would like to see what help we can count on from you, Albanus. Demetrio and Vegentius provide information. Melius and I provide gold to buy disorders in the street, and to pay brigands to burn good grain. You keep your plans to yourself and tell us about the magicks that will make Garian give the throne to you, if we do these other things as well. I, too, want to see these magicks."

The others seemed somewhat abashed that she had brought the promised sorcery out into the open, but Albanus merely smiled.

Rising, he tugged a brocade bellpull on the wall before moving to a table at the end of the room, a table where a cloth covered certain objects. Cloth and objects alike Albanus had placed there with his own hands.

"Come," he told the others. Suddenly reluctant, they moved to join him slowly.

With a flourish he whisked the cloth aside, enjoying their starts. He knew that the things on that table—a statuette in sapphire, a sword with serpentine blade and quillons of ancient pattern, a few crystals and engraved gems—were, with one exception, practically useless. At least, he had found little use prescribed for them in the tomes he had so plainfully deciphered. Items of power he kept elsewhere.

Ten years earlier, slaves on one of his estates north of Numalia had dug into a subterranean chamber. Luckily he had been there at the time, been there to recognize it as the storehouse of a sorcerer, been there to see that the luckless slaves were buried in that chamber once he had emptied it.

A year it had taken him just to discover how ancient that cache was, dating back to Acheron, that dark empire ruled by the vilest thaumaturgies and now three millenia and more gone in the dust. For all those years he had studied, eschewing a tutor for fear any sorcerer of ability would seize the hoard for his own. It had been a wise decision, for had he been known to be studying magicks he would surely have been caught up in Garian's purge of sorcerers from the capital. Garian. Thinking dark thoughts, Albanus lifted a small red crystal sphere from the table.

"I mistrust these things," Sephana said, shuddering. "Better we should rely on ways more natural. A subtle poison—"

"Would provoke a civil war for the succession," Albanus cut her off. "I don't want to tell you again that I have no intention of having to wrest the Dragon Throne from a half score of claimants. The throne will be given to me, as I have said."

"That," Vegentius grumbled, "I will believe when I see it."

Albanus motioned the others to silence as a serving girl entered. Blonde and pale of skin, she was no more than sixteen years of age. Her simple white tunic, embroidered about the hem with Albanus' house-mark, was slashed to show most of her small breasts and long legs. She knelt immediately on the marble floor, head bent.

"Her name is Omphale," the hawk-faced lord said.

The girl shifted at the mention of her name, but knew enough not to lift her head. She was but newly enslaved, sold for the debts of her father's shop, but some lessons were quickly learned.

Albanus held the red crystal at arm's length in his left hand, making an arcane gesture with his right as he intoned, *"An-naal naa-thaan Vas-ti no-entei!"*

A flickering spike of flame was suddenly suspended above the crystal, as long as a man's forearm and more solid than a flame should be. Within the pulsing red-and-yellow, two dark spots, uncomfortably like eyes, moved as if examining the room and its occupants. All moved back unconsciously except for Omphale, who cowered where she knelt, and Albanus.

"A fire elemental," Albanus said conversationally. Without changing his tone he added, "Kill Omphale!"

The blonde's mouth widened to scream, but before a sound emerged the elemental darted forward, swelling to envelop her. Jerkily she rose to her feet, twitching in the midst of an egg of flame that slowly opaqued to hide her. The fire hissed, and in the depths of the hiss was a thin shriek, as of a woman screaming in the distance. With the pop of a bursting bubble the flame disappeared, leaving behind a faint sickly sweet smell.

"Messy," Albanus mused, scuffing with a slippered foot at an oily black smudge on the marble floor where the girl had been.

The others' stares were stunned, as if he had transformed into the fabled dragon Xutharcan. Surprisingly, it was Melius who first regained his tongue.

"These devices, Albanus. Should we not have some of them as well as you?" His pouchy eyes blinked uncomfortably at the others' failure to speak. "As a token that we are all equals," he finished weakly.

Albanus smiled. Soon enough he would be able to show them how equal they were. "Of course," he said smoothly. "I've thought of that myself." He gestured to the table. "Choose, and I will tell you what powers your choice possesses." He slipped the red crystal into a pouch at his belt as he spoke.

Melius hesitated, reached out, and stopped with his hand just touching the sword. "What . . . what powers does this have?"

"It turns whoever wields it into a master swordsman." Having found that such was the extent of the blade's power, Albanus had researched no further. He had no interest in becoming a warrior-hero; he would be King, with such to do his bidding. "Take the blade, Melius. Or if you fear it, perhaps Vegentius. . . ." Albanus raised a questioning eyebrow at the square-faced soldier.

"I need no magicks to make me a bladesman," Vegentius sneered. But he made no move to choose something else, either.

"Demetrio?" Albanus said. "Sephana?"

"I mislike sorcery," the slender young man replied, openly flinching away from the display on the table.

Sephana was made of sterner stuff, but she shook her head just as quickly. "If these sorceries can pull Garian from the Dragon Throne, 'tis well enough for me. And they can not. . . ." She met Albanus' gaze for a moment, then turned away.

"I'll take the sword," Melius said suddenly. He hefted the weapon, testing the balance, and laughed. "I have no such scruples as Vegentius about how I become a swordsman."

Albanus smiled blandly, but slowly his face hardened. "Now hear me," he intoned, fixing each of them in turn with an obsidian eye. "I have shown but a small sampling of the powers that will gain me the throne of Nemedia, and grant your own desires. Know that I will brook no deviation, no meddling that might interfere with my designs. Nothing will stand between me and the Dragon Crown. Nothing! Now go!"

They backed from his presence as if he already sat on the Dragon Throne.

he tall, muscular youth strode the streets of Belverus, monument-filled and marble-columned capital of Nemedia, with a wary eye and a hand close to the well-worn leather-wrapped hilt of his broadsword. His deep blue eyes and fur-trimmed cloak spoke of the north country. Belverus had seen many northern barbarians in better times, dazzled by the great city and easily separated from their silver or their pittance of gold—though often, not understanding the ways of civilization, they had to be hauled away by the black-cloaked City Guard, complaining that they had been duped. This man, however, though only twenty-two,

walked with the confidence of one who had trod
the paving stones of cities as great or greater, of
Arenjun and Shadizar, called the Wicked; of
Sultanapur and Aghrapur; even the fabled cities
of far-off Khitai.

He walked the High Streets, in the Market District, not half a mile from the Royal Palace of
Garian, King of Nemedia, yet he thought he
might as well be in Hellgate, the city's thieves'
district. The open-fronted shops had display
tables out, and crowds moved among them
pricing cloth from Ophir, wines from Argos,
goods from Koth and Corinthia and even Turan.
But the peddlers' carts rumbling over the
paving stones carried little in the way of food-
stuffs, and their prices made him wonder if he
could afford to eat in the city for long.

Between the shops were huddled beggars,
maimed or blind or both, their wailing for alms
competing with the hawkers crying their wares.
And every street corner had its knot of toughs,
hard-eyed, roughly dressed men who fingered
swordhilts, or openly sharpened daggers or
weighed cudgels in their fists as their gazes
followed a plump merchant scurrying by or a
lissome shopkeeper's daughter darting through
the crowd with nervous eyes. All that was missing were the prostitutes in their brass and copper bangles, sheer shifts cut to display their
wares. Even the air had something of the cloying
smell he associated with a dozen slums he had
seen, a mixture of vomit, urine and excrement.

Suddenly a fruit cart crossing an intersection
was surrounded by half-a-dozen ruffians in
motley bits of finery mixed with rags. The
skinny vendor stood silent, eyes down and care-

worn face red, as they picked over his goods, taking a bite of this and a bite of that, then throwing both into the street. Stuffing the folds of their tunics with fruit, they started away, swaggering, insolent eyes daring anyone to speak. The well-dressed passersby acted as if the men were invisible.

"I don't suppose you'll pay," the vendor moaned without raising his eyes.

One of the bravos, an unshaven man wearing a soiled cloak embroidered with thread-of-gold over a ragged cotton tunic, smiled, showing the blackened stumps of his teeth. "Pay? Here's pay." His backhand blow split the skinny man's cheek, and the pushcart man collapsed sobbing across his barrow. With a grating laugh the bravo joined his fellows who had stopped to see the sport, and they shoved their way through the crowd of shoppers, who gave way with no more than a wordless mutter.

The muscular northern youth stopped a pace away from the pushcart. "Will you not call the City Guard?" he asked curiously.

The peddler pushed himself wearily erect. "Please. I have to feed my family. There are other carts."

"I steal not fruit, nor beat old men," the youth said stiffly. "My name is Conan. Will the City Guard not protect you?"

"The City Guard?" the old man laughed bitterly. "They stay in their barracks and protect themselves. I saw three of these scum hang a Guardsman by his heels and geld him. Thus *they* think of the City Guard." He wiped his hands shakily down the front of his tunic, suddenly realizing how visible he was talking to a barbarian in the middle of the intersection. "I have to go," he muttered. "I have to go." He bent to the handles of his pushcart without another glance at the young barbarian.

Conan watched him go with a pitying glance. He had come to Belverus to hire himself as a bodyguard or a soldier—he had been both, as well as a thief, a smuggler and a bandit—but whoever could hire his sword for protection in that city, it would unfortunately not be those who needed it most.

Some of the street-corner toughs had noticed his words with the peddler, and approached, thinking to have some fun with the outlander. As his gaze passed over them, though, cold as the mountain glaciers of his native Cimmeria, it came to them that death walked the streets of Belverus that day. There was easier prey elsewhere, they decided. In minutes the intersection was barren of thugs.

A few people looked at him gratefully, realizing he had made that one place safe for the moment. Conan shook his head, half angry with himself, half with them. He had come to hire his sword for gold, not to clear the streets of scum.

A scrap of parchment, carried by a vagrant breeze, fetched up against his boot. Idly he picked it up, read the words writ there in a fine round hand.

> King Garian sits on the Dragon Throne.
> King Garian sits to his feast alone.
> You sweat and toil for a scrap of bread,
> And learn to walk the streets in dread.
> He is not just, this King of ours,
> May his reign be counted in hours.

Mitra save us from the Dragon Throne,
And the King who sits to his feast alone.

He let the scrap go with the breeze, joining
still other scraps swirling down the street. He
saw people lift one to read. Some let it drop,
whitefaced, or threw it away in anger, but some
read and furtively tucked the bit of sedition into
their pouches.

Belverus was a plum ripe for the plucking. He
had seen the signs before, in other cities. Soon
the furtiveness would be gone. Fists would be
shaken openly at the Royal Palace. Stronger
thrones had been toppled by less.

Suddenly a running man pushed past him
with horror-stricken eyes, and on his heels came
a woman, her mouth open in a soundless
scream. A flock of children ran past shrieking
unintelligibly.

Down the street more screams and cries rose,
and the crowd suddenly stampeded toward the
intersection. Their fear communicated itself,
and without knowing why others joined the
stream. With difficulty Conan forced his way to
the side of the street, to a shop deserted by its
owner. What could cause this, he wondered.

Then the torrent of people thinned and was
gone, and Conan saw that the street they had
fled was littered with bodies, few moving. Some
had been trampled; others, further away, were
lacking arms or heads. And striding down the
center of the street was a man in a richly embroidered blue tunic, holding a sword with an
odd, wavy blade that was encarmined for its
entire length. A rope of spittle drooled from the
corner of his mouth.

Conan put his hand to his sword, then firmly took it away. For gold, he reminded himself, not to avenge strangers on a madman. He turned to move deeper into the shadows.

At that instant a child broke from a shop directly in front of the madman, a girl no more than eight years old, wailing as she ran on flashing feet. With a roar the madman raised his sword and started after her.

"Erlik's Bowels and Bladder!" Conan swore. His broadsword came smoothly from its worn shagreen sheath as he stepped back into the intersection.

The child ran screaming past without slowing. The madman halted. Up close, despite his rich garb, thinning hair and pouches beneath his eyes gave him the look of a clerk. But those muddy brown eyes were glazed with madness, and the sounds he made were formless grunts. Flies buzzed about the fruit the bravos had scattered.

At least, Conan thought, the man had some reason left, enough not to run onto another's blade. "Hold there," he said. "I'm no running babe or shopkeeper to be hacked down from behind. Why don't you—"

Conan thought he heard a hungry, metallic whine. An animal scream broke from the man's throat, and he rushed forward, sword raised.

The Cimmerian brought his own blade up to parry, and with stunning speed the wavy sword changed direction. Conan leaped back; the tip of the other's steel slashed across his belly, slicing tunic and the light chain mail he wore beneath alike as if they were parchment. He moved back another step to gain room for his own attack, but the madman followed swiftly, bloody blade slashing and stabbing with a ferocity beyond belief. Slowly the muscular youth gave ground.

To his shock he came to him that he was fighting a defensive battle against the slight, almost nondescript man. His every move was to block some thrust instead of to attack. All of his speed and cunning were going into merely staying alive, and already he was bleeding from half a dozen minor wounds. It came to him that he might well die on that spot.

"By the Lord of the Mound, no!" he shouted. "Crom and steel!" But with the clash of the blades ringing in his ears he was forced back.

Abruptly Conan's foot came down on a half-eaten plum, and with a crash he went down, flat on his back, silver-flecked spots dancing before his eyes. Fighting for breath he watched the madman's wavy blade go back for the thrust that would end his life. But he would not die easily. From his depths he found the strength to roll aside as the other lunged. The bloody blade struck sparks from the paving stones where he had been. Frantically he continued to roll, coming to his feet with his back against a wall. The madman whirled to follow.

The air was filled with a whir as of angry hornets, and the madman suddenly resembled a feathered pincushion. Conan blinked. The City Guard had arrived at last, a black-cloaked score of archers. They stayed well back, drawing again, for transfixed though he was, the madman still stood. His mouth was a gash emitting a wordless howl of bloodlust, and he hurled his sword at the big Cimmerian.

Conan's blade had no more than a hand's span

to travel to deflect the strange blade to clatter in
the street. The Guardsmen loosed their arrows
once more. Pierced through and through the
madman toppled. For a brief moment as he fell,
the look of madness faded to be replaced by one
of unutterable horror. He hit the pavement
dead. Slowly, weapons at the ready, the soldiers
closed in on the corpse.

The big Cimmerian slammed his blade home
in its sheath with a disgusted grunt. It was un-
necessary even to wipe a speck of blood from it.
The only blood shed had been his, and every one
of those cuts, insignificant as each was, ached
with the shame of it. The one attack he had
managed to meet cleanly, the thrown sword,
could have been met by a ten years' girl.

A Guardsman grabbed the dead man's shoulder and heaved him over onto his back, splintering half a dozen arrows on the stones of the
street.

"Easy, Tulio," another growled. "Like as not
our pay will be docked for those shafts. Why—"

"Black Erlik's Throne!" Tulio gasped. "It's
Lord Melius!"

The knot of mailed men stepped back, leaving
Tulio standing alone over the corpse. It was not
well to be too near a dead noble, most especially
if you had had a hand in killing him, and no
matter what he had done. The King's Justice
could take strange twists where nobles were
concerned.

A livid scar across his broad nose visible beneath the nasal of his helmet, the Guardsmen's
grizzled sergeant spat near the corpse. "There's
naught to be done for it now. Tulio!" That
Guardsman suddenly realized he was alone by

the body and jumped, his eyes darting frantically. "Put your cloak over the..., the noble
lord," the sergeant went on. "Move, man!" Reluctantly Tulio complied. The sergeant told off
more men. "Abydius, Crato, Jocor, Naso. Grab
his arms and legs. Jump! Or do you want to stay
here till the flies eat him?"

The four men shuffled forward, muttering as
they lifted the body. The sergeant started up the
street, and the bearers followed as quickly as
they were able, the rest of the troop falling in
behind. None gave a second look to Conan.

"Are you slowing that much, Cimmerian?" a
gruff voice called.

Conan spun, his angry retort dying on his lips
as he saw the bearded man leaning against a
shop front. "I'm still faster than you, Hordo, you
old robber of dogs."

Nearly as tall as Conan and broader, the
bearded man straightened. A rough leather
patch covered his left eye, and a scar running
from beneath the leather down his cheek pulled
that side of his mouth into a permanent sneer,
though now the rest of it was bent to a grin. A
heavy gold hoop swung from each ear, but if
they tempted thieves the well-worn broadsword
and dagger at his belt dissuaded them.

"Mayhap you are, Conan," he said. "But what
are you doing in Nemedia, aside from taking a
lesson on bladesmanship from a middle-aged
noble? The last I saw of you, you were on your
way to Aghrapur to soldier for King Yildiz."

Hordo was a friend, but he had not always
been so. The first time they met, the one-eyed
man and a pack of bandits had pegged Conan
out on the Zamoran plains at the orders of

Karela, a red-haired woman bandit known as the Red Hawk. Later they had ridden together to the Kezankian Mountains to try for treasure stolen by the sorcerer Amanar. From that they had escaped with naught but their lives. Twice more they had met, each time making a try at wealth, each time failing to gain more than enough for one grand carouse in the nearest fleshpots. Conan had to wonder if once again they would have a chance at gold.

"I did," Conan replied, "but I left the service of Turan a year gone and more."

"Trouble over a woman, I'll wager," Hordo chuckled, "knowing you."

Conan shrugged his massive shoulders. He always had trouble over women, it seemed. But then, what man did not?

"And what woman chased you from Sultanapur, Hordo? When last we parted you sat in your own inn with a plump Turanian wife, swearing never again to smuggle so much as a sweetmeat, nor set foot outside Sultanapur until you were carried out to your funeral pyre."

"It was Karela." The one-eyed man's voice was low with embarrassment. He tugged at his thick beard. "I could not give up trying to find word of her, and my wife could not cease nagging me to stop. She said I made a spectacle of myself. People talked, she said, laughed behind my back, said I was strange in the head. She would not have it said she married a man lacking all his brains. She would not stop, and I could not, so I said goodbye one day and never looked back."

"You still look for Karela?"

"She is not dead. I'm sure she lives." He grabbed Conan's arm, a pathetic urgency in his eyes. "I've heard never a whisper, but I'd know if she was dead. I'd know. Have you heard anything? Anything at all?"

Hordo's voice carried anguish. Conan knew that the Red Hawk had indeed survived their expedition into the Kezankians. But to tell Hordo would entail telling how last he saw her —naked and chained in a slave coffle on her way to the auction block. He could explain that he had had but a few coppers in his pouch, not even close to the price of a round-breasted, green-eyed slave in Turan. He could even mention the oath she had made him swear, that he would never lift a hand to save her. She was a woman of pride, Karela was. Or had been. For if Hordo had found no sign of her, it was more than likely the strap had broken her, and that she now danced for the pleasure of a dark-eyed master. And if he told the tale, he might well have to kill his old friend, the man who had always called himself Karela's faithful hound.

"The last I saw of her was in the Kezankians," he said truthfully, "but I'm sure she got out of the mountains alive. No pack of hillmen would have stood a chance against her with a sword in her hand."

Hordo nodded, sighing heavily.

People were venturing back into the street, staring at the bodies that still lay where they had been slain. Here and there a woman fell wailing across a dead husband or child.

Conan looked around for the sword the madman had been carrying. It lay before an open-fronted shop piled high with colorful bolts of cloth. The proprietor was gone, one of the dead or one of those staring at them. The Cimmerian picked up the sword, wiping the congealing blood from the serpentine blade on a bolt of yellow damask.

He hefted the weapon, getting the balance of it. The quillons were worked in a silver filigree that spoke of antiquity, and the ricasso was scribed with calligraphy that formed no words he had ever seen before. But whoever had made the weapon, he was a master. It seemed to become an extension of his arm. Nay, an extension of his mind. Still he could not help thinking of those it had just killed. Men. Women. Children. Struck from behind, or however they could be reached, as they fled. Slashed and hacked as they tried to crawl away. The images were vivid in his brain. He could almost smell their fear sweat and the blood.

He made a disgusted noise in his throat. A sword was a sword, no more. Steel had no guilt. Still, he would not keep it. Take it, yes—a sword was too valuable to be left behind—it would fetch a few silver pieces for his too-light purse.

"You're not keeping that?" Hordo sounded surprised. "The blade's tainted. Women and children." He spat and made the sign to ward off evil.

"Not too tainted to sell," Conan replied. On impulse he swung his fur-trimmed cloak from his shoulders and wrapped it around the sword. Its archaic pattern made it easily recognizable. Perhaps it would not be smart to carry it openly so soon after the death it had brought to Belverus.

"Are you that short of coin, man? I can let you

have a little silver, an you need it."

"I've enough." Conan weighed his purse again in his mind. Four days, if he stayed at an inn. Two weeks if he slept in stables. "But how is it you're rich to the point of handing out silver? Have you taken back to the bandit trade, or is it smuggling again?"

"Hsst!" Hordo stepped closer, casting his lone eye about to see if any had heard. "Speak softly of smuggling," he said in a voice meant for the big Cimmerian's ears alone. "The penalty now is slow impalement, and the crown pays a bounty for information that'd tempt your grandmother."

"Then why are you mixed in it?"

"I didn't say. . . ." The one-eyed man threw up his gnarled hands. "Hannuman's Stones! Yes, I'm in it. Have you no ear or eye that you don't know the prices in this city? The tariffs are more than the cost of the goods. A smuggler can make a fortune. If he lives."

"Maybe you need a partner?" Conan said suggestively.

Hordo hesitated. "'Tis not as it was in Sultanapur. Every cask of wine or length of silk that misses the King's Customs is brought in by one ring."

"For the whole of Nemedia?" Conan said incredulously.

"Aye. Been that way for more than two years, so I understand. I've only been here a year, myself. They're tight as a miser's fist about who they let in, and who they let know what. I get my orders from a man who gets his from somebody I've never seen, who likely gets his orders from somebody else." He shook his heavy head. "I'll try, but I make no promises."

"They can't be as tight as all that," Conan protested, "not if you're one of them after being here no more than a year."

Hordo chuckled and rubbed the side of his broad nose with a spatulate finger. "I'm a special case. I was in Koth, in a tavern in Khorshemish, because I'd heard a rumor . . . well, that's beside the point. Anyway, a fellow, Hassan, who works the Kothian end of the ring heard me asking questions. He had heard of the Red Hawk, admired her no end. When he found out I'd ridden with her, he offered me a job here in Belverus. I was about to the point of boiling my belt for soup, so I took it. If Hassan was here I could get you in in a fingersnap, but he stays in Koth."

"Strange," Conan mused, "that he wouldn't keep you there, too, since he admires the Red Hawk so. No matter. You do what you can. I'll make out."

"I'll try," Hordo said. He squinted at the sun, already well past its height, and shifted awkwardly. "Listen, there's something I have to do. The ring, you understand. I'd ask you along so we could swap lies, but they do not look kindly on people they don't know."

"We've plenty of time."

"Surely. Look you. Meet me at the Sign of the Gored Ox, on the Street of Regrets, just above Hellgate, half a glass or so after sunset." He laughed and clapped Conan on the shoulder. "We'll drink our way from one side of this city to the other."

"From top to bottom," Conan agreed.

As the one-eyed man left, Conan turned, the cloak-wrapped sword beneath his arm, and stopped. An ornate litter, scarlet-curtained, its frame and poles black and gold, stood a little way up the street, the crowd and even the toughs respectful enough to leave a cleared space about it. It was not the litter that arrested him—he had seen others in the streets, carrying fat merchants or sleek noblewomen—but as he had turned the curtain had twitched shut, leaving him with the bare impression of a woman swathed in gray veils till naught but her eyes showed. And he would have sworn, for all the briefness of that glimpse, that those eyes had been looking directly at him. Nay, not looking. Glaring.

Abruptly the front curtain of the litter moved, and apparently an order was passed, for the bearers set off swiftly up the street, away from the big Cimmerian.

Conan shook his head as he watched the litter disappear into the throng. 'Twas not a good way to begin in Belverus, imagining things. Aside from Hordo he knew no one. Taking a firmer grip on his cloak-wrapped bundle, he set out to wile away the time until his meeting with Hordo. He would learn what he could of this city wherein he hoped to forge some future for himself.

he Street of Regrets was the last street above Hellgate. It was the street where people hung on by their fingernails to keep from sliding down into the cauldron of the slum, people who knew despairingly that even if they managed to stay that one street above for their lives, their children would sink into the morass. A few had crawled there from Hellgate, stopping once they were safe above Crop-ear Alley, afraid to go further into a city they did not understand, ignoring the stench that told them how little distance they had come whenever the wind blew from the south. Those who truly escaped Hellgate did not stop on the Street of Regrets, not even for a day or an hour. But they were fewest of the few.

On such a street all folk desire to forget what lies ahead at the next turning, the next dawning, what lies behind on a thousand nights past. The Street of Regrets was a frantic, frenetic carnival. Corner musicians with lutes and zithers and flutes sent out frenzied music to compete with the laughter that filled the air, laughter raucous, drunken, hysterical, forced. Jugglers with balls and rings, clubs and flashing knives worked their art for the strumpets that strolled the street, half naked in brief silks, burnished brass bangles and stilted sandals, flaunting their wares for whoever had a coin. Their most lascivious wriggles and flagrant self-caresses, however, were offered to those well-dressed oglers from the Upper Town, standing out in the motley crowd as if they bore signs, come to witness what they thought was the depths of Hellgate depravity. And over it all floated the laughter.

The Sign of the Gored Ox was what Conan expected on such a street. At one end of a common room that reeked of stale wine was a small platform where three plumply rounded women in sheer yellow silk gyrated their hips and breasts to the sybaritic flutes. They were largely ignored by the men at the crowded tables, intent on drink or cards or dice. A brassy-haired trull, one strip of dark blue silk wrapped around and around her body in such a way as to leave much plump flesh bare, maintained a fixed smile as a fat Corinthian in striped robes stroked her as if attempting to calculate her price by the pound.

Another prostitute, her hair an impossible

red, eyed the breadth of Conan's shoulders and adjusted the gilded halter that supported her large round breasts. She swayed toward him, wetting her full lips suggestively, then stopped with a disappointed frown when he shook his head. He could see Hordo nowhere in the drunken mass; there would be time to find women when they were together.

There was one woman in the tavern who stood out from the rest. Seated alone against the wall, her winecup untouched in front of her, she seemed to be the only one there watching the dancers. Long black hair swirled below her shoulders, and large, hazel eyes and bee-stung lips gave her a beauty that outshone any of the doxies by far. Yet she was not of the sisterhood of the night. That much was certain from the simple robe of white cotton that covered her from neck to ankles. It was as out of place as she, that robe, not gaudy or revealing enough for a denizen of the Street of Regrets, lacking the ornate embroideries and rich fabrics of the women of the Upper Town who came to sample wickedness by sweating beneath one who might be a murderer or worse.

Women came later, he reminded himself. Shifting the cloak-wrapped sword beneath his arm, he looked about for an empty table.

From what seemed rather a bundle of rags than a man, a bony hand reached out to pluck at his tunic. A thin, rasping voice emerged from a toothless mouth. "Ho, Cimmerian, where go you with that strange blade of murder?"

Conan felt the hair stir on the nape of his neck. The old man, too emaciated to be wrinkled, had a filthy rag tied across where his eyes should be. But even had he had eyes, how could he have known what was in the cloak? Or that Conan was from Cimmeria?

"What do you know of me, old man?" Conan asked. "And how do you know it, without sight?"

The old man cackled shrilly, touching the bandage across his eyes with a crooked stick he carried. "When the gods took these, they gave me other ways of seeing. As I do not see with eyes, I do not see what eyes see, but . . . other things."

"I've heard of such," Conan muttered. "And seen stranger still. What more can you tell me of myself?"

"Oh, much and much, young sir. You will know the love of many women, queens and peasant girls alike, and many between in station. You will live long, and gain a crown, and your death will be shrouded in legend."

"Bull dung!" Hordo grunted, thrusting his head past Conan's shoulder.

"I was wondering where you were," Conan said. "The old man knew I'm Cimmerian."

"An earful of your barbarous accent, and he made a lucky guess. Let's get a table and a pitcher of wine."

Conan shook his head. "I didn't speak, but he knew. Tell me, old man. What lies weeks ahead for me, instead of years?"

The blind man had been listening with a pained expression, tilting his head to catch their words. Now his toothless smile returned. "As for that," he said. He lifted his hand, thumb rubbing his fingertips, then abruptly flattened it, palm up. "I am a poor man, as you can see, young sir."

The big Cimmerian stuck two fingers into the pouch at his belt. It was light enough, filled more with copper than silver, and little enough of either, but he drew out a silver queenshead and dropped it on the old man's leathery palm.

Hordo sighed in exasperation. "I know a haruspex and three astrologers would charge half that together, and give you a better telling than you'll find in this place."

The old man's fingertips drifted lightly over the face of the coin. "A generous man," he murmured. The coin disappeared beneath his rags. "Give me your hand. The right one."

"A palmist with no eyes," Hordo laughed, but Conan stuck out his hand.

As swiftly as they had moved over the coin the old man's fingers traced the lines of the Cimmerian's hand, marking the callouses and old scars. He began to speak, and though his voice was still thin, the cackle was gone. There was strength, even power in it.

"Beware the woman of sapphires and gold. For her love of power she would seal your doom. Beware the woman of emeralds and ruby. For her love of you she would watch you die. Beware the man who seeks a throne. Beware the man whose soul is clay. Beware the gratitude of kings." To Conan his voice grew louder, but no one else looked up from a winecup as he broke into a sing-song chant. "Save a throne, save a king, kill a king, or die. Whatever comes, whatever is, mark well your time to fly."

"That's dour enough to sour new wine," Hordo muttered.

"And makes little sense, besides," Conan added. "Can you make it no plainer?"

The old man dropped Conan's hand with a shrug. "Could I say my prophecies plainer," he said drily, "I'd live in a palace instead of a pigsty in Hellgate."

Stick tapping, he hobbled toward the street, deftly avoiding tables and drunken revelers alike.

"But mark my words, Conan of Cimmeria," he called over his shoulder from the doorway. "My prophecies always tell true." And he disappeared into the feverish maelstrom outside.

"Old fool," Hordo grumbled. "If you want good advice, go to a licensed astrologer. None of these hedge-row charlatans."

"I never spoke my name," Conan said quietly.

Hordo blinked, and scrubbed his mouth with the back of his calloused hand. "I need a drink, Cimmerian."

The scarlet-haired strumpet was rising from a table, leading a burly Ophirian footpad toward the stairs that led above, where rooms were rented by the turn of the glass. Conan plopped down on a vacated stool, motioning Hordo to the other. As he laid the cloak-wrapped sword on the table, the one-eyed man grabbed the arm of a doe-eyed serving girl, her pale breasts and buttocks almost covered by two strips of green muslin.

"Wine," Hordo ordered. "The biggest pitcher you have. And two cups." Deftly she slipped from his grasp and sped away.

"Have you yet spoken to your friends of me?" Conan asked.

Hordo sighed heavily, shaking his head. "I spoke, but the answer was no. The work is light here, Conan, and the gold flows free, but I am reduced to taking orders from a man named Eranius, a fat bastard with a squint and a smell like a dungheap. This bag of slime lectured me—imagine you me, standing still for a lecture?—about trusting strangers in these dangerous times. Dangerous times. Bah!"

" 'Tis no great matter," Conan said. Yet he had hoped to work again with this bearded bear of a man. There were good memories between them.

The serving girl returned, setting two leathern jacks and a rough clay pitcher half again the size of a man's head on the table. She filled the jacks and waited with her hand out.

Hordo rummaged out the coppers to pay, at the same time giving her a sly pinch. "Off with you, girl," he laughed, "before we decide we want more than you're willing to sell."

Rubbing her plump buttock she left, but with a steamy-eyed look at Conan that said she might not be averse to selling more were he buying.

"I told him you were no stranger," Hordo continued, "told him much of you, of our smuggling in Sultanapur. He'd not even listen. Told me you sounded a dangerous sort. Told me to stay away from you. Can you imagine him thinking I'd take an order like that?"

"I cannot," Conan agreed.

Suddenly the Cimmerian felt the ghost of a touch near his pouch. His big hand darted back, captured a slender wrist and hauled its owner before him.

Golden curls surrounded a face of child-like innocence set with guileless blue eyes, but the lush breasts straining a narrow strip of red silk named her profession, as did the girdle of copper coins low on her hips, from which hung panels of transparent red that barely covered the inner curves of her thighs before and the inner slopes of her rounded buttocks behind. Her fist above his entrapping hand was clenched tightly.

"There's a woman of sapphires and gold," Hordo laughed. "What's your price, girl?"

"Next time," Conan said to the girl, "don't try a man sober enough to notice how clumsy your touch is."

The girl put on a seductive smile like a mask. "You mistake me. I wanted to touch you. I'd not be expensive, for one as handsome as you, and the herbalist says I'm completely cured."

"Herbalist!" Hordo spluttered in his wine. "Get your hand off her, Conan! There's nine and twenty kinds of pox in this city, and if she's had one, she likely has the other twenty-eight yet."

"And tells me of it right away," Conan mused. He increased the pressure of his grip slightly. Sweat popped out on her forehead; her generous mouth opened in a small cry, and her fingers unclenched to drop two silver coins into Conan's free hand. In a flash he pulled her close, her arm held behind her back, her full breasts crushed against his massive chest, her frightened, sky-blue eyes staring into his.

"The truth, girl," he said. "Are you thief, whore, or both? The truth, and I'll let you go free. The first hint of a lie, and I'll take you upstairs to get my money's worth."

She wet her lips slowly. "You'll truly let me go?" she whispered. Conan nodded, and her shuddering breath flattened her breasts pleasantly against his chest. "I am no doxy," she said at last.

Hordo grunted. "A thief, then. I'll still wager she has the pox, though."

"It's a dangerous game you play, girl," Conan said.

She tossed her blonde head defiantly. "Who notices one more strumpet among many? I take only a few coins from each, and each thinks he spent them in his cups. And once I mention the herbalist none want the wares they think I offer." Abruptly she brought her lips to within a breath of his. "I'm not a whore," she murmured, "but I could enjoy a night spent in your arms."

"Not a whore," Conan laughed, "but a thief. I know thieves. I'd wake with purse, and cloak, and sword, and mayhap even my boots gone." Her eyes flashed, the guilelessness disappearing for an instant in anger, and she writhed helplessly within the iron band of his arm. "Your luck is gone this night, girl. I sense it." Abruptly he released her. For a moment she stood in disbelief; then his open palm cracking across her buttocks lifted her onto her toes with a squeal that drew laughter from nearby tables. "On your way, girl," Conan said. "Your luck is gone."

"I go where I will," she replied angrily, and darted away, deeper into the tavern.

Dismissing her from his mind he turned back to his wine, drinking deep. Over the rim of the leathern jack his eyes met those of the girl who had seemed out of place. She was looking at him with what was clearly approval, though not invitation, just as clearly. And she was writing on a scrap of parchment. He would wager there were not a handful of women on that entire street who could read or write so much as their own names. Nor many men, for that matter.

"Not for us," Hordo said, noticing the direction of his gaze. "Whatever she is, she's no daughter of the streets dressed like that."

"I care not what she is," Conan said, not entirely truthfully. She was beautiful, and he was willing to admit his own weakness for beautiful women. "At the moment I care about finding employment before I can no longer afford any woman at all. I spent the day walking through the city. I saw many men with bodyguards. There's not so much gold in it as in smuggling, but I've done it before, and I likely will again."

Hordo nodded. "There's plenty enough of that sort of work. Every man who had a bodyguard a year ago has five now. Some of the fatter merchants, like Fabius Palian and Enaro Ostorian, have entire Free-Companies in their pay. There the real money is to be made, hiring out your own Free-Company."

"If you have the gold to raise it in the first place," Conan agreed. "I couldn't buy armor for one man, let alone a company."

The one-eyed man drew a finger throug a puddle of wine on the table. "Since the trouble started, half of what we smuggle in is arms. Tariff on a good sword is more than the price used to be." He met Conan's gaze. "Unless I miscount, we could steal enough to outfit a company without anyone being the wiser."

"We, Hordo?"

"Hannuman's Stones, man! When they start telling me who my friends can be, I'm not much longer for smuggling."

"Then it's a matter of getting silver enough for enlistment bonuses. For, say, fifty men—"

"Gold," Hordo cut him off. "The going rate is a gold mark a man."

Conan whistled between his teeth. "It's not likely I'll see that much in one place. Unless you. . . ."

Hordo shook his head sadly. "You know me, Cimmerian. I like women, drink and dice too much for gold to stay long with me."

"Thief!" someone shouted. "We've caught a thief!"

Conan looked around to see the innocent-faced blonde struggling between a bulky, bearded man in a greasy blue tunic and a tall fellow with a weaselly look to his close-set eyes.

"Caught her with her hand in my purse!" the bearded man shouted.

Obscene comments rose amid the tavern's laughter.

"I told her her luck was gone," Conan muttered.

The blonde screamed as the bearded man ripped the strip of silk from her breasts, then tossed her up to the skinny man, who had climbed onto a table. Despite her struggles, he quickly tore away the rest of her flimsy garb and displayed her naked to the tavern.

The bearded man shook a dice cup over his head. "Who'll toss for a chance?" Men crowded round him.

"Let us go," Conan said. "I don't want to

watch this." He gathered up the cloak-wrapped sword and started for the street.

Hordo took one regretful look at the barely touched pitcher of wine, then followed.

At the door Conan caught the eye of the young woman in the plain cotton dress once more. She was staring at him again, but this time her face bore disapproval. What had he done, he wondered. Not that it mattered. He had more important concerns on his mind than women. Followed by Hordo, he ducked through the doorway.

Full dark was on the Street of Regrets, and the frenzy of its denizens had grown as if by motion they could warm themselves against the chill of night. Whores no longer strutted sensuously, but rather half-ran from potential patron to potential patron. Acrobats twisted and tumbled in defiance of gravity and broken bones as though for King Garian himself, receiving hollow, drunken laughter in payment, yet tumbling on.

Conan paused to watch a fire-juggler, his six blazing brands describing slow arcs above his bald head. A small ever-changing knot of people stood watching as well. Three came and two left even as the Cimmerian stopped. There were better shows that night on the street than a juggler. Conan fingered a copper out of his pouch and tossed it into the cap the quick-handed man had laid on the ground. There were only two in the cap to precede it. To Conan's surprise the juggler suddenly turned toward him, half-bowing as he kept the brands aloft, as if acknowledging a generous patron. As he straightened, he began to caper, legs kicking high, fiery batons spinning now so that it seemed his feet were always in the midst of the circles they described.

Hordo pulled at Conan's arm, drawing the muscular youth away down the street. "For a copper," the one-eyed man muttered disgustedly. "Time was, it'd have taken a silver piece to get that out of one of them. Maybe more."

"This city is gone mad," Conan said. "Never have I seen so many beggars this side of the Vilayet Sea. The poor are poorer, and more in number, than in any three other cities. Peddlers charge prices that would choke a Guild Merchant in Sultanapur, and wear faces like they were going bankrupt. More than half a silver queenshead for a pitcher of wine, but a juggler does his best trick for a copper. I haven't seen a soul who looks to care if tomorrow comes or no. What happens here?"

"What am I, Cimmerian? A scholar? A priest? 'Tis said the throne is cursed, that Garian is cursed by the gods."

Conan involuntarily made the sign against evil. Curses were nothing to fool with. Several people noticed and shied away from the big man. They had evil enough in their lives without being touched by the evil that troubled him.

"This curse," the big Cimmerian said after a time, "is it real? I mean, have the priests and astrologers spoken of it? Confirmed it?"

"I've heard nothing of that," Hordo admitted. "But it's spoken on every street corner. Everyone knows it."

"Hannuman's Stones," Conan snorted. "You know as well as I do that anything everyone knows is usually a lie. Is there any proof at all of a curse?"

"That there is, Cimmerian," Hordo said, poking a blunt finger at Conan for emphasis. "On the very day Garian ascended the Dragon Throne—the very day, mind you—a monster ran loose in the streets of Belverus. Killed better than a score of people. Looked like a man, if you made a man out of clay, then half melted him. Thing is, a lot of people who saw it said it looked something like Garian, too."

"A man made out of clay," Conan said softly, thinking of the blind man's prophecy.

"Pay no attention to that blind old fool," Hordo counseled. "Besides, the monster's dead. Wasn't those stay-in-the-barracks City Guards who did it, though. An old woman, frightened half out of her wits, threw an oil lamp at it. Covered it with burning oil. Left nothing but a pile of ash. The City Guard was going to take the old woman in, for 'questioning' they said, till her neighbors chased them off. Pelted them with chamber pots."

"Come," Conan said, turning down a narrow street.

Hordo hesitated. "You realize we're going into Hellgate?"

"We're being followed. Ever since the Gored Ox," Conan said. "I want to find out who. This way."

The street narrowed and twisted, and the laughter and the light of the Street of Regrets were quickly lost. The stench of offal and urine thickened. There was no paving here. The grate of their boots on gravel and the sounds of their own breathing where the loudest things to be heard. They moved through darkness, broken only occasionally by a pool of light from a window high enough for its owner to feel some safety.

"Talk," Conan said. "Anything. What kind of king is Garian?"

"Talk, he says," Hordo muttered. "Bel save us from your. . . ." He sighed heavily. "He's a king. What more is there? I hold no brief for any king. No more did you, last I saw you."

"Nor do I now. But talk. We're drunk, and too senseless to be silent while walking Hellgate in the middle of the night." He eased his broadsword in its scabbard. A hint of light from a window far above glinted on his face; his eyes seemed to gleam in the dark like those of a forest animal. A hunting animal.

Hordo stumbled over something that made ripe squelching sounds beneath his boots. "Vara's Guts and Bones! Let me see. Garian. At least he got rid of the sorcerers. I like kings better than I do sorcerers."

"How did he do that?" Conan asked, but his ear was bent for sounds from behind rather than the answer. Was that a foot on gravel?

"Oh, three days after he took the throne he executed all the sorcerers still at court. Gethenius, his father, had had dozens of them in the palace. Garian told no one what he intended. Some few did leave, giving one excuse or another, but the rest.... Garian gave orders to the Golden Leopards three glasses past midnight. By dawn every sorcerer still in the palace had been dragged out of bed and beheaded. Those who fled were true sorcerers, Garian said, and could keep their wealth. These, who couldn't even discover he intended their deaths, were charlatans and parasites. He had their belongings distributed to the poor, even in Hellgate. Last good thing he's done."

"Interesting," Conan said absently. In the dark his keen eyes picked out one shadow from another. There was a crossing alley ahead. And behind? Yes. That was the mutter of someone who had stepped in whatever had fouled Hordo's boots. "Say on," he said. His blade whispered on leather as it eased from its sheath.

The one-eyed man lifted his eyebrow at what Conan had done, then he, too, drew his sword. Both men walked with steel swinging easily in their fists.

"That curse," Hordo continued conversationally. "Gethenius took ill a fortnight after the planting, and as soon as he took to his bed the rains stopped. It rained in Ophir. It rained in Aquilonia. But not in Nemedia. The sicker Gethenius got and the closer Garian came to the throne, the worse the drought grew. The day he took the throne the fields were dry as powdered bone. And they gave about as much harvest. Tell me that's not proof of a curse."

They reached the alley; Conan side-stepped into its shadows, motioning Hordo to go on. The burly one-eyed man shambled on into the dark ahead, his words fading slowly.

"With the crops gone, Garian bought grain in Aquilonia, and raised tariffs to pay for it. Fool brigands on the border starting burning the grain wagons, so he raises tariffs again to hire more guards for the wagons, and to buy more grain, which the fools on the border still burn. High tariffs make for good smuggling, but I'd just as soon he. . . ."

Conan waited, listening. Briefly he considered unwrapping the madman's blade, but he could still feel the taint to it, even through the cloak. He propped it behind him against the wall. The following footsteps came closer, hurrying, yet hesitant. But one set, he was sure now.

A slight, cloak-shrouded shape moved into the alley crossing, pausing in the dark, all its attention on Hordo's faintly receding footsteps. Conan took a quick step forward, left hand coming down on the figure's shoulder. Spinning the shape, he slammed it against the wall. Breath whooshed out of his opponent. Blade across the figure's throat, he dragged it down to the alley to a pool of light. His mouth fell open as he saw the other's face. It was the girl who had seemed so out of place at the Gored Ox.

There was fear in her large, hazel eyes, but when she spoke her voice was under control. "Do you intend killing me? I don't suppose killing a woman would be beyond you, since you abandon them with such ease."

"What are you talking about?" he rasped.

"Are you working with footpads, girl?" He found it hard to believe she could be, but he had seen stranger things.

"Of course not," she replied. "I'm a poet. My name is Ariane. If you don't intend to cut my throat, could you take that sword away? Do you know what they were doing when I left? Do you have any idea?"

"Crom!" he muttered in confusion at her sudden torrent. Still, he lowered his blade.

She swallowed ostentatiously, and fixed him with a level gaze. "They were casting dice for who would have the first . . . turn with her. Every man there intended to take one. And in the meanwhile they were passing her about, beating her buttocks till they looked like ripe plums."

"The blonde thief," he exclaimed. "You're talking about the blonde thief. Do you mean to say you followed me into Hellgate just to tell me that?"

"I didn't know you were coming into Hellgate," she said angrily. "I do things on impulse. But what business is it of yours where I go? I'm not a slave. Certainly not yours. That poor girl. After you let her go I thought you had some sympathy for her, thought you might be different from the rest despite your rather violent appearance, but—"

"You knew she was a thief?" he broke in.

Her face turned defensive. "She has to live, too. I don't suppose you know about the things that drive people to become thieves, about being poor and hungry. Not you with your great sword, and your muscles, and—"

"Shut up!" he shouted, and immediately

dropped his voice, taking a quick look up and down the alley. It was well not to attract attention in a place like Hellgate. When he looked back at her she was staring at him, openmouthed. "I know about being poor," he said quietly, "about being hungry, and about being a thief. I was all of them before I was old enough to shave my face."

"I'm sorry," she said slowly, and he had the irritating feeling that it was as much for his youthful hunger as for what she had said.

"As for the girl. She threw away the chance I gave her. I told her her luck was gone, and it was, if I caught her, and you saw her."

"Maybe I should have spoken to her when I saw her," Ariane sighed.

Conan shook his head. "What kind of woman are you? A poet, you say. You sit in a tavern on the Street of Regrets, worrying about thieves. You dress like a shopkeeper's virgin daughter, and speak with the accents of a noblewoman. You chase me into Hellgate to upbraid me." He laughed, deep in his chest. "When Hordo returns we'll escort you back to the Street of Regrets, and may Mitra save the doxies and cut purses from you."

A dangerous light kindled in her eyes. "I *am* a poet, and a good one. And what's wrong with the way I dress? I suppose you'd rather I wore a few skimpy strips of silk and wriggled like—"

He clamped a hand over her mouth, not breathing while he listened. Her eyes were large and liquid on his face. It came again, that sound that had pricked his ear. The rasp of steel sliding from a sheath.

Shoving the girl further up the narrow confines of the dark alley, Conan spun just as the first man rushed him. The Cimmerian's blade slashed out his throat even while his sword was going up.

The first of the three following on his heels stumbled against the collapsing body, then shrieked as Conan's steel sought the juncture of shoulder and neck. From behind the men came a scream that ended in a gurgle, and a cry of "The Red Hawk!" told the Cimmerian youth that Hordo had joined the fray. The man facing Conan dropped into a guard position, nervously trying to see the combat behind him without taking his eyes from the massive youth.

Suddenly Conan shouted, shifting his shoulders as if he intended an overhand blow. His opponent's sword flashed up to block. Conan's lunge brought them face to face, the Cimmerian's blade projecting a foot through the other's back. He stared into the dying man's eyes, even in the darkness able to see the despair that came with the realization of death. Then only death was there. He tugged his blade free and wiped it on the dead man's cloak.

"Are you hurt, Conan?" Hordo called, stumbling past the bodies in the narrow alley.

"Just wiping my—" A foul odor filled Conan's nostrils. "Crom! What is that?"

"I slipped in something," Hordo replied sourly. "That's why I was so long getting back. Who's the wench?"

"I'm not a wench," Ariane said.

"Her name's Ariane," Conan said. He raised his eyebrows as he watched her slide a very efficient-looking little dagger inside her dress. "You didn't draw that against me, girl."

"I had it," she replied. "Perhaps I didn't think to need it with you. Are these friends of yours?"

"Footpads," he snorted.

Hordo straightened from examining one of the corpses. "Mayhap you ought to take a look, Conan. They're dressed well for Hellgate."

"Some of Hellgate's better citizens." The Cimmerian's nose wrinkled. "Hordo, as soon as we return Ariane to the Street of Regrets, you're going to find a bathhouse. That is, if you intend to keep drinking with me." Hordo muttered something under his breath.

"If it doesn't have to be a bathhouse," Ariane began, then stopped, chewing her full lower lip in indecision. Finally, she nodded. "It will be all right," she said half to herself. "There's an inn called the Sign of Thestis, just off the Street of Regrets. It has baths. You can come as my guests, for the night at least."

"Thestis!" Hordo crowed. "Whoever heard of an inn called after the goddess of music and such?"

"I have," Ariane said with some asperity. "If you are invited, the bed, food and wine are free, though you're expected to contribute if you can. You'll understand when you see it. Well? Do you come, or do you stink until you can pay two silver pieces to a bathhouse?"

"Why?" Conan asked. "You sounded not so friendly a minute or two gone."

"You interest me," Ariane said simply.

Hordo snickered, and Conan suddenly wished the one-eyed man smelled just a little better, so he could get close enough to thump him. Hastily the Cimmerian gathered up the ancient sword in the cloak.

"Let's get out of here," he said, "before we attract more vermin."

Hurriedly they picked their way back out of Hellgate.

Albanus angrily jerked the cord of his gold-embroidered dressing robe tight about his waist as he stalked into the carpeted antechamber of his sleeping apartments. Golden lamps cast a soft light on the walls, where bas-relief depicted scenes from the life of Bragoras, the ancient, half-legendary King of Nemedia from whom Albanus claimed pure and unsullied descent through both his father and mother.

The hawk-faced lord had left orders to be called from his bed whenever the two men now awaiting him arrived. Neither Vegentius nor Demetrio appeared to have slept at all. The soldier's surcoat, worked with the Golden Leopard, was wrinkled and damp with sweat, while the eyes of the slender youth were haggard.

"What have you discovered?" Albanus demanded without preliminary.

Demetrio shrugged and sniffed at his ever-present pomander.

Vegentius stiffened in tired anger at the peremptory tone, and spoke harshly. "Nothing. The sword's gone. Let it be. We don't need it, and you've already gotten Melius killed, giving him the thing in the first place. Though, Mitra knows, the man is little enough loss."

"How was I to know the accursed blade would seize his mind?" Albanus broke out. Hands knotted to keep them from shaking, he managed to regain control. "The sword," he said in a somewhat calmer voice, "must be recovered. Another incident like today, another man going berserk with that blade in his hands, and Garian will know there's sorcery loose in Nemedia again. Even with his dislike of majicks he might well bring his own sorcerer to court, for protection. Do you think I'll so easily let my plans be thwarted?"

"Our plans," Demetrio reminded gently from behind his pomander.

Albanus smiled slightly, a curving of the lips, nothing more. "Our plans," he agreed. Then even that slight softness was gone. "The Guardsmen were put to the question, were they not, Vegentius? After all, they did kill Lord Melius."

Vegentius gave a short nod. "All except their sergeant, who disappeared from the barracks when my Golden Leopards came to make the arrests. 'Twas guilt sent him running, mark my words. He knows something."

"Most likely," Demetrio murmured, "he knew what methods of questioning would be used."

"Unless he took the sword," Albanus said. "What did they say of that under the question?"

"Little enough," Vegentius sighed. "For the most part they begged for mercy. All they knew was that they were ordered to stop a madman who was slaughtering people in the Market District. They found him fighting a northern barbarian and killed him. When they discovered they'd slain a lord, they were so terrified they had no thought for the sword. They didn't even bring in the barbarian."

"He was still alive?" Albanus said, surprised. "He must be a master swordsman."

Vegentius laughed disparangingly. "Melius barely knew one end of a blade from the other."

"The skill is in the blade," Albanus said. "Six masters of the sword were slain in the making of it, their blood used for quenching, their bones burned to heat it, the essence of their art infused into its metal."

"Slash and hack, that's all Vegentius knows." Demetrio's voice dripped mockery. "But the art of steel. . . ." His blade whipped from its sheath. Knees bent, he danced across the colorfully woven carpet, his sword working intricate figures in the air.

"That fancy work may be good enough for first-blood duels among the gently born," Vegentius sneered, "but 'tis a different matter in battle, when your life hangs on your blade."

"Enough!" Albanus snapped. "Both of you, enough!" He drew a ragged breath. One day he would let them fight, for his entertainment, then have the winner impaled. But now was not the time. Thirty years he had worked for this. Too much time, too much effort, too much humiliating terror to allow it all to be ruined now. "That barbarian may have taken the sword. Find him! Find that blade!"

"I've already started," the square-faced soldier said smugly. "I sent word to Taras. He'll have had his alley rats hunting all night."

"Good." Albanus rubbed his hands together, making a sound like dry parchment rustling. "And you, Demetrio. What have you been doing to find the blade?"

"Asking ten thousand questions," the slender noble replied wearily. "From the Street of Regrets to the House of a Thousand Orchids. I heard nothing. If Vegentius had thought to let me know of this barbarian it would have made my searching easier."

Vegentius examined his nails with a complacent smile. "Who'd have thought to look for you in the House of a Thousand Orchids? They provide only women to their customers."

Demetrio slammed his sword back into its sheath as if he were driving it into the soldier's heart. Before he could open his mouth, though, Albanus spoke.

"There's no time for his petty bickering. Find that sword. Steal it, buy it, I care not, but get it. And without attracting attention."

"And if its possessor has discovered its properties?" Demetrio asked.

"Then kill him," Albanus said smoothly. "Or her." He turned to go.

"One more thing," Vegentius said abruptly. "Taras wants to meet with you."

Albanus turned back to face them, his eyes

black flints. "That scum dares? He should be licking the paving stones in gratitude for the gold he's given."

"He's afraid," Vegentius said. "Him and some of the others who know a little of what they really do. I can cow them, but even gold won't put their guts back unless they see you face to face and hear you tell them it all will happen as they've been told."

"Mitra blast them!" Albanus' eyes went to the bas-relief on the walls. Had Bragoras had to deal with such? "Very well. Arrange you a meeting in some out-of-the-way place."

"It will be done," the soldier replied.

Albanus smiled suddenly, the first genuine smile the others had ever seen on his face. "When I am on the throne, this Taras and his daggermen will be flayed alive in the Plaza of Kings. A good king should be seen to protect his people against such as they." He barked a laugh. "Now get you gone. When next I see you, bear a report of success."

He left with as little ceremony as he had come, for already he began to feel beyond the courtesies ordinary men offered one another. They were fools in any case, unable to realize that he saw them no differently than he saw Taras. Or that he would deal with them as harshly in the end. And if they would betray one king, they would betray another.

Inside his dimly lit bedchamber he strode impatiently to a large square sheet of transparent crystal hung on the wall. The thin crystal was undecorated save for odd markings around its outer edge, markings that lay entirely within the crystal. In the light from a single, small gold

tripod lamp the markings were almost invisible,
but from long practice Albanus' fingers touched
the proper ones in the proper sequence, intoning
words in a language three millenia dead.

As his finger lifted from the last, the crystal
darkened to a deep silvery blue. Slowly pictures
formed within it. In the crystal men moved and
gestured, talking though no sound could be
heard. Albanus gazed on Garian, who thought
himself safe in the Royal Palace, conferring with
long-bearded Sulpicius and bald Malaric, his
two most trusted councelors.

The King was a tall man, heavily muscled still
from a boyhood spent with the army, but now
beginning to show a smooth layer of fat from
half a year of inactivity on the throne. His
square-jawed face with its deep-set dark eyes
had lost some of the openness it had once had.
Sitting on the throne was responsible for that
change as well.

Albanus' hands moved around the rim of the
crystal again, and Garian's face swelled until it
filled the entire square.

"Why do you do that so often?"

The blonde who spoke watched him with
sapphire cat eyes from the satin cushions of his
bed. She stretched langorously, her skin gleaming like honeyed ivory in the dimness, her
dancer's legs seeming even longer as she
pointed her toes. Her large, pear-shaped breasts
lifted as she arched her slender back. Albanus
felt his throat thicken.

"Why do you not speak?" she asked, her voice
all pure innocence.

Bitch, he thought. "It's as if he were here,

Sularia, watching his mistress writhe and moan beneath me."

"Is that all I am to you?" Her tone was sultry now, caressing like warm oil. "A means of striking at Garian?"

"Yes," he said cruelly. "An he had a wife or a daughter, they would take their turns with you in my bed."

Her eyes drifted to the face in the crystal. "He has no time for a mistress, much less a wife. Of course, you are responsible for the many troubles that take his time. What would your fellows think, an they knew you took the risk of seducing the King's mistress to your bed?"

"Was it a risk?" His face hardened dangerously. "Are you a risk?"

She shifted in the cushions so that her head was toward him, her hips twisted to emphasize their curve against the smallness of her waist. "I am no risk," she said softly. "I wish only to serve you."

"Why?" he persisted. "At first I meant you only for my bed, but of your own will you began to spy in the palace, coming to kneel at my feet and whisper of who did what and who said what. Why?"

"Power," she breathed. "It is an ability I have, to sense power in men, to sense men who will have power. I am drawn to such men as a moth to the flame. I sense the power in you, greater than the power in Garian."

"You sense the power." His eyes lidded, and he spoke almost to himself. "I can feel the power inside, too. I've always felt it, known it was there. I was born to be king, to raise Nemedia to an empire. And you are the first other to realize it. Soon the people will take to the streets of Belverus with swords in hand to demand that Garian abdicate in my favor. Very soon. And on that day I will raise you to the nobility, Sularia. Lady Sularia."

"I thank my king."

Suddenly he unbelted his dressing robe and threw it off, turning so that the man in the crystal—if he were actually able to see from it— would have a clear view of the bed. "Come and worship your king," he commanded.

Mouth curving in a wet-lipped smile, she crawled to him.

As Conan made his way down to the common room at the Sign of Thestis the next morning, he wondered again if he had fallen into a nest of lunatics. Two lyres, four zithers, three flutes and six harps of assorted sizes were being played, but by musicians scattered about the room, and no two playing the same tune. One man stood declaiming verse to a wall with full gesticulations, as if performing for a wealthy patron. A dozen young men and women at a large table covered with bits of sculpture shouted over the music, telling one another in detail what was wrong with everyone else's work. Three men at the foot of the stairs also shouted at one another, all three simultaneously, about when morally reprehensible action was morally required. At least, that was what he thought they were shouting about. All the men and women in the room, none past their mid-twenties, were shouting about one thing or another.

He and Hordo had been made welcome the night before, after a fashion. There had been but a score of people in the inn then. If it was an inn. That was another thing the Cimmerian doubted. The lot of them had stared as if Ariane had brought back two Brythunian bears. And among that lot, with no more weapons than a few belt knives for cutting meat, perhaps they had seemed so.

While Hordo had gone out back to the baths—wooden tubs sitting on the dirt in a narrow court, not the marble palaces to cleanliness and indolence found elsewhere in the city—the odd youths had crowded around Conan, refilling his cup with cheap wine whenever it was in danger of becoming empty and prodding him to tell stories. And when Hordo returned they pressed him, too, for tales. Long into the night and the small hours of the morning, Conan and the one-eyed man had vied to top the other's last tale.

Those strange young men and women—artists, some said they were, others musicians, and still others philosophers—listened as if hearing of another world. Oft times those who called themselves philosophers made comments more than passing strange, not a one of which Conan had understood. It had taken him a while to realize that none of the others understood them either. Always there was a tick of silence punctuating each comment while the rest watched him who made it to see if they were supposed to nod solemnly at the pontification or laugh at the witticism. A time or two Conan had thought one of them was making fun of him, but he had done nothing. It would not have been proper to kill a man when he was not sure.

At the foot of the stairs he pushed past the philosophers—none of the three even noticed his passing—and stopped in astonishment. Ariane stood on a table in the corner of the room. Naked. She was slim, but her breasts were pleasantly full, her waist tiny above sweetly rounded hips.

He swung his cloak from his shoulders—the wavy-bladed sword was safely hidden in the tiny room he had been given for the night—and stalked across the room to thrust the garment up to her.

"Here, girl. You're not the sort for this kind of entertainment. If you need money, I've enough to feed both of us for a time."

For a moment she looked down at him, hands on hips and eyes unreadable, then astounded him by throwing back her head and laughing. His face reddened; he little enjoyed being laughed at. Instantly she dropped to her knees on the table, her face a picture of contrition. The way her breasts bounced within a handspan of his nose made his forehead suddenly grow beads of sweat.

"I'm sorry, Conan," she said softly, or what passed for softly in the din. "That may have been the nicest thing anyone has ever said to me. I shouldn't have laughed."

"If you want to exhibit yourself naked," he replied gruffly, "why not go to a tavern where there's a bit of money in it?"

"Do you see those people?" She pointed out three men and two women seated near the table, each with a piece of parchment fastened to a board and a bit of charcoal in hand, and each glaring impatiently at the girl and him. "I pose for them. They don't have the money to hire someone, so I do them a favor."

"Out in front of everybody?" he said incredulously.

"There isn't much room, Conan," she said, amusement plain in her voice. "Besides, everyone here is an artist of one sort or another. They do not even notice."

Eyeing her curves, he was willing to wager differently. But all he said was, "I suppose you can do what you want."

"You suppose right."

She waved to the people sketching and hopped down from the table, producing any number of interesting jiggles and bounces. He wished she would stop leaping about like that while she had her clothes off. It was all he could do not to throw her over his shoulder and take her back up to his room. Then he noticed a twinkle in her eye and a slight flush on her cheek. She knew the effect she had on him.

Deftly she took the cloak out of his hands and wrapped it chastely around her. "At the moment I would like to have some wine. With you." He looked at the cloak, raising an eyebrow questioningly, and she giggled. "It's different up there. There I'm posing. Down here I'm just naked. Come, there's a table emptying."

She darted away, and he followed, wondering

what difference the distance from the table to the floor made, wondering if he would ever understand women. As he slid onto a stool across a small, rough-topped table from her, someone thrust a clay jug of wine and two battered metal cups in front of them, disappearing while Conan was still reaching for his pouch.

He shook his head. " 'Tis the first tavern I've ever seen, where payment was not demanded before a cup was filled."

"Did not anyone explain last night?" she laughed.

"Perhaps they did. But there was more than a little wine being passed around."

"Did you really do all you talked about last night?" She leaned forward with interest, the top of the cloak gaping to expose the upper slopes of her cleavage. A part of his brain noted that that glimpse was almost as erotic as her fully exposed bosom had been. He wondered if she knew that and did it on purpose.

"Some of them," he answered cautiously. In truth he did not remember which stories he and Hordo had told. There had been *much* more than a little wine. He filled their cups from the clay jug.

"I thought so," she said in tones of satisfaction. "As to the money, you give what you can. Everyone staying here does, though some who only come in the day give nothing. Some of us receive money from our families, and of course we all put that in. They don't approve—the families that is—but they approve less of having us nearby to embarrass them. Whatever we have left over we use to distribute bread and salt to the hungry in Hellgate. It's little enough," she sighed, "but a starving man appreciates even a crumb."

"Some of these have families rich enough to give them money?" he said, looking around the room in disbelief. Suddenly her cultured accents were loud in his head.

"My father is a lord," she said defensively. She made it sound a crime, both being a lord and being the daughter of one.

"Then why do you live here, on the edge of Hellgate, and pose naked on tables? Can you not write poetry in your father's palace?"

"Oh, Conan," she sighed, "don't you understand that it's wrong for nobles to have gold and live in palaces while beggars starve in hovels?"

"Mayhap it is," Conan replied, "but I still like gold, though I've had little enough of it. As for the poor, were I rich, unless I misdoubt me I'd fill many a belly with what I spent."

"What other answer did you expect?" a lanky man said, pulling up a stool. His long face wore a perpetual scowl, made deeper by thick eyebrows that grew across the bridge of his nose. He scooped up Ariane's cup and drank half her wine.

"It is an honest answer, Stephano," Ariane said. Stephano snorted.

Conan remembered him now. The night before he had named himself a sculptor, and been free with his hands with Ariane. She had not seemed to mind then, but now she took back her winecup angrily.

"He is a generous man, Stephano, and I think me he'd be generous were he rich." She shifted her direct gaze back to Conan. "But can you not see that generosity is not enough? In Hellgate are those who lack the price of bread, while nobles sit safe in their palaces and fat merchants grow richer by the day. Garian is no just king. What must be done is clear.''

"Ariane!" Stephano said sharply. "You tread dangerous ground. School your tongue."

"What leave have you to speak so to me?" Her voice grew more heated by the word. "Whatever is between us, I am none of your property."

"I have not named you so," he replied, matching heat for heat. "I ask but that you let yourself be guided by me. Speak not so to strangers."

Ariane tossed her pretty head contemptuously, her big eyes suddenly cold. "Art sure there is no part of jealousy in your words, Stephano? No intent to rid yourself of a rival?" The sculptor's face flamed red. "Stranger he may be," she continued remorselessly, "yet he is the kind of man we seek. A warrior. Have I not heard Taras speak so to you a hundred times? We must needs have fighters if—"

"Mitra's mercy!" Stephano groaned. "Have you mind at all for caution, Ariane? He is a northern barbarian who likely never knew his father and would sell his honor for a silver piece. Guard your tongue!"

With his left hand Conan slid his broadsword free of its scabbard, just enough so that the edge of the blade below the hilt rested against the side of the table. "When I was still a boy," he said in a flat voice, "I saw my father die with a blade in his hand. With that blade I killed the man who slew him. Care you to discuss it further?"

Stephano's eyes goggled at the sword, his scowl momentarily banished. He touched his lips with his tongue; his breath came in pants. "You see, Ariane? You see what kind of man he is?" His stool scraped on the floor as he rose. "Come away with me, Ariane. Leave this man now."

She held out her winecup to Conan. "May I have some more wine?" She did not look at Stephano, or acknowledge his presence. Conan filled the cup, and she drank.

Stephano looked at her uncertainly, then took a step backwards. "Guard your tongue!" he hissed, and darted away, almost crashing into another table in his haste.

"Will you guard your tongue?" Conan asked quietly.

She peered into her wine a time before answering. "From the stories you told, your sword goes where the gold is. Do you choose only by who can pay the most gold?"

"No," he told her. "I've ridden away from gold rather than follow unjust orders." Sighing, he added truthfully, "But I do like gold."

Clutching his cloak about her, she rose. "Mayhap . . . mayhap we'll speak of it later. They wait for me to finish posing."

"Ariane," he began, but she cut him off.

"Stephano thinks he has a claim on me," she said quickly. "He has not." And she left almost as quickly as Stephano had.

Conan emptied his cup with a muttered curse, then turned to watch her drop his cloak and climb back to her pose on the table. After a moment her eyes shifted to him, then away, quickly. Again she met his gaze and tore hers away. Her rounded breasts rose and fell as her breathing became agitated. Spots of red appeared on her cheeks, growing, her face flushing hotter and hotter. Abruptly she uttered a small cry and leaped down, snatching up the cloak from the floor without looking again at Conan. She pulled the fur-trimmed garment about her as she ran, darting between the tables, feet flashing up the stairs.

The Cimmerian smiled complacently as he poured more wine from the clay jug. Perhaps things were not as bad as they seemed.

Hordo dropped onto the stool across the table, a frown creasing his eye. "Have you listened to what's said in this place?" he asked quietly. "Was there a Guardsman about, there'd be heads on pikes for sedition before many more dawns."

Conan looked casually to see if anyone was listening. "Or for rebellion?"

"This lot?" the one-eyed man snorted derisively. "They might as well march to the block and ask to have their heads chopped. Not that the city's not ripe for it, mind. But these have as much chance as a babe sucking a sugar-tit."

"But what if they had money? Gold to hire fighting men?"

Hordo had raised his cup as Conan spoke; now he choked on the wine. "Where would this lot get gold? If one of them had a patron, you can wager your stones he'd not be living on the rim of Hellgate."

"Ariane's father is a lord," Conan said quietly. 'And she told me some of the rest come of rich men, too."

The one-eyed man chose his words carefully. "Do you tell me they actually plan rebellion? Or think they do?"

"Stephano and Ariane, between them, as much as told me so."

"Then let us be gone from here. They may have some talents, but rebellion is not among them. If they met you last night and tell so much today, what have they told others? Remember, our heads can decorate pikes as easily as theirs."

Conan shook his head slowly, although Hordo was right, on the face of it. "I like it here," was all he said.

"You like a round-bottomed poet," Hordo said heatedly. "You'll die for a woman yet. Remember the blind soothsayer."

"I thought you said he was a fool," the Cimmerian laughed. "Drink, Hordo. Rest easy. We'll talk of our Free-Company."

"We've no gold yet that I can see," the other said sourly.

"I'll find the gold," Conan said with more confidence than he felt. He had no idea whence it might come. Still, it would be well to have his plans in order. A delay of days could mean the difference between being sought after and all who could afford such companies already having hired. "I'll find it. You say we can, ah, borrow weapons from the storehouses of the smuggling ring you serve. Are they serviceable? I've seen smuggled mail so eaten with rust it fell apart in a good rain, and blades that snapped at the first blow."

"Nay, Cimmerian. These are of good quality, and of any sort you want. Why, there are as many kinds of sword bundled in those storehouses as I've ever heard named. Tulwars from Vendhya, shamshirs from Iranistan, macheras in a dozen patterns from the Corinthian city-states. Fifty of this sort and a hundred of that. Enough to arm five thousand men."

"So many?" Conan murmured. "Why would they keep so much in their storehouses, and in such variety? There's no profit in storing swords."

"I bring what I'm told from the border to Belverus, and I'm paid for it in gold. I care not if they grow barley in the storehouses, so long as I get a fat purse each trip." Hordo tipped the jug over his cup; a few drops fell. "Wine!" he roared, a blast that brought dead silence to the room.

Everyone turned to stare in amazement at the two burly men. A slender girl in the same sort of plain neck-to-ankles cotton robe that Ariane wore approached hesitantly and placed another clay jug on the table. Hordo fumbled in the purse at his belt and tossed her a silver piece.

"The rest is for you, little one," Hordo said.

The girl stared at the coin, then laughed delightedly and dropped a mockingly deep curtsey before leaving. Conversation slowly resumed among those at the tables. The musicians struck up their various tunes, and the poet orated to the wall.

"Pretty serving girls," Hordo muttered as he refilled his battered metal cup, "but they dress like temple virgins."

Conan hid a smile. The one-eyed man had drunk deeply the night before. Well, he would discover soon enough that he did not have to pay for his wine. In the meantime, let him contribute for the both of them.

"Consider, Hordo. Such a motley collection of

weapons is just the sort of thing these artists would put together."

"That again?" the other man grumbled. "In the first place, whoever runs the ring, I can't see him wanting Garian overthrown. Those fool tariffs might be starving the poor, but they make good profits for smuggling. In the second place. . . ." His face darkened, the scar below his patch standing out whitely. "In the second place, I've been through one rebellion with you. Or have you forgotten riding for the Venhyan border half a step in front of the headsman's sword?"

"I remember," Conan said. "I've said naught of joining their rebellion."

"Said naught, but thought much," Hordo growled. "You're a romantic fool, Cimmerian. Always were, likely always will be. Hannuman's Stones, man, you'll not mix me in another uprising. Keep your mind fixed on the gold for a Free-Company."

"I always keep my mind on gold," Conan replied. "Mayhap I think on it too much."

Hordo groaned, but Conan was saved having to say more by the appearance of the slender girl who had brought the wine jug. Tilting her head to one side, she favored the big Cimmerian with a look, half shyness, half invitation, that made the room suddenly too warm.

"What's your name, girl?" Hordo asked. "You're a pretty little bit. Get rid of that cotton shift, deck yourself with a little silk, and you could work in any tavern in Belverus."

She tossed her head, laughing gaily, silken brown hair rippling about her shoulders. "Thank you, kind sir, and for your generous contribution." Hordo frowned in uncomprehension. "My name is Kerin," she went on, her soft brown eyes shifting to Conan like a light-fingered caress. "And by those shoulders, you must be the Conan Ariane spoke of. I work in clay, though I hope to have my sculpture cast in bronze some day. Would you pose for me? I can't pay you, but perhaps. . . ." Her mouth softened, full lower lip dropping slightly, and her eyes left no doubt what sort of arrangement she wanted with the muscular barbarian.

Conan had barely listened after the mention of posing. An image flashed in his brain of Ariane, posing on the table, and he was uncomfortably aware of his face growing hot. Surely she did not mean. . . . She could not want. . . .

He swallowed hard and cleared his throat. "You mentioned Ariane. Did she send a message?"

"Why did she see you first?" Kerin sighed. "Yes, she did. She's waiting in your room. To tell you something very important, she said." She ended with a slight smirk.

Conan scraped back his stool.

"Girl," Hordo said as the Cimmerian rose, "what is this posing? I might well do it." Kerin slipped into the seat Conan had vacated.

All the way across the common room Conan waited for Hordo's outraged shout, but when he looked back from the foot of the stairs the one-eyed man was nodding slowly, a delighted grin on his face. Laughing, Conan ran up the stairs. It seemed his friend would receive more than good value for his silver piece.

Upstairs the narrow hall was lined with many doors, most crudely made, for the original chambers had been roughly partitioned into more. When Conan pushed open his own rude plank door, Ariane was standing below the small window high in the wall. His cloak was still wrapped tightly around her, her fists showing at the neck where she held it together. He closed the door behind him and leaned back against it.

"I pose," she said without preamble. Her eyes glinted with something he could not quite read. "I pose for my friends, who cannot hire models. I do it often, and never have I felt embarrassment. Never until today."

"I merely looked at you," he said quietly.

"You looked at me." She uttered a sound halfway between a laugh and a sob. "You looked at me, and I felt like one of those girls at the Gored Ox, wriggling to a flute for drooling men. Mitra blast your eyes! How dare you make me feel like that!"

"You are a woman," he said. "I looked at you as a man looking at a woman."

She closed her eyes and addressed the cracked ceiling. "Hama All-Mother, why must I be stirred by an untutored barbarian who thinks with his sword?" A smug smile grew on his face, to be quashed almost immediately by a glare from her large hazel eyes. "A man may take as many women as he wishes," she said fiercely. "I refuse to have less freedom than a man. If I choose to have but one man at a time to my mat, and have no other till he leaves or I do, that is my affair. Can you accept me as I am?"

"Did your mother never tell you a man likes to do the asking?" he laughed.

"Mitra blast your heart!" she snarled. "Why

do I waste my time?" Muttering to herself she stalked toward the door, cloak flaring in her haste.

Conan reached out one massive arm, curling it around her waist beneath the cloak. She had time for one strangled squawk before he lifted her, the cloak floating to the floor, to crush her soft breasts against the hard expanse of his chest.

"Will you stay with me, Ariane?" he asked, looking into her startled eyes.

Before she could speak he tangled his free hand in her hair and brought her lips to his. Her small fists bruised themselves against his shoulders; her feet kicked futilely at his shins. Slowly her struggles subsided, and when a satisfied murmur sounded in her throat he released her hair. Panting, she let her head drop onto his broad chest.

"Why did you change your mind?" she managed after a time.

"I didn't change it," he replied. She looked up, startled, and he smiled. "Before you asked. This time I did the asking."

Laughing throatily, she let her head fall back. "Hama All-Mother," she cried, "will I never understand these strange creatures called men?"

He laid her gently on his sleeping mat, and for a long time thereafter only sounds passion-wrought passed her lips.

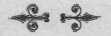

he Street of Regrets in the morning hours fit well Conan's mood. The paving stones were littered with the tawdry refuse of the previous night's revelry; those few people to be seen were stumbling home bleary eyed and hollow faced. Conan kicked rubbish from his path as he strode along, and gave growl for growl to the stray dogs that scavenged among the leavings.

The ten nights past had been an idyll at the Sign of the Thestis, wrapped in Ariane's arms, her passions and appetites feeding his own even as they sated them. Stephano brooded much in jealousy and wine, yet the memory of the Cimmerian's anger kept his tongue between his teeth. Hordo, drawn by the attractions of the slender Kerin, had moved his few belongings from an inn three streets away, and of an evening they drank and told each other lies till the charms of Ariane and Kerin parted them. Those were the nights. Days were another matter.

Conan paused at the sound of running boots behind him, then continued on as Hordo joined him.

"Ill luck this morrow, too?" the one-eyed man asked, eyeing the Cimmerian's face.

Conan nodded shortly. "When I had defeated all three bodyguards now in his service, Lord Heranius offered three gold marks for me to take service as their chief, with two more every tenday."

"Ill luck?" Hordo exclaimed. "Mitra! That's twice the usual rate for bodyguards. I'm tempted to give up smuggling. At least there'd be no danger of the headsman's block."

"And I must swear bond-oath before the City Magistrates not to quit his service without leave for two years."

"Oh."

Conan's right fist cracked into the other palm with a sound like a club striking leather. A drunk, stumbling his way home, jumped a foot in the air and fell in a puddle of vomit. Conan did not notice.

"Everywhere it is the same," he grated, "Free-Companies or single blade-fee alike. All demand the bond-oath, and some require three years, if they do not require five."

"Before the bond-oaths," Hordo mused.

"Some men changed masters every day, getting a silver piece more each time. Look you. Why not take service with whoever offers the most gold? This Lord Heranius, by the sound of it. When you're ready to go, if he won't release you, just go. An oath that makes a man a slave is no oath at all."

"And when I do, I must leave Belverus, perhaps all of Nemedia." He was silent for a time, his boots kicking broken clay wine-jars and soiled bits of abandoned clothing from his path. At last he said, "At first it was but talk, Hordo, this Free-Company that I would lead. Now it's more. I'll take no service until I ride at the head of my own company."

"It means so much to you?" Hordo said incredulously. He dodged a jar of slops thrown from a second-story window, hurling a curse at the thrower, already gone.

"It does," Conan said, ignoring the other's mutters about what had splashed on his boots. "In the final sum of it all, perhaps a man has no more than himself, naught but a strong right hand and the steel in it. And still, to rise, to make some mark in the world, a man must lead others. I was a thief, yet did I rise to command in the Army of Turan, and did well at it. I know not how far I may rise nor how far the path I follow may take me, yet do I intend to rise as high and go as far as my wits and a good sword will take me. I will have that Free-Company."

"When you do," the one-eyed man said drily, "be you certain they swear the bond-oath." They turned into the street that led to the Sign of Thestis.

As Conan laughed, three men stepped out to

spread themselves across the narrow street, broadswords in hand. The sound of boots behind made Conan glance quickly over his shoulder. Two more armed men stood there, cutting off retreat. The Cimmerian's blade whispered from its worn shagreen scabbard; Hordo, sword flickering free, pivoted to face those behind.

"Stand aside," Conan called to the three. "Find you easier meat elsewhere."

"Naught was said of a second man," the one to Conan's left muttered, his thin, rat-like face twitching.

The man to the right, shaven dome gleaming in the morning sun, hefted his sword uneasily. "We cannot take one without the other."

"You'll find but your deaths here," Conan said. With his left hand he unfastened the bronze pin that held his cloak, doubling the fur-lined garment loosely over that arm.

The leader, for the tall man in the center with his closely cropped beard was clearly so, spoke for the first time. "Kill them," he said, and his blade thrust for Conan's belly.

With pantherine grace the muscular Cimmerian moved aside, his cloak tangling the tall man's blade while his right foot planted itself solidly in the fellow's crotch. In the same move Conan's sword beat aside a thrust of the shavenhead. Gagging, the leader attempted to straighten; but Conan pivoted, his left foot taking the bearded man on the side of the head, knocking him under the feet of onrushing rat-face. Both went down in a heap.

The shaven-headed attacker hesitated, goggle-eyed at his companions on the ground, and died for it. Conan's slashing steel half-severed his throat. Bright red blood fountained as he went to his knees, then toppled onto his face in the muck of the street. Rat-face scrambled to his feet, and he tried a desperate overhead hack. Conan's blade rang against the other, bringing it into a sweeping downward circle, sliding his blade along his opponent's, thrusting it into the villain's chest.

A quick kick next to his blade freed the body to collapse alongside the other; and Conan spun to find the leader on his feet, his narrow, bearded face suffused with rage. He swung while the big Cimmerian was yet turning, staring with surprise as Conan dropped to a squat, buttocks on his heels. Conan's steel sliced a bloody line across his abdomen. The tall man screamed like a woman, dropping his sword as his frantic hands tried vainly to hold his intestines in. His eyes were glazed with death before he struck the filthy paving stones.

Conan looked for Hordo in time to see the one-eyed man's blade decapitate his second attacker. With the head still rolling across the pavement Hordo turned to glare at Conan, blood oozing from a gash on his sword arm and another, smaller, on his forehead.

"I'm too old for this, Cimmerian."

"You always say that." As he spoke, Conan bent to check the pouches of the men he had killed.

"It's true, I tell you," Hordo insisted. "If these hadn't been such fools as to talk and dither while we set ourselves, they might have chopped us to dog meat. As it was, my two nearly sliced my cods off. I'm too old, I say."

Conan straightened from the bodies with six new-minted gold marks. He bounced them on his palm. "Fools they may be, but they were sent after one of us. By somebody willing to pay ten gold marks for a death." He jerked his head at the two Hordo had killed. "You'll find each of them has a pair of these too."

Hordo muttered an oath and bent to the remaining bodies, straightening up with four fat coins. The one-eyed man closed his fist tightly on them. "Yon rat-face spoke of not expecting two. Mitra, who'd pay ten gold marks for either of us?"

A gangling boy shambled out of an alley not a dozen paces distant. At the sight of the bodies his jaw dropped open, and with a scream of pure terror he dashed away, his wail fading as he sped.

"Let us discuss it at the Thestis," Conan said, "before we gather an audience."

"With our luck," Hordo muttered, "this will be the one morning in half a year the City Guard has patrols out."

It was but a short distance down the twisting street to the inn, but obviously no one had heard the fighting. Only Kerin gave them a second glance when they walked in. In those morning hours there were few of the artists about, and none of the noise that would reverberate in the evening.

"Hordo," the slender girl said, "what happened to your arm?"

"I fell over a broken wine-jar," he replied sheepishly.

She gave him a sharp look and left, returning in a moment with a pile of clean rags and a jug of wine. Uncorking the wine, she began to pour it over the gash on Hordo's arm.

"No!" he shouted, snatching it from her hand.

An amused smile quirked her mouth. "It hurts not that much, Hordo."

"It hurts not at all," he growled. "But this is the proper way to use wine."

And he tipped the clay jug up to his mouth, with his free hand fending off her attempts to take it back. When finally he stopped for breath she jerked it away, pouring the little wine that remained over a cloth and dabbing at his forehead.

"Hold still, Hordo," she told him. "I will fetch you more wine later."

Across the common room Conan noticed a face strange to the inn. A handsome young man in a richly embroidered red velvet tunic sat at a table in a corner, talking to Graecus, a swarthy sculptor who spent considerable time in the company of Stephano.

After discovering that someone might want him dead, Conan was feeling suspicious of strangers. He touched Kerin's arm.

"That man," he said. "The one talking to Graecus. Who is he? He seems well dressed for an artist."

"Demetrio, an artist?" she snorted. "A catamite and a wastrel. They say he's a great wit, but I've never found him so. Betimes he likes to dazzle those among us who can be dazzled by his sort, when he is not rolling in the fleshpots."

"Think you it's him?" Hordo asked.

Conan shrugged. "Him, or anyone else."

"By Erebus, Cimmerian, I'm too old for this."

"What are you two talking about?" Kerin demanded. "No. I'd as lief not know." She rose, pulling Hordo behind her, a faun leading a bear. "That cut on your arm needs ointment. Wine-jar, indeed!"

"When I return," Hordo called over his shoulder to Conan, "we can begin looking for the men we want. Courtesy of our enemy, eh?"

"Done," Conan called back, rising. "And I'll fetch that sword. It should fetch a coin or two."

In his room abovestairs the Cimmerian pried up a loosened floor board and took out the serpentine blade. Light from the small window ran along the gleaming steel, and glinted on the silver work of the quillons. The feel of taint rose from it like a miasma.

As he straightened he wrapped his cloak, rent from the tall man's sword, about the blade. Even holding it in his bare hand made his stomach turn as the slaying of his first man had not.

When Conan returned to the common room, the man in the red velvet tunic was waiting at the foot of the stair, a pomander to his aquiline nose, his eyes lidded with langorous indolence, yet the Cimmerian noted that the hilt of his sword showed wear, and the hand that held the pomander had bladesman's calluses. Conan started past.

"A moment, please," the slender man said. "I am called Demetrio. I collect swords of ancient pattern, and I could not help but hear that you possess such a one, and wish to sell it."

"I remember nothing of calling it ancient," Conan replied. The man had a viperish quality the Cimmerian liked not. As if he could smile and clasp a hand, yet strike to the heart while doing so. Still, he found himself listening.

"Perhaps I but imagined you named it ancient," Demetrio said smoothly. "If it is not, I have no interest. But an it is, well might I buy." He eyed the cloak-wrapped bundle beneath the Cimmerian's arm. "You have it there?"

Conan reached into the cloak and drew forth the blade. "This is the sword," he said, and stopped as Demetrio jumped back, hand to his own sword. The Cimmerian flipped the sword over, proffering the hilt. "Perhaps you wish to try its heft?"

"No." The word was a shaky whisper. "I can see that I want it."

The flesh about Demetrio's mouth was tight and pale. The strange thought came to Conan that the slender man was afraid of the sword, but he dismissed the notion as foolish. He tossed the sword onto a nearby table. His hand felt dirty from holding it. And that was foolish too.

Demetrio swallowed, seeming to breathe more easily as he looked at the blade where it lay. "This sword," he said, not looking at the Cimmerian. "Has it any . . . properties? Any magicks?"

Conan shook his head. "None that I know." Such might add to the price he could demand, but any such claims would be easily disproved. "What will you give?"

"Three gold marks," Demetrio said promptly.

The big Cimmerian blinked. He had been thinking in terms of silver pieces. But if the sword had some value to this young man, it was time to bargain. "For a blade so ancient," he said, "many collectors would pay twenty."

The slender man gave him a searching look. "I

have not so much with me," he muttered.

Shocked, Conan wondered if the blade was that of some long-dead king; Demetrio had made not even a pretense of haggling. His practised thief's eye priced the amethyst-studded gold bracelet on Demetrio's wrist at fifty gold marks, and a small ruby pin on his tunic at twice that. The man would be good for twenty marks, he thought.

"I would be willing to wait," Conan began, when Demetrio pulled the bracelet from his wrist and thrust it at him.

"Will you take that?" the fellow asked. "I would not risk another buying while I am gone to get coin. It is worth more than the twenty marks, I assure you. But add in that cloak, for I would not carry a bare blade in the streets."

"Cloak and blade are yours," the Cimmerian said, and quickly exchanged the fur-trimmed garment for the bracelet.

He felt a surge of joy as his fist closed over the amethyst-studded gold. No need to make do now with the few men ten gold pieces would hire. His Free-Company was literally in his grasp.

"I would ask you," he added, "why this blade has such worth. Is it perhaps the sword of an ancient king, or hero?"

Demetrio paused in the act of carefully wrapping the cloak about the sword. Carefully, Conan thought, and as gingerly as if it were a dangerous animal.

"How are you called?" the slender man asked.

"I am called Conan."

"You are right, Conan. This is the sword of an ancient king. In fact, you might say this is the sword of Bragoras." And he laughed as if he had said the funniest thing he had ever heard. Still laughing, he gathered up the sword and cloak and hurried into the street.

Albanus paused at the door, the crude, fur-trimmed bundle beneath his arm out of place in the tapestry-hung room with its carpet-strewn marble floor. Sularia sat before a tall mirror, a golden silk robe about her creamy shoulders, a kneeling slave woman brushing the honey silk of her hair. Seeing his reflection Sularia let the robe drop, giving him a view of her generous breasts in the mirror.

The hawk-faced lord snapped his fingers. The slave looked around; at his gesture she bowed and fled on bare feet.

"You have brought me a gift?" Sularia said. "It is wrapped most strangely, an you have."

She examined her face in the mirror, and lightly stroked rouge onto her cheeks with a brush of fur.

"This is not for you," he laughed. "'Tis the sword of Melius."

With a key that hung on a golden chain about his neck, he unlocked a large lacquered chest standing against the wall, turning the key first one way then the other in a precise pattern. Were that pattern not followed exactly, he had told Sularia, a cunningly contrived system of tubes and air-chambers would hurl poison darts into the face of the opener.

Albanus swung back the lid and, tossing aside the tattered cloak, carefully laid the sword in the place he had prepared for it. The tomes of ancient Acheron, bound in virgins' skin, were there, well layered in silk, and those most vital thaumaturgical implements from the cache. His fingers rested briefly on a bundle of scrolls and rolled canvases. Not yet of any magical significance, they still deserved their place in the chest, those sketches and paintings of Garian. In a place of honor, resting on a silken cushion atop a golden stand, was a crystal sphere of deepest blue within which silver flecks danced and glittered.

Letting her robe drift to the floor, Sularia came to stand naked beside him. Her tongue touched her lips in small flickers as she stared down at the sword. "It was that blade which slew so many? Is it not dangerous? Ought you not to destroy it?"

"It is too useful," he said. "Had I but known what I know now, never would I have put it in the hands of that fool Melius. 'Twas those runes on the blade led me at last to its secret, buried in the grimoires."

"But why did Melius slay as he did?"

"In the forging of this weapon, the essences of six masters of the sword were trapped within the steel." He let his fingers brush lightly along the blade, sensing the power that had been required for its making. Such power would be his, power beyond the ken of mortal minds, power far beyond that of earthly kings. "And in that entrapment did madness come." He reached down as if to lift the sword, but stopped with his hand clawed above the hilt. "Let the same hand grasp this hilt but three times to use this blade, and the mind that controls that hand will be ripped away, merging with the madness of those ancient masters of the sword. Escape. Slay, and escape. Slay. Slay!"

Ending on a shout, he looked at Sularia. Her mouth hung open, and she stared at his hand above the sword with open fear in her blue eyes.

"How often have you used the sword?" she whispered.

He laughed and took his hand away. Instead of the sword he picked up the crystal sphere, holding it delicately in his fingers, almost reverently, though he knew no power under heaven could so much as chip its seemingly fragile surface.

"You fear the sword?" he asked softly. His adamantine gaze seemed to pierce to the heart of the cobalt sphere. "Here is that which is to be feared, for by this is summoned and controlled a being—a demon? a god?—I know not, yet a being of such power that even the tomes of Acheron speak of it in whispers full of awe."

And he would be its master, master of more power than all the kings of all the nations of the world. His breath quickened at the thought. Never yet had he dared that summoning, for that act held dangers for he who summoned, dangers that master might find himself slave, a mortal plaything for an immortal monster with eternity to amuse itself. Yet, was he not descended of Bragoras, ancient hero-king who had slain the dragon Xutharcan and bound the demon Dargon in the depths of the Western Sea?

Almost unbidden, the words of summoning began to roll from his lips. "*Af-far mea-roth, Omini deas kaan, Eeth-far be-laan Opheah cristi....*"

As the words came, the sky darkened above the city as though the sun had dimmed to twilight. Lightning cracked and forked across a cloudless sky, and, rumbling, the earth began to shake.

Albanus stumbled, looked around him in sudden panic at walls that quivered like cloth in the breeze. It was too soon for this. It was madness to have tried. And yet, he had not finished the incantation. There was a chance. Hastily he returned the sphere, glowing now, to its cushion within the lacquered chest. With great care he blanked his mind. There must be not even the merest thought of summoning. No thought at all. No thought.

Slowly the light in the crystal sphere faded, and the earth ceased to move. The lightnings faded and were gone. Light broke forth over the city as if at a new sunrise.

For a long time Albanus did not look at

Sularia. Did she say one word, he thought grimly, but one word of the spectacle of fool he had made himself, he would gut her and strangle her with her own entrails. But one word. He turned to face her with a face dark as that beneath an executioner's hood.

Sularia stared at him with eyes filled with pure lust. "Such power," she whispered. "You are a man of such power, almost I fear me it might blind me to look on you." Her breath came in pants. "Is it thus you will destroy Garian?"

His spirit soared, and his pride. "Garian is not worthy of such," he sneered. "I will create a man, give him life with my two hands. So will I bring the usurper to his doom."

"You are so powerful as that?" she gasped.

He waved it away. "A mere trifle. Already have I done so, and this time the errors of the last will not be repeated." Abruptly he tangled his hand in her hair, forced her to the floor, forced her though she would have gone willingly and more than willingly. "Nothing stands in my way," he said as he lowered himself atop her. She cried out, and he heard in it the cries of the people acclaiming their king, their god.

Sephana raised herself from the cushions of her bed, her lushly rounded body sweat-oiled from love making. Her full breasts swayed with the motion.

The man in her bed, a lean young captain of the Golden Leopards, lifted himself unsteadily on one elbow. His dark eyes were worshipful as he gazed at her. "Are you a witch, Sephana? Each time I think that I will die from the pleasure. Each time I think that I've had all the ecstacy there is in the world. And each time you give more than I could dream of."

Sephana smiled contentedly. "And yet, Baetis, I think you tire of me."

"Never!" he said fervently. "You must believe me. You are Derketo come to earth."

"But you refuse me such a small favor."

"Sephana," he moaned, "you know not what you ask. My duty. . . ."

"A small favor," she said again, walking slowly back to the bed.

His eyes followed her hungrily. She was no slender girl, but a woman of curves, a callimastean and callipygean marvel to put hunger in any man's eyes. He reached for her, but she stepped back.

"A door left unlatched, Baetis," she said softly. "A passage left unguarded. Would you deny your king a surprise, the same delights you now enjoy?"

The young captain breathed heavily, and his eyes closed. "I, at least, must be there," he said at last.

"Of course," she said swiftly, and moved to kneel astride him. "Of course, Baetis, my love." Her smile was vulpine, the light in her violet eyes feral. Let Albanus make his long, drawn-out plans. She would strike while he still planned. It was a pity that Baetis had to die along with Garian. But that was in the future. Sighing contentedly, she gave herself over to pleasure.

The straw butts were each the size of a man's torso. Conan set the last of them in place, and swung into the saddle to gallop the hundred and fifty paces back to the men he and Hordo had gathered in the five days past. He wished the one-eyed man were with him, but Hordo was yet keeping his contacts with the smugglers, and he was seeing to the shifting of goods from a storehouse before the Kings Customs made a supposed surprise inspection. They could never tell, Hordo maintained, when those contacts might prove useful.

The Cimmerian reigned in his big Aqilonian black before the two score mounted men, holding up a short, heavy bow before the men. "This is a horse bow."

The bows had been a lucky find, for mounted archery was an art unknown in the west, and Conan counted on this skill to add to his Free-Company's appeal to patrons. The bows had been lying unstrung in the smugglers' store-house, thought too short and of too heavy a draw to be wanted. Each of the forty now wore other acquisitions from the storehouse: metal jazeraint hauberks over padded tunics, and spiked helms. A round shield hung at each saddle, and a good Turanian scimitar, bearing the proof-mark of the Royal Foundry at Aghra-pur, swung at each hip.

Conan hoped their armor was unfamiliar enough to Nemedia to give them a foreign flavor. Men usually believed that foreigners knew strange tricks of fighting. With the horse bows, they might believe correctly. As he and Hordo had chosen only men already possessing a horse—they had gold enough only for signing bonuses, not for buying horses—so had they chosen men who knew something of archery. But none knew mounted archery. That was why Conan had brought them to this clearing outside of Belverus.

"You're all accustomed to using a bow-ring on your thumb," he went on, "but when you fight mounted, you must be able to shift from bow to sword to lance and back, quickly. A bow-ring encumbers the grip."

"How do you draw the thing at all?" asked a grizzled man with a livid scar across his broad nose. He held the short bow out at arm's length and attempted to draw it. The cord moved no more than a handspan, producing laughter from some of the others.

The grizzled man's name was Machaon. Though he did not recognize Conan, the Cimmerian knew him for the sergeant who had commanded the City Guards in killing Lord Melius.

"Use a three-fingered grip on the cord," Conan said once the laughter had died, "and draw thusly."

The muscular Cimmerian notched an arrow and, placing the bowstring to his cheek, pushed the short, powerful bow out to draw it. As he did so, he pressed with his knees, bringing the war-trained black around. The straw butts seemed to swing before his eyes; he loosed. With a solid thud the shaft struck square in the center of the middle butt. A surprised murmur went up from the men.

"Thus is it done," Conan said.

"'Tis more than passing strange," a tall, hollow-cheeked man muttered, "this archery from horseback." His black eyes were sunken, and he looked as though he had been ravaged by disease, though those among the company who knew him said he had no sickness but a doleful spirit. "If it is a thing of use, why do we not see it among the armies of Nemedia or Aquilonia or any other civilized land?"

Conan was saved answering by Machaon.

"Open your mind, Narus," the grizzled man said, "and for once let not your mournful mood color what you see. Think you. We can appear, strike and be gone while foot-archers rush to plant their sharpened stakes against the charge they expect, while pikemen and ordinary infantry yet prepare to close ranks against the mounted attacks they know. Enemy cavalry will be but lowering their lances to countercharge when our arrows strike to their hearts. Put off your dolorous countenance, Narus, and smile at the surprise we will give our enemies."

Narus deliberately showed his teeth in a grin that made him look more the plague victim than ever. A ripple of laughter and obscene comment greeted his attempt.

"Machaon has seen the right of it," Conan announced. "I name him now as sergeant of this Free-Company."

A surprised and thoughtful look appeared on Machaon's scar-nosed face, and a murmur of approval rose from the rest. Even Narus seemed to think it a good choice, in his mournful way.

"Now," Conan continued, "let each man take a turn at the butts. First with the horse unmoving."

For three full turns of the glass the Cimmerian kept them at it, progressing to shooting with their mounts at a walk, thence to firing at the gallop. Every man knew horsemanship and the bow, if not together, and they made good advance. By that time's end, did they not use their horse bows so well as Turanian light cavalry, yet was their skill enough to surprise and shock any of these western lands. Machaon, to no one's surprise, and Narus, to everyone's, were the best after Conan.

After that time the Cimmerian led them back into Belverus, to one of the stables that lined the city's wall, where he had arranged for their horses to be tended. After each man had given his mount into the care of a stable slave he left to go his own way until the morrow, when Conan had commanded them to meet again at the stable, for such was the custom of Free-Companies when not in service. It was about that last that Machaon spoke as Conan was leaving.

"A moment, captain," the grizzled man said, catching Conan at the heavy wooden doors of the stable. Machaon had been handsome as a youth, but aside from the scar that cut across his broad nose his face was a map of his campaigns. On his left cheek was a small tattoo of a six-pointed star from Koth; three thin gold rings from Argos dangled from the lobe of his right ear, and his hair was cut short in front and long in back after the style of the Ophirian border.

"It would be well, captain, if you were to put the company into service soon. Though it's been but a few days since we swore the bond-oath yet have I heard some complain openly that we earn no gold, and speak of the ease of taking a second bond-oath using another name before another Magistrate."

"Let them know that we'll take service soon," Conan replied, though he wondered himself why he had approached none of the merchants who might wish to hire a Free-Company. "I see that I made a good choice for sergeant."

Machaon hesitated, then asked quietly, "Know you who I am?"

"I know who you are, but I care not who you were." Conan met the man's dark-eyed gaze until Machaon finally nodded.

"I'll see to the men, captain."

From the stable Conan made his way to the Sign of Thestis through streets that seemed to have twice as many beggars and three times

as many toughs as a tenday past. No plump
merchant or stern-faced noble now made his
way in even the High Streets without a hard-
eyed escort, and no slave-borne curtained litter,
whether it contained a noble's sleek daughter or
the hot-eyed courtesan who served him, traveled
shorn of its bevy of armed and armored guar-
dians. The City Guard were nowhere to be seen.

The Thestis when Conan entered was filling,
as it always did of a midday, with youthful
artists in search of a free meal from the inn's
stewpot. Their arguments and musical instruments blended into a cacophony that the Cimmerian had learned to ignore.

He grabbed Kerin's arm as she rushed past, a
clay wine-jug in each hand. "Has Hordo returned?" he asked.

She set one of the jugs down hard enough to
crack it, ignoring the wine spreading across the
table top and the yelps of those seated there.
"He sent a message by a boy," she said coldly.
"You are to meet him at the Sign of the Full
Moon, on the Street of Regrets, a glass past the
sun's zenith."

"Why there? Did he say why he does not come
here?"

Kerin's eyes narrowed to slits, and she spoke
through clenched teeth. "There was some
mention of a dancer, with breasts. . . . Enough!
If you would learn more, learn it from that
miserable one-eyed goat!"

The Cimmerian suppressed a smile until she
had flounced away. He hoped this dancer was
all that Hordo thought, for the one-eyed man
was surely going to pay for his pleasures when

he again came in reach of Kerin.

He was trying to decide if he had time for a bowl of stew—it was assuredly better than that served on the Street of Regrets—before leaving to meet Hordon, when Ariane approached and put a small hand on his arm. He smiled, suddenly thinking of a better use for his time than a bowl of stew.

"Come up to my room," he said, slipping an arm around her. He pulled her close and tried out his best leer. "We could discuss poetry."

She tried to suppress a giggle, and almost succeeded. "If by poetry you mean what I think you mean, you want to do more than talk about it." Her smile faded, and her eyes searched his face. "There's something more important to speak of now, but I must have your oath never to repeat a word of what is said to you. You must swear."

"I do so swear," he said slowly.

Abruptly he knew why he had not hired his Free-Company out. Without a doubt, a company in service to merchant or noble would be expected to support the throne in a rebellion. But he wanted no part of crushing Ariane and her friends. Most especially not Ariane.

"I've wondered," he went on, "when you would speak to me of this revolt of yours."

Ariane gasped. "You know," she whispered. Quickly she put her fingers on his lips to prevent him speaking. "Come with me."

He followed her through the tables into the back of the inn. There, in a small room, Stephano slouched scowling against the flaking wall, and Graecus, the stocky sculptor, straddled a bench, grinning. Leucas, a thin man with a big nose who called himself a philosopher, sat cross-legged on the floor chewing his lower lip.

"He knows," Ariane said as she closed the door, and they all jumped.

Conan casually put his hand to his sword hilt.

"He knows!" Stephano yelped. "I told you he was dangerous. I told you we should have nothing to do with him. This is not our part of it."

"Keep your voice down," Ariane said firmly. "Do you want to tell everyone in the inn?" He subsided sulkily, and she went on, addressing the others too. "It's true that recruiting men like Conan was not part of what we were supposed to do, but I've heard each one of you complain that you wanted to take a more direct part."

"At least you can write poetry taunting Garian," Graecus muttered. "All I can do is copy what you write and scatter it in the streets. I can't do a sculpture to rouse the people."

"King Garian sits on the Dragon Throne," Conan said suddenly. They all stared at him. "King Garian sits to his feast alone. I saw that one. Did you write it, Ariane?"

"Gallia's work," she said drily. "I write much better than that."

"This is all beside the point," Stephano shrilled. "We all know why you trust him, Ariane." He met Conan's icy blue stare and swallowed hard. "I think what we do is dangerous. We should leave hiring this sort of . . . this sort of man to Taras. He knows them. We don't."

"We know Conan," Ariane persisted. "And we all agreed—yes, you too, Stephano—that we should take a part in finding fighting men, whatever Taras says. With Conan we get not one, but forty."

"If they'll follow him," Graecus said.

"They will follow me wherever there is gold," Conan replied.

Graecus looked a little unsettled at that, and Stephano laughed mockingly, "Gold!"

"Fools!" Ariane taunted. "How many times have we talked of those who claimed that revolution should be kept pure, that only those who fought for the right reasons should be allowed to take part? How many of them went to the impaling stake for their purity?"

"Our cause is just," Stephano grated. "We taint it with gold."

Ariane shook her head wearily. "Time and again we have argued this. The time for such argument is long past, Stephano. How think you Taras gathers fighting men? With gold, Stephano. Gold!"

"And from the start did I oppose it," the lanky sculptor replied. "The people—"

"Would follow us and rise," she cut him off. "They would follow us and, none of us knowing aught of weapons or war, would be cut down."

"Our ideals," he muttered.

"Are not enough." She glared at each of her fellow conspirators in turn, and they shifted uneasily beneath her gaze. Of them all, Conan realized, the strongest will was housed within her sweet curves.

"What I want," Graecus announced, "is a chance to hold a sword in my hand. Conan, can I ride with you on the day?"

"I have not said I would join you," Conan replied slowly.

Ariane gasped, clutching her hands beneath her rounded breasts, her face a picture of dismay. Graecus sat open-mouthed.

"I told you he was not to be trusted," Stephano muttered.

"My men will follow me," the Cimmerian went on, "but not if I lead them only to the headsman's block or the impaling stake. I cannot join you without some idea of your chances of success, and to know that I must know your plans."

"He could betray us," Stephano said quickly.

"Be quiet, Stephano," Ariane said, but she studied the Cimmerian's face without speaking further.

"I am not civilized enough," Conan told her softly, "to betray my friends."

She nodded shakily. Stephano tried to cut her off, but she ignored him. "Taras hires warriors. He says that we need at least a thousand, but he will soon have that many. Our strength, though, is the people. Their anger is so great now, and their hunger, that they would pull Garian down with their bare hands, could they. Some know they will receive weapons. Others will follow. We have weapons for ten thousand, weapons smuggled across the border. Some no doubt by your friend, Hordo."

"*Ten* thousand?" Conan said, remembering Hordo's estimate of five.

"Ten," Graecus said. "I've seen them. Taras showed me a storehouse full."

And let him count them, too, Conan thought drily. "It takes a great deal of gold to arm ten thousand, even poorly. And more to hire a thousand already armed. You provided this gold?"

"Some part of it, yes," Ariane said defensively. "But, as you know, we earn no great amounts, and most of what we have from our . . . our other sources goes to this inn."

"There are some," Stephano said loftily, "who despite their wealth believe that we are right and Garian will destroy Nemedia. They furnish Taras with what is needed to acquire arms and men."

"Who are they?" Conan asked. "Will they support you openly, put their names behind you once you take to the streets?"

"Of course," Stephano said, but almost immediately his loftiness fell into uncertainty. "That is, I suppose they will. You see, they prefer to remain anonymous." He laughed shakily. "Why, not even any of us here has ever seen them. Their money goes directly to Taras."

"What Stephano means," Ariane said as the sculptor sank into silence, "is that they're affrighted we will fail, and fear to find themselves upon the headsman's block. 'Tis likely they think to manipulate us, and the revolution, to increase their own wealth and position. But if they do, they forget that we command the people. And a thousand armed men."

A thousand armed men who had taken gold from these mysterious benefactors, Conan thought wearily. "But what is your plan? Not just to rush into the streets handing swords out to the people?"

Graecus smiled broadly. "We are not such fools as you might think us, Conan. Those of us who distribute the bread in Hellgate have found men who can be trusted, marked out those who will follow when the word is given. These will receive the weapons. We will lead them to surround the Royal Palace, while Taras takes the thousand to seize the city gates and lay seige to the City Guard in their barracks."

"What of the Free-Companies, and the bodyguards?" Conan asked. "There must be three thousand such in the city, and those who have paid them will most certainly support the king."

"Yes," Ariane said, "but each will also keep his bodyguard close about him till he sees what happens. We can ignore them. If necessary, they can be rooted out later, one by one. A Free-Company of a hundred may be overrun by a thousand from the gutter to whom death is no more than an escape from hunger."

She looked ready to lead such an assault herself, small head erect, shoulders back outthrusting her breasts to strain the fabric of her shift, eyes alight with hazel fire. Conan knew her words were true. Men who welcomed death were fearsome opponents in the assault, though more easily dealt with in the long campaign. Whatever the outcome of this meeting, he must keep his company ready to move at all times with no more than an instant's warning.

What he said, though, was, "What of the army?"

It was Graecus again who answered. "The closest troops are a thousand at Heranium and two at Jeraculum. They would take five days to reach Belverus, once they have been commanded to march, but will be too few to do anything to effect while we hold the city gates.

As to the forces on the Aquilonian border, they will still have to decide to abandon the border, worrying all the while of what Aquilonia will do."

"Ten days' march from the border for a sizeable force," Conan said thoughtfully. "Two days hard riding for a message to get there. So you can count on twelve days before you must face seige machinery and soldiers in numbers to assault the city walls. Perhaps it will be longer, but 'tis best to count on no more."

"You have an eye for such things," Graecus said approvingly. "We plan based on twelve days."

"And will have no need for them," Stephano pronounced with a dismissing wave of his hand. "Long before then, the downtrodden of the city will have risen to join us. A hundred thousand men will line the walls of the city, shoulder to shoulder. We will have called on Garian to abdicate—"

"Abdicate!" Conan shouted. The others started, staring at the walls as if they could see them listening. He went on in a lower tone. "You raise a rebellion, then call on Garian to abdicate? 'Tis madness. The Golden Leopards could hold the Royal Palace for half a year of siege, perhaps more. You have twelve days."

"'Tis none of my idea," Ariane said disgustedly. "From the first have I said we must sweep over the Palace in the first hour."

"And slaughter everyone there!" Stephano said. "Then we are no better than Garian, our beliefs and ideals so much rhetoric."

"I do not remember," Graecus said slowly, "who it was first suggested we demand that

Garian abdicate. On first thought, perhaps it seems best to do as Ariane wishes, attack the Palace while the Golden Leopards yet believe it is no more than another disturbance in the streets. But we cannot totally abandon the very ideals for which we fight. Besides," he finished with a smile, as if he had found the solution, "it is well known that the hill on which the Royal Palace sits is riddled with a hundred passages, any one of which will take us inside its defenses."

"Everyone may know of these passages," Ariane said, her voice dripping acid, "but do you know where to find one of them? Just one?"

"We could dig," the stocky man suggested weakly. Ariane snorted, and he subsided.

Conan shook his head. "Garian will not abdicate. No king would. You will but waste time you do not have to waste."

"If he will not abdicate," Stephano said, "then the people will storm the Royal Palace and tear him to pieces with their bare hands for his crimes against them."

"The people," Conan said, staring at the dark-browed man as if he had never seen his like before. "You talk of preventing a slaughter that will tarnish your ideals. What of the thousands who will die taking the Palace? If they can?"

"We compromised our ideals by hiring swordsmen for gold," Stephano maintained stubbornly. "We cannot compromise them further. All who die will be martyrs to a just and glorious cause."

"When is this glorious day?" Conan asked sarcastically.

"As soon as Taras has gathered his thousand

men," Graecus replied.

"In effect, then this Taras gives the word for your uprising?" Graecus nodded slowly, a suddenly doubtful look on his face, and Conan went on. "Then I must speak to Taras before I decide whether to join you."

Ariane's eyes grew wide. "You mean that you still may turn aside from us? After we have opened ourselves to you?"

"We have told him all!" Stephano cried, his voice growing more shrill by the word. "He can betray everything! We have given ourselves to this barbarian!"

His face suddenly hard, Conan gripped his sword with both hands, pulling it up so that the hilt was before his face. Stephano stumbled back with a shriek like a woman, and Graecus scrambled his feet. Ariane's face was pale, but she did not move.

"By this steel," Conan said, "and by Crom, Lord of the Mound, I swear that I will never betray you." His icy blue eyes found Ariane's and held them. "I will die first."

Ariane stepped forward, her face full of wonder, and placed a hesitant hand on the Cimmerian's cheek. "You are like no other man I have ever known," she whispered. Her voice firmed. "I believe him. We will arrange a meeting for him with Taras. Agreed, Stephano? Graecus?" The two sculptors nodded jerkily. "Leucas? Leucas!"

"What?" The skinny philosopher started as if he had been asleep. "Whatever you say, Ariane. I agree with you wholeheartedly." His eye lit on Conan's bared blade, and his head jerked back to thump against the wall. He remained like that, staring at the steel with horrified eyes.

"Philosophers," Ariane murmured laughingly.

"I must go," Conan said, returning his sword to its scabbard. "I must meet Hordo."

"I will see you tonight, then," Ariane said. Stephano suddenly looked as if his stomach pained him. "And, Conan," she added as he turned for the door, "I trust you with my life."

With her life, the Cimmerian thought as he left the inn. Yet was she involved to the heart in the conspiracy and uprising. It could succeed. If Taras had in fact the thousand trained and armed men he claimed. If the people rose, and followed, and did not flee when faced with the interlocked shields and steady tread of infantry, the armored charge of heavy cavalry and the roof-rending crash of monstrous seige engines. If the rebels in their pride could be convinced to let their ideals wait on victory and seize the Palace while the Golden Leopards yet stood unaware. Too many ifs. Her life was bound with a doomed cause. Yet in the pride of his youth Conan swore another oath, this to himself. While holding to his oath not to betray, he would save her life despite her.

IX

By one glass past midday the Street of Regrets had begun its revelry, though slowly, yet building for the climax of night. A hundred jugglers tossed balls, batons, rings, knives and flaming wands where a thousand soon would. A hundred strumpets, rouged, perfumed and bangled, lightly draped with brightly colored silks, postured where two thousand would strut at dark. Through them strolled scores of richly tunicked nobles and merchants, each convoyed by his sword-bearing man or pair, vanguard for the multitudes to follow. Litters in dozens, borne by well-muscled slaves, bounded by armored guards, carried sleek, hot-breathed women seeking in advance of their sisters the vices offered by the desperate. And among them all the beggars wheedled in their rags.

Conan, making his way down the street, indifferent to its sights and sounds, found himself laughing when at last he spied the Sign of the Full Moon. On a slab of wood hanging above the entrance was painted a naked woman, kneeling and bent, her back to the viewer, and her buttocks glowing as if reflecting the sun. This spoke of the raucous delights that Hordo would choose.

Suddenly one of the litters caught his eye, scarlet curtained, its black poles and framing worked with gold. Of a certainty it was the litter he had seen his first day in Belverus, the litter of the veiled woman who had looked at him so strangely. The scarlet curtain twitched aside, and once again he was looking into the eyes of the woman veiled in gray. Over that distance he could discern not even so much as their color, yet those tilted eyes were familiar to him. Hauntingly so; if he could but bring back the memory.

He shook his head. Memory and imagination played tricks. A hundred women he had known and a thousand he had not could have eyes exactly alike. He turned to enter the Full Moon.

From behind, sweeping over the murmur of the street, came a sound, a woman's laugh, half sob. He spun, an icy chill running up his spine. That laugh had seemed so familiar that he was almost sure if he opened his mouth a name would emerge to match it. But no woman was there, save the whores. The litter was swallowed up in the throng.

The Cimmerian eased sword and belt dagger in their sheaths, as if that easing would ease his mind. He was too much on edge for worry of Ariane, he told himself. It would do good to lose himself for a time with Hordo in drink and ogling of this fabulous dancer. He plunged into the Full Moon.

The common room of the Full Moon smelled of sour wine and stale perfume. The rough wooden tables were no more than a third filled at this hour, with men who hunched over their drinks, nursing their wine and their own dark fears together. Seven women danced to two shrill flutes and a zither, each carrying a strip of transparent red silk used now to cover the face, now to conceal bare breasts. From thin gilded girdles worn low on rounded hips depended curved brass plates that covered the juncture of their thighs, each plate marked with the price for which she who wore it could be enjoyed in the rooms above.

Though all the dancers were nicely curved, Conan saw none he believed would have excited Hordo's imagination the way the message indicated. Perhaps they had other dancers, he thought, who would appear later. As he took a table close to the narrow platform where the dancers writhed, a plump serving wench appeared at his elbow, a single twist of muslin about her hips.

"Wine," he said, and she darted away.

As he settled to enjoying the women on the stage he became aware of someone staring at him. Hesitantly the thin philosopher, Leucas, approached his table.

"I need . . . may I talk with you, Conan?"

The thin man looked about him nervously as he spoke, as though afraid of being overheard. The only other men not concentrating on their wine were three dark-skinned Kothians, their hair braided into metal rings and Karpashi daggers strapped to their forearms. They appeared to be arguing as to whether the dancers were worth the prices they bore. Still, Leucas half fell onto the stool across from Conan, leaning across the table and pitching his voice in an urgent whisper as if he expected someone to stop him, violently, at any second.

"I had to talk to you, Conan. I followed. Your sword. When I saw it, I knew. You're the one. You are the kind of man who can do this sort of thing. I . . . I am not. I'm just not a man of action." Sweat poured down his narrow face, though the tavern was shadowed and cool. "You do understand, don't you?"

"Not a word," Conan said.

Leucas squeezed his eyes shut, muttering under his breath, and when he opened them he seemed to have gotten a grip on himself. "You agree that Garian must be removed, do you not?"

"That's what you're planning," Conan replied noncommittally.

"But . . ." Leucas' voice rose alarmingly; he pulled it down with visible effort. "But that has to be changed, now. We can wait no longer. What happened these few days past. The sun darkening. The ground trembling. The gods have turned their faces from Nemedia. That was a sign, a warning that we must remove Garian before they remove him, and with him all of Belverus."

Conan's own god, Crom, Dark Lord of the Mound, gave a man life and will and nothing more. Conan had seen little evidence that other gods did any more. As for the darkened sky and the trembling ground, it was his opinion that someone in Belverus worked at sorcery, despite Garian's prohibitions. He had no love of such, but for once he was not involved, and he intended to remain that way.

All he said was, "You think your plans should be advanced, then? But why speak to me of it?"

"No, you don't understand. Not those plans. Something different. More immediate." The thin man's face had a sheen now, from the sweat that covered it, and his voice shook, though he kept it low. "We are to be introduced into the palace, you see. With knives. Garian must die. Immediately. But I cannot. I am not that sort of man. You are a man of violence. Take my place."

"I'm no assassin," Conan growled.

Leucas yelped, eyes darting frantically. "Keep your voice down," he almost sobbed. "You don't understand. You have to—"

"I understand what you ask," Conan said coldly. "Ask again and I'll give you my fist in your teeth." A sudden thought struck him. "Does Ariane know of this?"

"You must not tell her. You must not tell anyone. I should never have spoken to you." Abruptly Leucas stumbled to his feet. Backing away from the table, he made vague and futile gestures. "Consider it, Conan. Will you do that? Just consider it."

The Cimmerian made as if to rise, and with a yelp the philosopher scrambled away, almost diving into the street.

Conan's mouth twisted angrily. How dare the man consider him so, an assassin, a murderer? He had killed, surely, and likely would again, but because he had to, not because he had been paid to. But more important than his feelings was Ariane. Conan could see no way for a man like Leucas, smelling of fear-sweat, to enter the Royal Palace without being taken. And once given a whiff of hot irons and pincers, the philosopher would babble every name he knew back to his mother. The Cimmerian could escape if worse came to worst, but Ariane would be a fawn in a snare. Would Hordo appear, he decided, they would find Ariane, and he would warn her about Leucas.

Thinking of Hordo reminded him of his wine. Where could that serving girl be? Nowhere in sight, that was certain. In the entire tavern no one was moving except the dancers and the three Kothians, apparently ambling closer for a better inspection of the wares.

Conan started to rise to go in search of the girl, and as he did one of the Kothians suddenly shouted at him, "I told you she is my woman, barbar!"

With practiced moves the three crossed their wrists and drew their forearm daggers. The flutes ceased their play, and the dancers ran screaming as the Kothians plunged at the muscular Cimmerian, a blade in each fist.

One-handed, Conan heaved his table over to crash before them. "Fools," he shouted as he sprang to his feet, "you have the wrong man."

Two of the Kothians danced aside, but one fell, rolling to his knees before Conan, daggers stabbing. Conan sucked in his belly, and the blades skittered off his jazeraint hauberk, one to either side. Before the attacker could move, Conan's knee had smashed into his bony chin, splintering teeth in a spray of blood. Even as the man's blades fell from nerveless hands, and he followed them unconscious to the filthy floor, Conan's own steel was in his grasp, broadsword and belt dagger held low at the ready.

"You have the wrong man," he said again. The remaining two split, gliding in the feline crouch of experienced knife fighters. Noise picked up at the tables as men took wagers on the outcome. "I've never seen you before, nor your woman."

The two men continued to move, flanking the Cimmerian, blades held low for the thrust that would slip under the overlapping metal plates of his hauberk.

"You are he," one said, and when Conan's eyes flickered to him, the other attacked.

The Cimmerian had been expecting it, though. Even as his eyes shifted, so had his sword slashed. The attacking Kothian screamed, a fountain of blood where his right hand had been. Desperately clutching the stump of his wrist, the man staggered back, sinking to the floor with the front of his tunic staining deeper red with every spurt.

Conan spun back to face the third man, but that one was of no mind to continue the business. Dismay writ large on his dark face, he stared at his two fellows on the floor, one senseless and one bleeding to death.

The big Cimmerian pointed at him with his sword. "Now. You will tell me—"

Suddenly the door of the tavern was filled with City Guardsmen, a dozen of them, crowding through with swords in hand. The first one pointed at Conan. "There he is!" he shouted. In a mass the Guardsmen surged forward, plowing through onlookers and toppling tables in their haste.

"Crom!" Conan muttered. They looked to have no mind for asking who had begun the fighting, or why. Springing onto the narrow stage, he dashed for the door the dancers had used. It was latched.

"Take him!" a Guardsman howled. "Cut him down!" Bursting through the tavern's patrons—most of whom would gladly have gotten out of the way had they been given a chance—the Guardsmen rushed for the stage.

Conan took a quick step back and hurled himself against the rough wooden door, smashing through in a shower of splinters. Dancers, shrieking now again, huddled in the narrow passage, at the end of which he saw a doorway letting onto the outside. Hurriedly he forced his way through the scantily clad dancers. At the doorway he paused, then turned, waving his sword overhead, and roared, making the most horrible face he could. Screaming with renewed energy, the dancers stampeded back onto the stage. Shouts of consternation rose as the Guardsmen found themselves caught in a deluge of hysterical female flesh.

That should hold them, Conan thought. Sheathing his steel he hurried out into an alley behind the tavern. Little wider than his shoulders and twisting like a snake, it smelled of old vomit and human excrement. He chose a direction and started off through the buzzing flies.

Before he reached the first turning, a shout rose behind him. "There he goes!"

A glance over his shoulder confirmed that the Guardsmen were pouring into the alley. The gods must have tainted his luck, he thought, to send him the only Guardsmen in Belverus with a mind for duty. Perhaps they did not like women. Shouting and slipping in the filth, the black-cloaked squad rushed after him.

Conan set out at a run, keeping his balance as best he could, half falling against the walls at every twisting of the alley, his massive shoulders knocking more stucco from the flaking, mildewed buildings. Another alley serpentined across the one he followed; he dodged down it. Still another passage appeared, winding cramped between dark walls, and he turned into that. Behind the curses of his pursuit followed.

As he ran he realized that he was in a warren, a maze of ancient passages in an area surrounded by more normal roadways. The buildings seemed ready to topple and fill those passages with rubble, for though they had begun long years past with but single stories, as years and needs demanded more room that could not be got by building outward, extra rooms had been constructed atop the roofs, and more atop those, till they resembled nothing so much as haphazard stacks of stuccoed and gray-tiled boxes.

In such a region, running like a fox before hounds, it would be a matter of luck if he found his way to the outside before his pursuers seized

him. And it seemed his luck was sour that day.
But there was another option, for one who had
been born among the icy crags and cliffs of Cimmeria.

With a mighty leap he caught the edge of a
roof, and swung himself up to lie flat on the
slate tiles. The curses and shouts of the Guardsmen came closer, were below him, were moving
off.

"He's up there!" a man shouted below. "I see
his foot!"

"Erlik's Bowels and Bladder!" Conan muttered. His luck was not sour. Verily it had
rotted.

As the Guardsmen struggled to climb, the
Cimmerian darted across the slates, hoisted
himself onto a higher level, scrambled over it
and leaped to a lower roof. With a great crack
the tiles gave way beneath his feet, and he
plummeted into the room below.

Dazed, Conan struggled to his feet in a welter
of broken slate. He was not alone, he realized. In
the shadows against the far wall, face obscured,
a large man in an expensive cloak of plain blue
uttered a startled oath in the accents of the
gutter. Another man, short beard circling a face
pocked with the marks of some disease, stared
in disbelief at Conan.

It was the third man, though, a gray cloak
pulled over his scarlet tunic, who drew the eye.
Hawk-faced and obsidian-eyed, his dark hair
slashed at the temples with white, he looked
born to command. And now he issued one. "Kill
him," he said.

Crom, Conan thought, reaching for his sword.

Did everyone in Belverus want him dead? The pock-faced man put hand to sword hilt.

"Down there!" came a shout from above. No muscle moved in the room save a twitching of the pock-faced man's cheek. "That hole in the roof! A silver piece to the man who first draws blood!"

Visage dark as death, the hawk-faced man raised a clawed hand, as if he could strike Conan across the breadth of the room. There were thuds above as men dropped to the roof. "No time," the hawk-faced one snarled.

Turning, he stalked from the room. The other two vanished behind him.

Conan had no mind either to greet the Guardsmen or to follow on the heels of those three. His eye lit on a tattered cloth, hung against the wall like a tapestry. As if it hid something. He jerked it aside to reveal a door. That let onto another room, full of dust and empty of else, but from there another door opened into a hall. As Conan closed that one softly behind him, he heard the thumps of men dropping through the hole in the roof.

For a wonder, after the maze of the alleys, the corridor ran straight to a street, and for its length the Cimmerian saw no one save one aging blowze who cracked a door and gave him a gaptoothed smile of invitation. Shuddering at the thought, he hurried on.

When he got back to the Thestis, the first person he saw was Hordo, scowling into a mug of wine. He dropped onto a stool across from him.

"Hordo, did you send a message telling me to

meet you at the Sign of the Full Moon?"

"What? No." Hordo shook his head without looking up from his mug. "Answer me this, Cimmerian. Do you understand any part of women? I walked in, told Kerin she had the prettiest eyes in Belverus, and she slapped my face and said she supposed I thought her breasts weren't big enough." He sighed mournfully. "And she won't say another word to me."

"Mayhap I can illumine your problem," Conan said, and in a low voice he told of the message purporting to come from the one-eyed man, and what had occurred at the Full Moon.

Hordo caught the import at once. "Then 'tis you they're after. Whoever 'they' are. Did the knifemen not take you, the Guardsmen were meant to."

"Aye," Conan said. "When the Guardsmen followed so doggedly, I knew their palms had been crossed with gold. But I still know not who did the crossing."

Hordo drew a line through a puddle of spilled wine with a spatulate finger. "Have you thought of leaving Belverus, Conan? We could ride south. Trouble brews in Ophir, too, and there's no dearth of hiring for Free-Companies. I tell you, this business of someone you know not seeking your death sits ill with me. I knew you should have heeded that blind soothsayer."

"You knew. . . ." Conan shook his head. "An I ride south, Hordo, I lose the company. Some would not leave the gold to be had here, and I have not the gold to pay the rest until we find service in Ophir. Besides, there are things I must attend to here first."

"Things? Conan, tell me you're not involving us in this . . . this hopeless children's revolt."

"Not exactly."

"Not exactly," Hordo said hollowly. "Tell me what it is you are doing. Exactly."

"Earn a little gold," Conan replied. "Discover who means to have me dead, and deal with them. Oh, and save Ariane from the headsman's axe. You don't want Kerin's pretty head to fall, do you?"

"Perhaps not," the one-eyed man said grudgingly.

Looking around the room until he spotted Kerin, Conan waved for her to come to the table. She hesitated, then came over stiffly.

"Is Ariane here?" he asked her. The first part of saving her head was to let her know about Leucas, so she could stop him.

"She went out," Kerin said. She looked straight at the big Cimmerian as if Hordo did not exist. "She said she had to arrange a meeting for you."

"About that message this forenoon," Hordo said suddenly.

Casually Kerin leaned over and tipped his winemug into his lap. He leaped to his feet, cursing, as she left.

"Beheading's too good for her," he growled. "Since we've both been abandoned, as it seems, let us go to the Street of Regrets. I know a den of vice so iniquitous that whores blush to hear it mentioned."

"Not the Sign of the Full Moon, I trust," Conan laughed.

"Never a bit, Cimmerian." Hordo broke into

song in a voice like a jackass in pain. "Oh, I knew a wench from Alcibies, her nipples were like rubies. Her hair was gold, but her rump was cold, and her...." A sudden, shocked silence had descended on the common room. "You're not singing, Conan."

Laughing, Conan got to his feet, and roaring the truly obscene second verse they marched out to horrified gasps.

re you certain?" Albanus demanded.
Golden lamps suspended on chains from the
arched ceiling of the marble-columned hall cast
shadows on the planes of his face, making him
look the wolf he was fiercer cousin to.

Demetrio bristled sulkily, half at the doubting
tone and half for having been made to wait on
Albanus in the entry hall. "You wanted Sephana
watched," he muttered. "I had her watched. And
I'm certain. Would I have come in the night were
I not?"

"Follow me," Albanus commanded, speaking
as to a servant.

And he no more noticed the young catamite's

127

pale lips and clenched fists than he would have those of a servant. Demetrio followed as commanded; that was all that was important. Albanus had slipped already into his persona of king. After all, it was now but a matter of days. His last essential acquisition had been made that very day.

The dark-eyed lord went directly to the chamber where he so often sported himself with Sularia, but the woman was not there now. He tugged the brocaded bell-pull on the wall in a particular fashion, then went straight to his writing desk.

"When?" he demanded, uncapping the silver inkpot. Taking quill and parchment before him, he scribbled furiously. "How long have I before she acts?"

"I was not privy to her planning," Demetrio answered with asperity. "Is it not enough that she gathers her myrmidons about her this night?"

"Fool!" Albanus grated.

With quick movements the hawk-faced lord sprinkled sand across the wet-inked parchment from a silver cellar, then lit the flames beneath a small bronze wax-pot. A slave entered, his short white tunic embroidered at the hem with Albanus' house-mark. Albanus ignored him, pouring off the sand and folding the parchment, sealing it with a drop of wax and his signet.

"Had all Sephana's conspirators come, Demetrios, when your watcher brought word to you?"

"When the third arrived, he came to me immediately. She would not have three of them together if she did not mean to strike tonight."

Cursing, Albanus handed the parchment to the slave. "Put this in the hands of Commander Vegentius within a quarter of a glass. On pain of your life. Go."

The slave bowed and all but ran from the room.

"If all have not yet come," Albanus said as soon as the slave had gone, "there may yet be time to stop her before she reaches the Palace." He hurried to the lacquered chest, unlocking it with the key that hung about his neck. "And stop her I will."

Demetrio eyed the chest and its contents uneasily. "How? Kill her?"

"You have not the stuff of kings in you," Albanus laughed. "There is a subtle art in shaping punishment to fit the crime and the criminal. Now stand aside and be silent."

The slender young noble needed no second warning. He buried his nose in his pomander—was it not said that all sorceries had great stenches associated with them?—and wished most fervently that he were elsewhere at that moment.

Carelessly sweeping a priceless bowl of Ghirgiz crystal from a table to shatter on the floor, Albanus laid in its place a round silver tray graven with an intricate pattern that pained the eye which tried to follow it. With hurried movements he pushed back the flowing sleeves of his deep blue tunic, opened a vial and traced a portion of that pattern in scarlet liquid, muttering incantations beneath his breath as he did. The liquid followed the precise lines worked in the silver, a closed rubiate intricacy that did not spread or alter.

A packet containing powdered hair from Sephana's head—her serving maids had been easily bribed to provide the gleanings of her brush—was emptied into a mortar wrought from the skull of a virgin. Certain other ingredients were minutely measured on burnished golden scales and added to the skull, the mixture then ground by a pestle made of an infant's thigh bone.

With this concoction he traced other lines of that scribing on the tray. Powder and liquid each formed a closed figure, yet though no part of one touched the other, some portions of each shape seemed to be within the other. But those portions were not always the same, and the eye that looked on them too long spun with nausea and dizziness.

For a bare moment Albanus paused, anticipating, savoring. There had been the matter of the droughts, but this was the first time that he had struck so at a human being. The power of it seemed to course through his veins, building like the pleasure of taking a woman. Every instant of prolonging made the pleasure greater. But he knew there was no time.

Spreading his arms he began to chant in a long-dead tongue, his voice invoking, commanding. Powder and liquid began to glow, and his words became more insistent.

Demetrio moved back as the arcane syllables pierced his brain, not stopping until he stood against the wall. He understood no single one of them, yet all had meaning in the depths of his soul, and the evil that he cherished there knew itself for a lighted spill beside a dark burning mountain. He would have screamed, but terror had him by the throat; his screams echoed in the sunless caverns of his mind. .

Albanus' voice grew no louder, yet his words seemed to shake the walls. Tapestries stirred as if at an unseen, unfelt wind. The glow from the silver tray grew, brighter, ever brighter, till it sliced through closed eyelids like razors of fire. Then powder and liquid alike were no more, replaced by burning mist that still held the shape of that pattern and seemed more solid that those first substances had been.

A clap sounded in the room, as thunder, and the mist was gone, the graven silver surface clear. The glow lingered a moment longer, behind the eyes, then it, too, faded.

Albanus sighed heavily, and lowered his arms. "Done," he muttered. " 'Tis done." His gaze rose to meet that of Demetrio; the slender young man shivered.

"My Lord Albanus," Demetrio said, long unattempted humility cloying in his throat, yet driven by his fear, "I would say again that I serve you to the best of my abilities, and that I wish no more than to see you take your rightful place on the Dragon Throne."

"You are a good servant?" Albanus said, his mouth curling with cruel amusement.

The young noble's face flushed with anger, but he stammered, "I am."

Albanus' voice was as smooth and as cutting as the surgeon's knife. "Then be silent until I have need for you to serve me again."

Demetrio's face went pale; Albanus noted it, but said nothing. The youth was beginning to learn his proper place in the scheme of things. He had his uses in gathering information. Perhaps, an he learned his place well enough, he could be allowed to live.

Carefully the cruel-eyed lord relocked the lacquered chest. "Come," he said, turning from the chest. "We have little time to meet the others."

He saw the question—what others?—trembling on Demetrio's lips. When it did not come, he allowed himself a smile. Such was the proper attitude toward a king, to accept what was given. How sweet it would be to have all of Nemedia so. And perhaps beyond Nemedia. Why should borders decided by others deter him?

In short order they had donned heavy cloaks against the night and left the palace. Four slaves carried torches, two before and two behind. Ten armed and armored guards, mail and leather creaking, surrounded Albanus as he made his way through the dark streets. That they surrounded Demetrio as well was incidental.

They saw no one, although scurrying feet could often be heard as footpads and others who lurked in the night hurried to be out of the way, and from time to time some glimmer of sound from the Street of Regrets came to them as the wind shifted. Elsewhere, those who could not afford to hire bodyguards slept ill at ease, praying that theirs would not be among the houses ravaged that night.

Then, as they approached Sephana's palace, where fluted marble columns rose behind the alabaster wall enclosing her garden, a procession of torches appeared down the street. Albanus stopped some distance from the palace gate, waiting in silence for a proper greeting.

"Is that you, Albanus?" came Vegentius' growl. "A foul night, and a foul thing to have to slit the throat of one of my own captains."

Albanus' mouth twisted. This one would not live, not an he were a hundred times as useful. He waited to speak until Vegentius and his followers, a score of Golden Leopards, their cloaks thrown back to give sword arms free play, half bearing torches, were close enough to be seen clearly.

"At least you managed to dispose of Baetis. Have you yet found the barbarian?"

"Taras has sent no word," the big soldier said. "'Tis likely, pursued as he was, that he's no more than a common thief or murderer. Naught to concern us."

Albanus favored him with a scornful glance. "Whatever disrupts a meeting like that concerns me. Why did the Guard pursue him so? Long time has passed ere they were known for such enthusiasm."

"This matter differs from that of Melius. I have no pretext to ask questions of the Guard."

"Make one," Albanus commanded. "And now force me this gate."

Vegentius spoke quietly to his men. Six of them moved quickly to the wall, dividing into two groups. In each trio two men linked hands to lift the third, who laid his cloak across the jagged shards of pottery set in the top of the wall and scrambled over to drop on the far side. From thence a startled cry was heard, then cut significantly short. With a rattle of stout bars being lifted, the gates swung open.

Albanus marched in, sparing not a glance for the guard who lay in the light spilling from the small gatehouse, surrounded by a spreading pool of blood.

Vegentius told off two more men to remain at the gate. The rest followed the hawk-faced lord through the landscape gardens to the palace itself, with its pale columns and intricately worked cornices, and up broad marble stairs to a spacious portico. Some ran to throw back the tall bronze-hung doors with a crash.

In the columned entry hall, half a dozen men started, and stared as soldiers rushed in to surround them with bared blades.

"Dispose of them," Albanus ordered without slowing. He went straight to the alabaster stairs, Demetrio trailing after.

Behind him men began shouting for mercy as they were herded away.

"No!" a skinny, big-nosed man screamed. "I would not have done it. I—" Vegentius' boot propelled him beyond hearing.

Albanus made his way to Sephana's bedchamber along halls he once had traversed for more carnal purposes. But not, he thought as he opened the door, for more pleasurable ones.

Demetrio followed him diffidently into the room, peering fearfully for the destruction the magick had wrought. There seemed to be none. Sephana lay on her bed, though to be sure she did not move or acknowledge their presence. She was naked, a robe of blue silk clutched in her hand as if she had been on the point of donning it when she decided instead to lie down. Albanus chuckled, a dry sound like the rattle of a poisonous serpent.

The slender youth crept forward. Her eyes were open; they seemed to have life, to see. He touched her arm, and gasped. It was as hard as stone.

"She still lives," Albanus said suddenly. "A living statue. She will not have to worry about losing her beauty with age now."

Demetrio shivered. "Would it not have been simpler to kill her?"

The hawk-faced lord gave him a glance that was all the more frightening for its seeming benevolence. "A king must think of object lessons. Who thinks of betraying me will think next on Sephana's fate and wonder at his own. Death is much more easily faced. Would you betray me now, Demetrio?"

Mouth suddenly too dry for words, the perfumed youth shook his head.

Vegentius entered the room laughing. "You should have heard their crying and begging. As if tears and pleas would stay our steel."

"They are disposed of, then?" Albanus said. "All who were under this roof? Servants and slaves as well?"

The big square-faced man drew a broad finger across his throat with a crude laugh. "In the cesspool. There was one—Leucas, he said his name was, as if it mattered—who wept like a woman and said it was not he, but one named Conan who was to do the deed. Anything to— What ails you, Albanus?"

The hawk-faced lord had gone pale. His eyes locked with those of Demetrio. "Conan. 'Twas the name of he from whom you bought the sword." Demetrio nodded, but Albanus, though looking at him, saw other things. He whispered, uttering his thoughts unaware. "Coincidence? Such is the work of the gods, and when they tangle the skeins of mens' fates so it is for cause. Such cause could be murderous of ambition. I dare not risk it."

"It cannot be the same man," Vegentius protested.

"Two with such a barbarous name?" Albanus
retorted. "I think not. Find him." His obsidian
glare drilled each man in turn, turning them to
stone with its malignancy. "I want this Conan's
head!"

Conan poured another dipperful of water over his head and peered blearily about the courtyard behind the Thestis. The first thing his eye lit on was Ariane, arms crossed and a disapproving glint in her eye.

"If you must go off to strange taverns," she said firmly, "drinking and carousing through the small hours, you must expect your head to hurt."

"My head does not hurt," Conan replied, taking up a piece of rough toweling to scrub his face and hair dry. His face hidden, he winced into the toweling. He hoped fervently that she would not shout; if she did his skull would surely explode.

"I looked for you last night," she went on. "Your meeting with Taras is arranged, though he wished no part of it at first. You have little time now. I'll give you directions."

"You are not coming?"

She shook her head. "He was very angry at our having approached you. He says we know nothing of fighting men, of how to choose good from bad. After I told him about you, though, he changed his mind. At least, he will meet you and decide for himself. But the rest of us are not to come. That is to let us know he's angry."

"Mayhap." Conan tossed aside the toweling and hesitated, choosing his words. "I must speak to you of something. About Leucas. He is putting you in danger."

"Leucas?" she said incredulously. "What danger could he put me in?"

"On yesterday he came to me with some goat-brained talk of killing Garian, of assassination. An he tries that—"

"It's preposterous!" she broke in. "Leucas is the last of us ever to speak for any action, especially violent action. He cares for naught save his philosophy and women."

"Women!" the big Cimmerian laughed. "That skinny worm?"

"Yes, indeed, my muscular friend," she replied archly. "Why, he's accounted quite the lover by those women he's known."

"You among them?" he growled, his massive fists knotting.

For a moment she stared, then her eyes flared with anger. "You do not own me, Cimmerian. You have no leave to question me of what I did or did not do with Leucas or anyone else."

"What's this of Leucas?" Graecus said, ambling into the courtyard. "Have you seen him? Or heard where he is?"

"No," Ariane snapped, her face coloring. "And what call have you to skulk about like some spy?"

Graecus seemed to hear nothing beyond her denial. "He's not been seen since last night. Nor Stephano, either. When I heard his name mentioned. . . ." He laughed weakly. "Perhaps we could stand to lose a philosopher or three, but if they're taking sculptors this time as well. . . ." He laughed again, but his face was a sickly green.

Ariane was suddenly soothing. "They will return." She laid a concerned hand on the stocky man's shoulder. "Why, like as not they wasted the night in drink. Conan, here, did the same."

"Why should they not return?" Conan asked.

Ariane shot him a dagger look, but Graecus answered shakily. "Some months past some of our friends disappeared. Painters and sketchers, they were. But two were never seen again, their bodies found in a refuse heap beyond the city walls, where Golden Leopards had been seen to bury them. We think Garian wishes to frighten us into silence."

"It sounds not like the way of a king," Conan said, frowning. "They frighten with public executions and the like."

Graecus suddenly looked ready to vomit.

Arian scowled at Conan. "Should you not be making ready to meet Taras?" Without waiting for an answer, she turned to Graecus, uttering soothing sounds and stroking his brow.

Disgruntled, Conan tugged on his padded

under-tunic and jazeraint hauberk, muttering to himself on the peculiarities of Ariane. As he buckled his sword belt about him, she spoke again.

"Do you need to go so, as if armed for war?" Her tone was biting, her annoyance at him still high. "You'll not have to fight him."

"I have my reasons," Conan muttered.

Not for a sack of gold as big as a cask would he have told her that someone in the city was trying to kill him. In her present mood, she would think he was trying to shift her sympathy from Graecus to himself. Erlik take all women, he thought.

Setting his spiked helm on his head, he said coldly, "Give me your directions for finding this Taras." Her face as she gave them was just as cold.

The Street of the Smiths, whence Ariane's directions took him, was lined not only with the shops of swordsmiths and ironworkers, but also of smiths in gold, silver, copper, brass, tin and bronze. A cacophony of hammering blended with the cries of sellers to make the street a solid sheet of noise, reverberating from end to end. The Guilds made sure that a man who worked one metal did not work another, but so too did they hire the guards that patrolled the street. No bravos lurked on the Street of the Smiths, and shoppers strolled with an ease seen nowhere else in the city.

As he came closer to the place of the meeting —rooms reached by entering a narrow hall next to a coppersmith's shop and climbing the stairs at its end—the less he wished to enter it unprepared. He had no reason to foresee trouble, but too many times of late someone had tried to put a blade into him.

Short of the coppersmith's he began to dawdle, pausing here to heft a gleaming sword, there to finger a silver bowl hammered in an intricate pattern of leaves. But all the while he observed the building that housed the coppersmith with an eye honed by years as a thief.

A pair of Guild guards had stopped to watch him, where he stood before a silversmith's open-fronted shop. He raised the bowl he held to his ear and thumped it.

"Too much tin," he said, shaking his head and tossing the bowl back on the merchant's table. He strolled off pursued by the silversmith's frenzied imprecations, but the guards paid him no more mind.

Just beyond the coppersmith's was an alley, smelling as much of mold and old urine as any other in the city. Into this he slipped, hurrying down its narrow length. As he had hoped, damp air and mold had flaked away most of the mud plastered over the stones of the building.

A quick glance showed that no one was looking down the alley from the street. His fingers sought cracks amid the poorly dressed and poorly mortared stone. Another might have found such a climb impossible, most especially in heavy hauberk and boots, but to one of the Cimmerian mountains the wide chinks in the stone were as good as a highway. He scrambled up the side of the building so quickly that someone who had seen him standing on the ground and looked away for a moment might well have thought he had simply disappeared.

As he heaved himself onto the red clay tiles of the roof, a smile lit his face. Set in the roof was a skylight, a frame stretched with panes of fish-skin. It was, he was certain, situated above the room he sought.

Carefully, so as not to dislodge loose tiles—and perhaps send himself hurtling to the street below—he made his way to the skylight. The panes were clear enough to allow some light through, but not for seeing. It was the work of a moment with his belt dagger to make a slit, to which he put his eye.

The room below was narrow, and ill lit even with the skylight and two brass lamps on a table. In it four men stood, two with cocked crossbows in hands, watching the door through which he was supposed to walk.

The big Cimmerian shook his head, in anger and wonder at the same time. It was one thing to be wary of trouble where none was expected, another to find it waiting there.

"Is he coming, or not?" one of the men without a crossbow asked irritably. He had a deep scar across the top of his head, where someone had caught him a blow that should have killed him.

"He'll come," the other man with no crossbow replied. "The girl said she'd send him right to this room."

Conan froze. Ariane. Could she have sent him here to die?

"What will you tell her?" the horribly scarred man asked. "She has influence enough to cause trouble, Taras."

"That I hired him," Taras laughed, "and sent

him out of the city to join the others she thinks I've hired. That should keep her quiet."

Lying on the roof, the big Cimmerian heaved a sigh of relief. Whatever Ariane had done, she had done unknowingly. Then the rest of what Taras had said penetrated. The others she thought he had hired. It was as he had feared. The young rebels were being duped. Conan had a great many questions for Taras. His broad-sword slipped from its sheath, steel rasping on leather.

"Be you sure," Taras told the crossbowmen, "to fire the instant he steps into the room. These barbars die hard."

"Even now is he a dead man," one of the pair replied. The other laughed and patted his cross-bow.

A wolfish grin came to Conan's face. It was time to see who would die in that room. Like silent death he rose, and leaped.

"Crom!" he roared as his feet tore through the skylight.

The men below had only time to start, then Conan's boots struck one of the crossbowmen squarely atop his head, bearing him to the floor with a crunch of snapping vertebrae. The second crossbowman desperately swung his weapon, trying to bring it to bear. Conan kept his balance with cat-like skill, and pivoted, dagger darting over the swinging crossbow to transfix the bow-man's throat. With a gurgling scream he who had named the Cimmerian a dead man himself died, squeezing the trigger-lever as he did. Abruptly the scar-topped man, sword half drawn, coughed once and toppled, the crossbow quarrel projecting from his left eye.

Using the dagger as a handle Conan hurled the sagging body of the bowman at Taras, and as he did he recognized that pock-marked face. Taras had been at that other meeting he had interrupted by coming through the roof.

The pocked man staggered, clawing for his sword, as the corpse struck him. "You!" he gasped, getting his first clear look at the Cimmerian's face.

Snarling, Conan struck, his blade clanging against the hilt of the other's partially drawn sword. Taras shrieked, severed fingers dropping to the floor. And yet he was no man to go down easily. Even while blood flowed from his mutilated right hand, his left snatched his dagger from its sheath. With a cry of rage, he lunged.

It would have been easy for Conan to kill the man then, but he wanted answers more than he wanted Taras' death. Sidestepping Taras' lunge, he clubbed his fisted hilt against the back of the pock-faced man's neck. The lunge became a stumble, and, yelling, Taras fell over the scarred man's body and crashed to the floor. He twitched once, emitting a long sigh, and did not rise.

Cursing, Conan heaved the man onto his back. Taras' limp fingers slid away from his dagger, now embedded in his own chest. His sightless eyes stared at the Cimmerian.

"Erlik take you," Conan muttered. "I wanted you alive."

Wiping his blade on Taras' tunic, he returned the sword to its scabbard, thinking furiously all the while. The man was condemned out of his own mouth of duping the young rebels. Yet he had had that meeting with two who, by their clothing and bearing, were men of wealth and position. He had to assume that that meeting had a related purpose, and that someone did indeed intend to move against Garian, using Ariane and the rest as tools. And tools had a way of being broken and discarded once their use was done.

As Conan tugged his dagger from the crossbowman's throat, the door suddenly swung open. He crouched, dagger at the ready, and found himself staring across the corpse at Ariane and Graecus.

The stocky sculptor seemed to turn to stone as his bulging eyes swept the carnage. Ariane met Conan's gaze with a look of infinite sadness.

"I did not think Taras had the right to exclude us from this meeting," she said slowly. "I thought we should be here, to speak up for you, to. . . ." Her words trailed off in a weary sigh.

"They intended my death, Ariane," Conan said.

She glanced from the shattered skylight frame on the floor to the opening in the roof. "Which of them leapt from above, Conan? It seems clear that one entered that way. To kill. I wondered so when you armored yourself and would not tell me why. Wondered, and prayed I was wrong."

Why did the fool girl have to take everything wrongly, he thought angrily. "I listened at the skylight, Ariane, and entered that way. After I heard them speak of slaying me. Think you they had cocked crossbows to slay rats?" She looked at him, levelly but with eyes lacking hope or life.

He drew a deep breath. "Hear me, Ariane. This man Taras has hired no armed men to aid your rebellion. I heard him say this. You must—"

"You killed them!" Graecus suddenly shouted. The stocky man's face was flushed, and he panted as if from great exertion. "It is as Stephano feared. Did you kill him also, and Leucas? Mean you to slay us all? You will not! You cannot! There are hundreds of us! We will slay you first!" Suddenly he glanced down the hall toward the stairs, and with a shrill cry dashed in the other direction. Ariane did not move.

Hordo appeared in the doorway, gazing briefly after the fleeing sculptor. His lone eye took in the bodies. "I returned to the Thestis in time to hear the girl and the other speak of following you. It looks well that I decided to follow them in turn."

Ariane stirred. "Will you murder me now, too, Conan?"

The Cimmerian rounded on her angrily. "Do you not know me well enough by now to know I would not harm you?"

"I thought I did," she said hollowly. Her eyes traveled from one corpse to the next, and she laughed hysterically. "I know nothing of you. Nothing!" Conan reached for her, but she shied away from his big hand. "I cannot fight you," she whispered, "but an you touch me, my dagger can yet seek my own heart."

He jerked back his hand as if it had been burnt. At last he said coldly, "Do not remain here o'erlong. Corpses attract scavengers, and those with two legs will see you as more booty." She did not look at him or make answer.

"Come, Hordo," he growled. The one-eyed man followed him from the room.

In the street, those who saw Conan's dark face and the ice of his blue eyes stepped clear of his sweeping strides. Hordo hurried to keep up, asking once they were clear of the clangor of the Street of the Smiths, "What occurred in that room, Cimmerian, to turn the girl so against you?"

Conan's look at Hordo was deadly, but in swift, terse sentences he told of how he had gone there, of what he had heard and what deduced.

"I am too old for this," Hordo groaned. "Not only must we watch for Graecus and the others to put knives in our backs, but, not knowing who among the nobles and merchants is embraced in this, with whom can we take service? Where do we go now, Cimmerian?"

"To the only place left for us," Conan replied grimly. "The King."

n the wide marble steps of the Temple of Mitra, a startled man dropped a cage of doves as the Free-Company made its way down the narrow, winding street. So surprised was he to see mounted and armed men in the Temple District that he watched them open-mouthed, not even noticing that his cage had broken and his intended sacrifices were beating aloft on white wings.

Hordo's saddle creaked as he leaned forward and whispered fiercely to Conan. "This is madness! 'Twill be luck if we are not met atop the hill by the whole of the Golden Leopards!"

Conan shook his head without answering.

He knew full well that approaching the Royal Palace unannounced with two score armed men was far from the proper way to appeal for entry into the King's service. He knew, too, that there was no time for more usual methods, such as bribery, and that left only enlistment in the Nemedian army. Or this.

In truth, it was not the Golden Leopards who troubled him so much as the young rebels. Desperate, believing he had betrayed them or was on the way to do so, they might try almost anything. And these winding streets that climbed the hill to the Royal Palace were a prime place for ambush.

Those streets were a remnant of ancient times, for once in the dim past what would become the Royal Palace had been a hilltop fortress, about which a village had risen, a village which over the centuries had grown into Belverus. But long after the hilltop fortress had become the Royal Palace of Nemedia, long after the rude village huts had been replaced by columned temples of alabaster and marble and polished granite, the serpentine streets remained.

The Palace itself retained much of the fortress about it, although its battlements were now of lustrous white marble, and towers of porphyry and greenstone rose within. The portcullises were of iron beneath their gilt, and drawbridges spanned a drymoat bottomed with spikes. Round about it all a sward of grass, close cropped as if in a landscaped garden, yet holding not the smallest growth that might shelter a stealthy approach, separated the Palace from the Temple District that encircled the hill below.

At the edge of the greensward Conan halted the company. "Wait here," he commanded.

"Gladly," Hordo muttered.

Alone, Conan rode forward, his big black stallion prancing slightly. Two pikemen in golden cloaks guarded the drawbridge, and a man in the crested helmet of an officer stepped out from the barbican as the big Cimmerian drew rein.

"What seek you here?" the officer demanded. He eyed the rest of the Free-Company thoughtfully, but they were distant and few in number.

"I wish to enter my company in the service of King Garian," Conan replied. "I have trained them in a method of fighting new to Nemedia, and to the western world."

The officer smiled in mockery. "Never yet have I heard of a Free-Company without some supposedly secret art of war. What is yours?"

"I will demonstrate," Conan said. "It is better in the showing." Inwardly, he breathed a sigh of relief. His one real fear beyond reaching the Palace had been that they would not so much as listen.

"Very well," the officer said slowly, eyeing the rest of the company once more. "You alone may enter and demonstrate. But be you warned, an this secret is something every recruit in the Nemedian army is taught, as are most Free-Company tricks, you will be stripped and flogged from the gates to the foot of the hill for the edification of your company."

Conan touched boots to the big stallion's flanks. The horse pranced forward a step; the pikemen leveled their weapons, and the officer looked wary. The Cimmerian allowed a cold smile to touch his mouth, but not his eyes. "'Tis nothing known to any Nemedian, though it may be taught to recruits."

The officer's mouth tightened at his tone. "I think others might like to see this, barbar." He stuck his head back into the gatehouse and muttered an order.

A golden-cloaked soldier emerged, gave Conan an appraising glance, and sped into the Palace. As Conan rode through the gate following the officer, other soldiers appeared from the barbican, some following behind. The Cimmerian wondered if they came to watch, or to guard that he did not take the Palace single-handed.

The Outer Court was paved in flagstone, four hundred paces in each direction, and surrounded by arcaded walks to the height of four stories. Beyond those walks directly opposite the gate could be seen the towers that rose in the gardens of the Inner Court, and the Palace proper, wherein King Garian and his court lived.

The soldiers who had followed dropped back deferentially as a score of officers, led by one as large as Conan himself, appeared. The officer who had brought Conan in bowed as this big man came near.

"All honor to you, Commander Vegentius," he said. "I hoped this barbar might provide some entertainment."

"Yes, Tegha," Vegentius said absently, his eye on Conan. And a strangely wary eye, the Cimmerian thought. Abruptly the big officer said, "You, barbar. Know I you, or you me?" His hand tightened on his sword as he spoke.

Conan shook his head. "I know you not, Commander." Though, as he thought on it, this Vegentius did look familiar, but vaguely, as one seen but briefly. No matter, he thought. The memory would come, an it were important.

Vegentius seemed to relax as the Cimmerian spoke. Smiling vigorously, he said, "Let us have this demonstration. Tegha, get the barbar what he needs for it."

"I need a straw butt," Conan told the officer, "or some other mark."

Laughter rose among the officers as Tegha chose out two soldiers to fetch a butt.

"Archery," one of them laughed loudly. "I saw that bow at his saddle, but thought it for a child."

"Mayhap he shoots it with one hand," another replied.

Conan kept his silence as the comments grew more ribald, though his jaw tightened. Removing the short weapon from its lacquered saddle-case, he carefully checked the tension of the string.

"A harp," someone shouted. "He plays it like a harp."

Conan fingered through the forty arrows in the quiver strapped behind the cantle of his saddle, making sure once again that each fletching was sound.

"He must miss often, to carry so many shafts."

"Nay, he uses the feathers to tickle women. Take her ankle, you see, and turn her. . . ."

The laughing comments droned on, some measure of silence falling only when the soldiers returned with a straw butt.

"Set it there," Conan commanded, pointing to a spot some fifty paces away. The soldiers ran to comply, as eager as their superiors to see the barbarian's discomfiture.

"Not a great distance, barbar."

"But it's a child's bow."

Breathing deeply to calm himself, Conan rode away from the bunched officers, stopping when he was a full two hundred paces from the butt. Nocking a shaft, he paused. This demonstration must proceed perfectly, and for that his concentration must be on the target, not clouded by anger at the chattering baboons who called themselves officers.

"Why wait you, barbar?" Vegentius shouted. "Dismount and—"

With a wild cry Conan swung the bow up and fired. Even as the shaft thudded home in the butt he was putting boot to the stallion's flanks, galloping forward at full speed, sparks striking from the flagstones beneath the big black's drumming hooves, firing as quickly as he could nock arrow to bowstring, shouting the ululating warcry that oft had wrung fear from the warriors of Gunderland and Hyperborea and the Bossonian Marches.

Arrow after arrow sped straight to the butt. At a hundred paces distant he pressed with his knee, and the massive stallion broke faultlessly to the right. Conan fired again and again, mind and eye one with bow, with shaft, with target. Again his knees pressed, and the war-trained stallion pivoted, rearing and reversing his direction within his own length. Still Conan fired, thundering back the way he had come. When at last he put hand to rein there were four arrows left in the quiver behind his saddle, and he knew, did anyone count the feathered shafts that peppered the butt, they would number thirty and six.

He cantered back to the now silent officers.

"What sorcery is this?" Vegetius demanded. "Have your arrows been magicked, that they strike home while you careen like a madman?"

"No sorcery," Conan replied, laughing. For it was, indeed, his turn to laugh at the stunned expressions worn by the officers. " 'Tis accounted a skill, though not a vast one, if a man can hit a running deer with a bow. This is but a step beyond. I myself had no knowledge at all of the bow when I was taught."

"Taught!" Tegha exclaimed, not noticing the glare Vegentius gave him. "Who? Where?"

"Far to the east," Conan said. "There the bow is the principal weapon of light cavalry. In Turan—"

"Whatever they do in these strange lands," Vegentius broke in harshly, " 'tis of no matter here. We have no need of outlandish ways. A phalanx of good Nemedian infantry will clear any field, without this frippery of bowmen on horses."

Conan considered telling him what a few thousand mounted Turanian archers would do to that phalanx, but before he could speak another group approached, and the officers were all bowing low.

Leading this procession was a tall, square-faced man, the crown on his head, a golden dragon with ruby eyes and a great pearl clutched in its paws proclaiming him to be King Garian. Yet Conan had no eyes for the king, nor the counselors who surrounded him, nor the courtiers who trailed him, for there was among them a woman to seize the eye. A long-legged, full-breasted blonde, she was no gently born lady, not wearing transparent red silk held by pearl clasps at her shoulders and snugged about her slender waist by entwined ropes of pearls set in gold. But an she were someone's leman, he paid her not the attention he ought. For she returned Conan's stare, if not so openly as he, yet with a smoky heat that quickened his blood.

Conan saw that Garian was approaching him, and doffed his helm hoping the King had not seen the direction of his gaze.

"I saw your exhibition from the gallery," Garian said warmly, "and I have never seen the like." His brown eyes were friendly—which meant he had not noticed Conan's gaze—though not so open as the eyes of one who did not sit on a throne. "How are you called?"

"I am Conan," the Cimmerian replied. "Conan of Cimmeria." He did not see the blood drain from Vegentius' face.

"Do you come merely to entertain, Conan?"

"I come to enter your service," Conan said, "with my lieutenant and two score men trained to use the bow as I do."

"Most excellent," Garian said, clapping a hand against the stallion's shoulder. "Always have I had an interest in innovations of warfare. Why, from my childhood I as much as lived in the army camps. Now," a trace of bitterness crept into his voice, "I have not even time to practice with my sword."

"My King," Vegentius said deferentially, "this thing is no better than trickery, an entertainment, but of no use in war." As he spoke his eyes drifted to Conan. The Cimmerian thought, but could not believe, it was a look of hatred and fear.

"No, good Vegentius," Garian said, shaking his head. "Your advice is often sound on matters military, but this time you are wrong." Vegentius opened his mouth; Garian ignored him. "Hear me now, Conan of Cimmeria. An you enter my service, I will give each man of yours three gold marks, and three more each tenday. To yourself, ten gold marks, and another each day you serve me."

"It is meet," Conan said levelly. No merchant would have paid more than half so well.

Garian nodded. "It is done, then. But you must practice the sword with me for a full glass each day, for I see by the wear of your hilt that you have some knowledge of that weapon aş well. Vegentius, see that Conan has quarters within the Palace, and let them be spacious."

In the way of kings, having issued his commands Garian strode away without further words, soldiers bowing as he left, courtiers and counselors trailing in his wake. The blonde went, too, but as she went her eyes played on Conan's face with furnace heat.

From the corner of his eye Conan saw Vegentius moving away. "Commander Vegentius," he called, "did not the King say my company was to be quartered?"

Vegentius almost snarled his reply. "The King said you were to receive quarters, barbar. He said naught of that rag-tag you call a company. Let them quarter in the gutter." And he, too, stalked away.

Some of Conan's euphoria left him. He could not run whining to Garian, asking that Vegentius be made to quarter his men. There were inns aplenty at the foot of the hill, but in even the cheapest of them, he would have to supplement the men's pay from his own purse. That would strain even his new-found resources. Yet it was not the worst of his worries. Why did Vegentius hate him? He must discover the answer before he was forced to kill the man. And he would have to keep the blonde from getting him beheaded. While enjoying her favors, if possible. But then, when had one born on a battlefield sought a life free of troubles?

Laughing, he rode to the gate to tell the others of their fortune.

he high domed ceiling of plain gray
stone was well lit by cressets brass-hung about
the bare walls, in which there was no window
and but a single door, and that well guarded on
the outside. Albanus would allow no slightest
risk to that which the room housed. Even but
gazing on it, he felt the power that would come
to him from it. Centered in the room was a circular stone platform, no higher than a step from
the floor, and on it sat a large rectangular block
of peculiarly beige clay. It was that clay that
would give Albanus the Dragon Throne.

"Lord Albanus, I demand again to know why I
am brought here and imprisoned."

Albanus schooled his face to a smile before turning to the scowling, bushy-browed man who confronted him with fists clenched. "A misapprehension on the part of my guards, good Stephano. I but told them to fetch to me the great sculptor Stephano, and they overstepped themselves. I will have them flogged, I assure you."

Stephano waved that last away as unimportant, though Albanus noted he did not ask for the guards to be spared their promised flogging.

"You have heard of me?" the sculptor asked instead, his chest puffing.

"Of course," Albanus replied, hard put not to laugh. This man was read as easily as a page of large script. "'Tis why I want you to sculpt this statue for me. As you can see, your implements are all provided." He gestured a low table that held every sort of sculptor's tool.

"'Tis all wrong," Stephano said with overbearing condescension. "Clay is used for small figures. Statues are of stone or bronze."

Albanus' lips retained their smile, but his eyes were frozen coals. "The clay is brought all the way from Khitai." He could think of no more distant land to serve as a source. "When fired, it has the hardness of bronze, yet is lighter than the damp clay. On the table are sketches of he whom the statue is to portray. Examine them."

Looking doubtfully at the block of clay, Stephano took up the parchments, unrolled them, and gasped, "Why, this is Garian!"

"Our gracious king," Albanus agreed unctuously, though he near choked on the words. "'Tis to be a present for him. A surprise."

"But how is the work to be clothed?" the

sculptor asked, ruffling through the drawings.
"In all of these is he naked."

"And so is the sculpture to be." Albanus fore-
stalled the surprise on Stephano's face by adding, "Such is the custom of Khitai with statues
of this clay. They are clothed in actual garments,
this raiment being changed from time to time so
that the figure is clothed always in the latest
fashion." He was pleased with himself for that
invention. He wondered if it might not be
amusing to have a statue done so of himself once
he ascended the throne.

Stephano laughed suddenly, a harsh sound
like the scraping of slates. "And what would be
done with a naked statue of Garian, were Garian
no longer on the throne?"

"An unlikely event," Albanus said blandly.

Stephano looked startled, as if not realizing
he had spoken aloud. "Of course. Of course."
His face hardened, thick brows drawing down.
"Yet why should I accept the offer of this commission, following as it does a night spent
locked in your cellars?"

"A grievous error for which I have apologized.
Shall we say a thousand gold marks?"

"I have no interest in gold," the sculptor
sneered.

"To be distributed to the poor," Albanus continued smoothly. "I have heard much of the
good charities you do in Hellgate." Stephano's
face did not soften, but the hawk-faced lord saw
the way. His voice became a mesmeric whisper.
"Think of all the good that you could do with a
thousand pieces of gold. Think of your fellows
following you as you distribute it. I would

wager none of them has ever had the hundredth part so much to give." Stephano nodded slowly, staring at the wall as if he saw a scene there. "How they would laud you, following in your steps with their praises. How great you would be in their eyes." Albanus fell silent, waiting.

Stephano seemed to stand straighter. Abruptly he shook himself and gave an embarrassed laugh. "Of a certainty, great good could come from so much gold. I was lost in thought of those I could help."

"Of course." The cruel-faced lord smiled, then his voice became brisker. "This must be a surprise to Garian. To that end, none may know that you are here. Food and drink will be brought to you. And women, should you desire. Daily will you have leave of the gardens, an you remember your caution. Now get you to your labor, for time presses."

When Albanus had left that room, he stood, trembling, between the guards who stood with bared swords to either side of the door. His stomach roiled with nausea. That he should have to treat one such as Stephano as near an equal! It was ill to be borne. Yet such could not be driven to their work by threat or even torture, as he had discovered to his regret, for the works they then produced were fatally flawed.

A deferential touch on the sleeve of his tunic brought him erect, teeth bared in a snarl.

The slave who had touched him cowered back, his head bent low. "Forgive me, master, but Commander Vegentius awaits, much exercised, and bids me beg your presence."

Albanus thrust the man aside and strode

down the hall. He had every detail planned. Had the soldier contrived to foul some part of the scheme, he would geld him with his own hand.

Vegentius was in the columned entry hall, pacing, his face beaded with sweat. He began to speak as soon as Albanus appeared.

"Conan. The barbar who fought Melius and took his sword after. He whom Leucas named part of Sephana's plot. Now one of that name has caught Garian's eye, and taken service with him. And I recognize him; it is he who broke into our meeting with Taras. Four times has he tangled himself in our planning, Albanus, and I like it not. I like it not. 'Tis an ill omen."

"Do the gods join in my affairs?" Albanus whispered, not realizing that he spoke. "Do they think to contend with me?" Louder, he said, "Speak not of ill omens. This very morning a soothsayer told me that I would wear the Dragon Crown at my death. I had him slain, of course, to still his tongue. With such a prophecy of success, what omen can one barbarian be?"

The square-faced soldier bared a handspan of his blade. "Easily could I slay him. He is alone in the Palace, with none to guard his back."

"Fool!" Albanus grated. "A murder within the Palace, and Garian will think strongly to his safety. We do not need him on his guard."

Vegentius sneered. "His safety lies in my hand. One in three of the Golden Leopards answers to me, not to the Dragon Throne."

"And two in three do not. Nor does any part of my plan call for blades to be drawn within the walls of the Palace. I must be seen to save Nemedia from armed rabble rising in the streets."

"Then he is to live?" Vegentius blurted incredulously.

"Nay, he dies." Could this Conan be some weapon of the gods, lifted against him? No. He was destined to wear the Dragon Crown. He was born to be a king, and, with the power of the blue sphere, a living god. "Taras has been so commanded," he continued. "But make it known to him that the man must die well away from the Palace, in some place where his death may be placed to a drunken brawl."

"Taras seems to have vanished, Albanus."

"Then find him!" the cruel-eyed lord snapped irritably. "And remember, within the Palace walls let this barbarian be watched but inviolate. When he ventures out, slay him!"

teel rang in the small courtyard as Conan blocked the descending blade and smoothly moved back to a guard position. Sweat oiled his massive chest, but his breathing was controlled, his eye firm, his blade steady.

Garian circled to his left about the big Cimmerian. He also was stripped to the waist, and but slightly smaller, though his muscles were covered by the fat of recent inactivity. Sweat rolled down his sloping shoulders, and his blade wavered, if but a hair's breadth.

"You are good, barbar," the king panted.

Conan said nothing, moving only enough to keep his face to the other man. Fighting, even in practice, was not the time to talk.

"But you say little," the king continued, and as he spoke his sword darted for the Cimmerian's middle.

Conan barely moved. His mighty wrists pivoted, his blade arced down to clash against the king's, carrying it safely to one side. Instead of forcing taking the other's blade further out of line, as was the favored tactic, Conan dropped suddenly, squatting on his right leg with his left extended to the side. His steel slid off the other blade, swung forward and stopped as it touched Garian's stomach. Before the startled king could react, Conan flowed back to his feet and to guard.

A disgusted expression on his face, Garian stepped back. "'Tis enough for today," he said grimly, and strode away.

Conan picked up his tunic and began to wipe the sweat from his chest.

When Garian had disappeared through the arched courtyard gate, Hordo stepped out from the shadows beneath a balcony, shaking his shaggy head. "'Tis well he knew not that I was here, Cimmerian, else we both might find ourselves in the dungeons beneath these stones. But then, kings dislike being bested, even when there are no others to see."

"Did I accept defeat in practice, then soon defeat would find me when it was not practice."

"But still, man, could you not hold back a little? He is a king, after all. No need for us to be dismissed before we get as much of his gold as we can."

"I know no other way to fight, Hordo, save to win. How fare the men?"

"Well," Hordo replied, seating himself on a

coping stone. "'Tis an easy life, drinking and wenching away their gold."

Conan pulled his tunic over his head and scabbarded his sword. "Have you seen any sign that Ariane and the others are ready to call their people into the streets?"

"Not a whisper," the one-eyed man sighed. "Conan, I do not say betray them—Kerin's shade would haunt me, an I did—but could we not at least say to Garian that we have heard talk of uprising? He'd give us much gold for such a warning, and there'd be no rising were he on his guard. I like not to think of Kerin and Ariane dying in the gutters, but so they will an they rise. I . . . I could not ride against them, Cimmerian."

"Nor I, Hordo. But rise they will, if Garian is on his guard or no, or I misread the fire in Ariane. To stop them we must find who uses them. That man who met with Taras could tell me much."

"I've given orders, as you said, to watch for a hawk-face man with white at his temples, but 'twill be a gift of the gods an we find him so."

Conan shook his head disgustedly. "I know. But we can do only what we can. Come. Let us to my chamber. I've good wine there."

Palaces far more opulent stood in Turan and Vendhya, but this one was no mean place. Many were the courtyards and gardens, some small, holding perhaps a marble fountain in the form of some fanciful beast, others large, in which rose alabaster towers with gilded corbeled arches and golden cupolas. Great obelisks rose to the sky, their sides covered with hieroglyphs and telling the legends of Nemedian kings for a thousand years and more.

While walking down a cool arcade beside a garden where peacocks cried and golden-feathered pheasants strutted, Conan suddenly stopped. Ahead, a woman swathed in gray veils had come out of a door and, seemingly not noticing them, was walking the other way. The Cimmerian was certain it was the woman he had twice seen in her litter. Now, he decided, was a good time to discover why she had looked at him with such hatred. But as he started forward, Hordo grabbed his arm, pulling him aside behind a column.

"I want to speak to that woman," Conan said. He spoke softly, for voices carried in those arcades. "She does not like me, of that I'm sure. And I have seen her before, without those veils. But where?"

"I, too, have seen her," Hordo replied in a hoarse whisper, "though not without the veils. She is called Lady Tiana, and 'tis said her face is scarred by some disease. She will not allow it to be seen."

"I'll not ask to see her face," Conan said impatiently.

"Listen to me," the one-eyed man pleaded. "Once I followed Eranius when he left us to get his orders. Always, I knew, he went to the Street of Regrets, each time to a different tavern. This time he left the city entire, and in a grove beyond the wall met this Lady Tiana."

"Then she is part of the smuggling," Conan said. "That may provide a lever, if she proves difficult about answering my questions."

"You do not understand, Cimmerian. I was not close enough to hear what was said, yet did I see Eranius all but grovel before her. He would not do so unless she were high, very high, in the ring. Bother her, and you may find ten score smugglers in this city, hard men all, seeking your head."

"Mayhap they do already." Assuredly someone did; why not a woman who seemed to hate him, for whatever reason? He shrugged off Hordo's hand. "She will be gone if I do not go now."

But Conan paused, for as the Lady Tiana reached the end of the arcade, the blonde who had accompanied Garian appeared before her. Sularia, he had learned her name was, and she was indeed Garian's mistress. The veiled woman moved to go past, but Sularia, in golden breastplates and a golden silk skirt no wider than a man's hand front or rear, sidestepped in front of her.

"All honor to you, Lady Tiana," Sularia said, a malicious smile playing over her sensual lips. "But why are you covered so on such a bright day? I know you would be lovely, could we but persuade you into bangles and silks."

The veiled woman's hand flashed out, cracking across Sularia's face in a backhand blow that sent the blonde crumpling to the ground. Conan was stunned at the blow; it had taken no common woman's strength.

Sularia stumbled to her feet, rage twisting her face into a mask. "How dare you strike me?" she spat. "I—"

"To your kennel, bitch!" a third woman snapped, appearing beside the other two. Tall and willowy, she was as beautiful as Sularia, but with silken black hair and imperious dark eyes in a haughty face. Her blue velvet robe, sewn with tiny pearls, made the blonde look a tavern girl.

"Speak not so to me, Lady Jelanna," Sularia answered angrily. "I am no servant, and soon. . . ." She stopped suddenly.

Jelanna's mouth curled in a sneer. "You are a slut, and soon enough Garian will decide so for himself. Now, get you gone before I summon a slave to whip you hence."

Sularia trembled from head to foot, her face venomous. With an inarticulate cry of rage, she sped away from the two women, past where Conan and Hordo stood behind the column.

Conan watched her go; when he turned back, Jelanna and Tiana were gone. Scowling, he leaned against the stone.

"In this place I could search a tenday and not find her," he growled. "I should have spoken straight off, instead of letting you draw me away like a frightened boy."

"Mitra, Conan, let us ride from this city." Hordo's single eye fixed the Cimmerian with entreaty. "Forget Lady Tiana. Forget Garian, and his gold. There's gold in Ophir, and when we take blade-fee there, at least we'll know who wants to kill us."

Conan shook his head. "Never have I run away from my enemies, Hordo. 'Tis a bad habit to form. Go you on to the taverns. I go to my chamber to think on how to find this Tiana. I'll find you later, and match you two drinks to one."

As the Cimmerian started away, Hordo called

after him. "Always before you knew who your enemies were!"

But Conan walked on. A wise man did not leave an unknown enemy behind him, but rather sought that enemy out. Better to die than flee, for once flight began how could it end? The enemy would come at last, and victory or death would be decided then at a time and place of the foe's choosing. While there was yet life and will, the enemy must be sought.

Reaching his chamber, Conan put his hand to the door; it shifted at his touch. The latch had been drawn. Warily he drew his blade and stepped aside. With swordpoint he thrust the door open. It swung back to crash against the wall, but there was no other sound, no hint of movement within.

Snarling, the big Cimmerian threw himself through the open door in a long dive, tucking his shoulder under as he hit the floor to roll to his feet, sword at the ready.

Sularia sat up on his bed, crossing her long legs sensuously beneath her and clapping her hands with delight. "Horseman, bowman, swordsman, and now tumbler. What other tricks have you, barbarian?"

Keeping a tight rein on his anger, Conan closed the door. He was no man to enjoy making a fool of himself before a woman, most especially not a beautiful woman. When he turned back to her his eyes were blue glacier ice.

"Why are you here, woman?"

"How magnificent you are," she breathed, "with the sweat of combat still on you. You defeated him, didn't you? Garian could not stand against one such as you."

Hastily he searched the room, flipping aside each tapestry on the wall, putting his head out of the window to make sure no assassin clung to the copings. Even did he look under the bed, before her amused smile made him throw the coverlet back down with an oath.

"What do you look for, Conan? I have no husband to jump out accusing."

"You have a king," he growled. One look at her, golden breastplates barely containing her swelling orbs, narrow strips of golden silk tangled about her thighs, proved she could carry no weapon greater than a pin.

"A king who can talk of nothing but tariffs and grain and things even more boring." A sultry smile caressed her lips, and she let herself fall backwards on the bed, breathing deep. "But you, barbarian, are not boring. I sense power in you, though afar as yet. Will you become a king, I wonder?"

Conan frowned. That sequence of words seemed to touch some deeply buried memory. Power. That he would be a king. He thrust it all from his mind. A fancy for children, no more.

He laid his sword across the bed above Sularia's head. It would be close to hand there, let come who would. The blonde twisted to gaze at the bare blade, wetting her lips as if its closeness excited her. Conan clutched the golden links that joined her breastplates in his fist and tore them from her. Her eyes darted back to him, the icy sapphire of his commanding the smouldering blue of hers.

"You have played a game with me, woman,"

he said softly. "Now 'tis my turn to play."

Neither of them saw the door move ajar, nor the woman in gray veils who stood there a time, watching them with eyes of emerald fire.

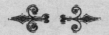

As Conan walked through the Palace the next afternoon, Hordo ran to join him.

" 'Tis well to see you, Cimmerian. I had some niggling fears when I did not meet you in the taverns last night."

"I found something else to do," Conan smiled.

Hurrying slaves thronged the corridors, keeping near the walls to leave the center free for strolling lords and ladies, of which there were some few in richly embroidered velvets and satins, hung about with gold chains and emeralds and rubies on necks and wrists and waists. Nobles gave the warrior pair curious looks, men haughtily disdainful, women thoughtful.

Hordo eyed them all suspiciously, then dropped his voice and leaned closer to Conan as they walked. "Mayhap you took time last night to reconsider what occurred yesterday. Even now Garian's torturers may be heating their irons. Let us to horse and away while we can."

"Cease this foolish prattle," Conan laughed. "Not two glasses ago I exercised at swords with Garian, and he said no ill word to me. In fact, he laughed often, except when his head was thumped."

The one-eyed man's stride faltered. "Cimmerian, you didn't.... Mitra! You do not crack the pate of a king!"

"I cracked no pate, Hordo. Garian's foot slipped on leaves blown by the breeze, and he struck his face with his own hilt in falling. A bruise, no more."

"What men like you and me account a bruise," Hordo said, raising a finger like one of the philosophers at the Thestis, "Kings account a mortal insult to dignity."

"I fear you are right," Conan sighed. "You do grow old."

"I am too," Hordo began, and snapped his mouth shut with a glare as he realized what the big Cimmerian had said.

Conan suppressed the laughter that wanted to escape at the look on the bearded man's face. Hordo might call himself old, but he was very ready to thump anyone else who named him so. Then the Cimmerian's mirth faded.

They had come on a courtyard in which a score of the Golden Leopards stood in a large circle about Vegentius, all including the Commander stripped to the waist. A small knot of nobles stood discreetly within an arcade on the far side, watching. Apart from them, but also among those columns so she should not seem to watch, was Sularia.

Vegentius turned within the circle, arms flexing over his head. "Who will be next?" he called to the men around him. "I've not worked up a sweat as yet." His bare chest was deep, his shoulders broad and covered with thick muscle. "Am I to get no exercise? You, Oaxis."

A man stepped forward, dropping into a crouch. As tall as Vegentius, he was not so heavily muscled, though no stripling. Vegentius laughed, crouching and circling. Oaxis circled with him, but not laughing.

Abruptly they rushed together, grappling, feet shuffling for position and leverage. Conan could see that the slighter man had knowledge, and agility. Even as the Cimmerian thought, Oaxis slipped an arm free, his fist streaking for Vegentius' corded stomach. Perhaps he remembered who it was he struck, for at the last instant the blow slowed, the impact bringing not even a grunt from the grinning Vegentius.

The bigger man was under no such restraints. His free hand axed into the side of Oaxis' neck with a sound like stone striking wood. Oaxis staggered and sagged, but Vegentius held him up yet a moment. Twice his fist rose and fell, clubbing the back of the other's neck. The first time Oaxis jerked, the second he hung limp. Vegentius released him to crumple in a heap on the flagstones.

"Who comes next?" the huge Commander of the Golden Leopards roared. "Is there none among you to give me a struggle?"

Two of the bare-chested soldiers ran out to drag their companion away. None of them seemed anxious to feel Vegentius' power. The big man continued turning, smiling his taunting smile, until he found himself facing Conan. There he stopped, his smile becoming grim.

"You, barbar. Will you try a fall, or has that northern cold frozen all the guts out of you?"

Conan's face tightened. He became aware of Sularia's gaze on him. The arrogance of a prideful man under the eyes of a beautiful woman spurred him. Unfastening his swordbelt, he handed it to Hordo. A murmur rose among the nobles; wagers began to be made.

"You've more courage than sense," the one-eyed man grumbled. "What gain you, an you defeat him, except a powerful enemy?"

"He is my enemy already," Conan replied, and added with a laugh, "One of them, at least."

The Cimmerian pulled his tunic over his head and, dropping it to the ground, approached the circle of men. The nobles measured the breadth of his shoulders, and the odds changed. Vegentius, sure that the barbarian's laughter had held some slur against him, waited with a snarl on his face. The soldiers moved back, widening the circle as Conan entered.

Abruptly Vegentius charged, arms outstretched to crush and destroy. Conan's massive fist slammed into the side of his head, jarring him to a halt. Crouching slightly, the Cimmerian dug his other fist under the big soldier's ribs, driving breath from him. Before Vegentius could recover Conan seized him by throat and belt, heaving him into the air, swinging the bulk of the man over his head to send him crashing to his back.

Awe grew in the eyes of the watching soldiers. Never had they seen Vegentius taken from his feet before. Among the nobles the odds changed again.

Conan waited, breathing easily, well balanced on his feet, while Vegentius staggered up, shock writ clear on his face. Then rage washed shock away.

"Barbar bastard!" the big soldier howled. "I spit on your mother's unmarked grave!" And he swung a blow that would have felled any normal man.

But Conan's face was painted now with rage, too. Eyes like icy, windswept death, too full of fury to allow thought of defense, he took the blow, and it rocked him to his heels. Yet in that same instant his fist splintered teeth in Vegentius' mouth. For long moments the two huge men stood toe to toe, giving and absorbing blows which would have been enough to destroy an ordinary man.

Then Conan took a step forward. And Vegentius took a step back. Desperation came on the soldier's face; on Conan's eyes was the cold glint of destruction. Back the Cimmerian forced the other. Back, fists pounding relentlessly, toward the arcade where an ever-growing crowd of nobles watched, dignity forgotten as they yelled excitedly. Then, with a mighty blow, he sent the brawny man staggering.

Struggling to remain on his feet, Vegentius stumbled back, nobles parting before him until he stopped at last against the wall in the shadows of the arcade. Straining, he pushed himself erect, tottered forward and fell at the edge of the arcade. One leg moved as if some part of his brain still fought to rise, and then he was still.

Cheering soldiers surrounded Conan, unheeding of their fallen Commander. Smiling nobles, men and women alike, rushed forward, trying to touch him diffidently, as they might reach to stroke a tiger.

Conan heard none of their praise. In that brief instant when Vegentius had stood within the shadows of the arcade, he had remembered where he had seen the man before. He pushed free of the adulation and acclaim, gathering his tunic and returning to Hordo.

"Do you remember," he asked the one-eyed man quietly, "what I told you of first seeing Taras, when I fell through the roof into his secret meeting, and the big man who stood in the shadows?"

Hordo's eye darted to Vegentius, now being lifted by his soldiers. The nobles were drifting away. "Him?" he said incredulously.

Conan nodded, and the bearded man whistled sourly.

"Cimmerian, I say again that we should ride for Ophir, just as soon as we can assemble the company."

"No, Hordo." Conan's eyes still held the icy grimness of the fight, and his face wore the look of a wolf on the hunt. "We have the enemy's trail, now. It's time to attack, not run."

"Mitra!" Hordo breathed. "An you get me killed with this foolishness, I'll haunt you. *Attack?*"

Before Conan could reply, a slave girl appeared, bending knee to the Cimmerian. "I am to bid you to King Garian with all haste."

The one-eyed man stiffened.

"Be at ease," Conan told him. "Was it my head the King sought, he'd not send a pretty set of ankles to fetch me." The slave girl suddenly eyed him with interest.

"I trust no one," Hordo grumbled, "until we find out who wants you dead. Or until we leave Nemedia far behind."

"I'll tell you when it is time to ride for the border," Conan laughed. "Lead on, girl." She darted away, and the Cimmerian followed.

King Garian waited in a room hung with weapons and trophies of the chase, but his mind was not on the hunt. Scrolls and sheets of parchment littered the many tables that dotted the room, and even the floor. As Conan entered, Garian hurled a scroll across the room with a sound of disgust. The bruise on his cheek stood out against the angry flush of his countenance.

"Never ask to be a king, Conan," were his first words.

Taken aback, Conan could only say, "And why not?"

Garian's bluff face was a picture of loathing as he swept his arms about to indicate all of the scrolls and parchments. "Think you these are the plans for some grand campaign? Some magnificent ceremony to honor my father's name and memory? Think you so?"

Conan shook his head. More times than one his life had been altered by the plans and strategies of one king or another, but he had never been party to those plannings. He eyed a parchment, lying almost at his feet. The sheet seemed covered with columns of numbers.

Garian stalked about the room lifting scrolls from tables, hurling them to the floor. "The city drains must be cleared or, so the Physicians' Guild claims, the miasmas will bring on a plague. It is recommended the ancient passages beneath the Palace be located and filled, to make the Palace more secure. Part of the city wall must be rebuilt. The army's pay is in arrears. Grain to be bought. Always more grain." He stopped, scowling at the spreading antlers of a great stag on the wall. "I took that in the wilderness on the Brythunian border. How I wish I were back there now."

"Can your counselors not deal with those things?" Conan asked.

The King laughed bitterly. "So they could, were it not for the gold. Gold, Conan. I am reduced to grubbing for it like a greedy merchant."

"The Treasury—"

"—is well nigh bare. The more grain I must buy in Ophir and Aquilonia, the higher the price goes, and I must try to replace an entire crop, with insane brigands burning those wagons that do not travel under army escort and many that do. Already have I ordered some ornaments to be melted, but even an I strip the Palace bare it would be barely enough."

"What will you do?" Conan asked. Always had he imagined the wealth of kings to be limitless. This was a new thing for him, that a king might have to worry about gold no less than he, if in greater amounts.

"Borrow," Garian replied. "A number of

nobles and merchants have wealth to rival my own. Let them take a hand in preventing our nation from starving." He rooted among the parchments until he found one folded and sealed with the Dragon Seal of Nemedia. "You will carry this to Lord Cantaro Albanus. He is among the richest men in Nemedia, and so will be among the first to be asked to contribute." Face hardening, he handed the parchment to Conan and added, "Or be taxed if they will not lend."

The King motioned for Conan to go, but the big Cimmerian remained where he stood. It was a delicate thing he was about to do, but he was not a man used to delicacy, and he felt an unaccustomed awkwardness. Garian looked at him in obvious surprise that he did not leave.

"How well do you trust Vegentius?" Conan blurted finally.

"Well enough to retain him as Commander of the Royal Bodyguard," Garian replied. "Why ask such a question?"

Conan took a deep breath and began the tale he had planned on his way to this room. "Since coming here I have thought that I had seen Vegentius before. Today I remembered. I saw him in a tavern in the city in close converse with a man called Taras, one who has been known to say that some other would be better on the throne than you."

"A serious charge," Garian said slowly. "Vegentius has served me well, and my father before me for many years. I cannot think he means me harm."

"You are the king, yet one lesson of kingship I know. A man who wears a crown must be ever wary of others' ambitions."

Garian threw back his head and laughed. "A good swordsman you may be, Conan, but you must leave being king to me. I have somewhat more experience with wearing a crown than you. Now go. I would have that message to Lord Albanus quickly."

Inclining his head, Conan left. He hoped that he had planted some seed of suspicion, yet this fighting with words pleased him not at all. To face an enemy with steel was his way, and he hoped that it came soon.

When Conan reached the Palace gate, he found Hordo waiting with his horse. And twenty men, among them Machaon and Narus. The Cimmerian looked at Hordo questioningly, and the one-eyed man shrugged.

"I heard you were to carry a message to some lord," he told Conan. "Mitra! For all you know he could be the other man at that meeting with Taras. Or the one who wants you dead. Or both."

"You grow as suspicious as an old woman, Hordo," Conan said as he swung into the saddle.

Vegentius, battered but in full armor and red-crested helmet, appeared suddenly in the gate with half-a-score Golden Leopards at his heels.

When his eyes fell on Conan's mounted men, he stopped, glaring. Abruptly he spun and, angrily pushing through the soldiers, stormed back into the Palace.

"Mayhap I am suspicious," Hordo said quietly, "but at least I've sense enough to remember that some of your enemies have faces we know. Besides, you'll find the city changed in the last few days."

As Conan led his twenty into the empty streets, the changes were evident. Here and there a dog with ribs protruding sniffed warily around a corner. Occasionally a man could be seen hurrying down a side street, as if pursued, though no one else was about. Windows were shuttered and doors were barred; no shop was open nor hawker's cry heard. A deathly silence hung palpable in the air.

"Soon after we rode to the Palace it began," Hordo muttered. He looked around and hunched his shoulders uneasily, as if riding among tombs. "First people abandoned the streets to the toughs, the beggars and the trulls. The last two went quickly enough, with none to give or buy, and the bravos had the city to themselves, terrorizing any who dared set foot out of doors. Yesterday, they disappeared too." He looked at Conan significantly. "All in the space of a glass."

"As if they had orders?"

The one-eyed man nodded. "Maybe Taras hired armed men after all. Of a sort."

"But not for the purpose Ariane believed." The big Cimmerian was silent for a time, staring at the seemingly deserted buildings. "What is the news of her?" he asked finally.

Hordo had no need to ask who he meant. "She's well. Twice I've been to the Thestis; the others look at me as they'd look at a leper come to their dinner. Kerin has taken up with Graecus."

Conan nodded without speaking, and they rode in silence to the gates of Albanus' palace. There Conan dismounted, pounding on the barred gate with his fist.

A flap no bigger than a man's hand opened in it, and a suspicious eye surveyed them. "What do you seek here? Who are you?"

"My name is Conan. Open the gate, man. I bear a message to your master from King Garian himself."

There was a moment's whispered conversation on the other side of the gate. Then came the rattle of a bar being drawn, and the gate opened enough for one man to pass.

"You can enter," the voice from inside called, "but not the others."

"Conan," Hordo began.

The Cimmerian quieted him with a gesture. "Rest easy, Hordo. I could not be safer in a woman's arms." He slipped through the opening.

As the gate closed behind him with a solid thud, Conan faced four men with drawn swords; another snugged the point of his blade under the Cimmerian's ribs from the side.

"Now, who are you?" rasped the swordsman who pricked Conan's tunic.

Wishing he had had sense enough to don his hauberk before leaving the Royal Palace, Conan turned his head enough to make out a narrow face with wide-set eyes and a nose with the tip gone. "I told you." He reached beneath his tunic, and froze as the sword point dug deeper. "I want only to show you the message. What trouble can I mean with a sword in my ribs?"

To himself, he thought that clip-nose stood too close. The man should never have touched blade to tunic unless he meant to thrust. One quick sweep of the arm would knock that sword aside, then clip-nose could be hurled at his fellow, and. . . . The big Cimmerian smiled, and the others shifted uneasily, wondering what he found to smile about.

"Let me see this message," clip-nose demanded.

From beneath his tunic Conan produced the folded parchment. Clip-nose reached, but he moved it beyond the man's grasp. "You can see the seal from there," he said. "It's meant for Lord Albanus, not you."

"'Tis the Dragon Seal, in truth," clip-nose muttered. His sword left Conan's ribs with obvious reluctance. "Follow me, then, and do not stray."

Conan shook his head as they started up the stone walk toward the palace proper, a massive structure of fluted columns, with a great gilded dome that hurled back the sun. Suspicion on the guards' part had been warranted, given the state of the city, but the surliness should have faded when they learned he was a Royal Messenger. That it had not spoke ill for Garian's plans. Often men absorbed the attitudes of their master without either man or master realizing.

In the many-columned entry hall, clip-nose conferred, well out of Conan's hearing, with a gray-bearded man whose tunic was emblazoned with Lord Albanus' house-mark backed by a great key. Clip-nose left, returning to his post at the gate, and the gray-bearded man approached Conan.

"I am Lord Albanus' chamberlain," he said, giving neither name nor courtesy. "Give me the message."

"I will place it in Lord Albanus' hands," Conan replied flatly.

He had no real reason not to give it to the chamberlain, for such a one was his master's agent in all things, yet he was irked. A messenger from the King should have been given chilled wine and damp towels to take the dust of the street from him.

The chamberlain's face tightened, and for a moment Conan thought the man would argue. Instead he said curtly, "Follow me," and led the Cimmerian up marble stairs to a small room. "Wait here," he commanded Conan, and left after casting an eye about as if cataloguing the room's contents against a light-fingered visitor.

It was no mean room for all its smallness. Tapestry-hung and marble-floored, its furnishings were inlaid with mother-of-pearl and lapis lazuli. An arch led onto a balcony overlooking a garden fountain. But still there were neither towels nor wine. It boded ill indeed for Garian, such insult to his messenger.

Muttering to himself, Conan walked to the balcony and looked down. Almost he cried out in surprise, slights forgotten for the moment. Stephano staggered drunkenly through the garden, half supported by two girls in skimpy silks.

The sculptor bent to dabble his fingers in the

fountain and near fell in. "No water," he laughed at the girls, as they drew him back. "Want more wine, not water." Giggling together, they wound a shaky way from the fountain and into the exotic shrubs.

Someone cleared his throat behind Conan, and the Cimmerian spun.

A plump man of middling height stood there, one hand clutching his ill-fitting velvet tunic at the neck. "You have a message for me?" he said.

"Lord Albanus?" Conan said.

The plump man nodded shortly and thrust out his hand. Slowly Conan gave him the sealed parchment. The plump man's hand closed on it like a trap. "Now go," he said. "I have the message. Go!"

Conan went.

The gray-bearded chamberlain was waiting immediately outside to conduct him to the door, and there clip-nose waited with another man to escort him to the gate.

As he emerged, Hordo brought his horse forward, a relieved grin wreathing his scarred face. "Almost was I ready to come over that wall after you."

"I had no trouble," Conan said as he mounted. "I carried the King's message, remember. When next you see Ariane, tell her that Stephano is not dead, as she feared. He dwells within, sporting himself with serving girls."

"I mean to see her this day," Hordo replied. He stared at the gate thoughtfully. " 'Tis odd he sent no message to his friends that he is well."

"Not so odd as a lord with broken nails and work-calloused hands," the Cimmerian said.

"A swordsman—"

"No, Hordo. I know work-wrought calluses when I see them. Still, 'tis none of our concern. Vegentius is, and this very night I mean to have private conversation with the good Commander." Grimly he rode from the gate, the others galloping in two columns behind.

Albanus thrust the plump man, now dressed in nought but a filthy breechclout, to his knees, face to the marble floor.

"Well, Varius?" Albanus demanded of his chamberlain, his cruel face dark with impatience. He snatched the parchment, crumpled it in his fist. "Did he seem suspicious? Did he accept this dog as me?" He prodded the kneeling man with his foot. "Did he think you a lord, dog? What did he say?"

"He did, master." The plump man's voice was fearful, and he did not lift his face from the floor. "He asked only if I was Lord Albanus, then gave me the parchment and left."

Albanus growled. The gods toyed with him, to send this man whose death he sought beneath his very roof, where he could not touch the barbarian, lest suspicion be drawn straight to him, and where he must hide to escape recognition. Beneath his own roof! And on this, the first day of his triumph. His eye fell on the kneeling man, who trembled.

"Could you not have found someone more presentable to represent me, Varius? That even a barbarian should take this slug for me offends me."

"Forgive me, my lord," the chamberlain said,

bowing even more deeply in apology. "There was little time, and a need to find one who would fit the tunic."

Albanus' mouth curled. "Burn that tunic. I'll not wear it again. And send this thing back to the kitchens. The sight of it disgusts me."

Varius made a slight gesture; the kneeling man scurried from the room, hardly rising higher than a crouch. "Will that be all, my lord?"

"No. Find that drunken idiot Stephano, and hasten him to the workroom. But sober him, first."

Albanus waved Varius from the room, and turned to the message from Garian. Curious as to what it could be, he split the seal.

> Our Dear Lord Cantaro Albanus,
> All honor to you. We summon you before the Dragon Throne that you may advise Us on matters near Our heart. As one who loves Us, and Nemedia, well, We know you will make haste.
>
> GARIAN, NEMEDIA PRIMUS

A feral gleam lit Albanus' black eyes as he wadded the parchment in clawed hands. "I will come to you soon enough," he whispered. "My love I will show with chains and hot irons till on your knees you will acknowledge me King. Albanus, First in Nemedia. You will beg for death at my hand."

Tossing the crumpled sheet aside, he strode to the workroom. The four guards before the door stiffened respectfully, but he swept past them without notice.

On the stone circle in the center of the room stood the clay figure of Garian, complete at last. Or almost, he thought, smiling. Perfect in every detail, just slightly larger than the living man—Stephano had made some quibble about that, saying it should be either exactly life size or of heroic proportions—it seemed to be striding forward, mouth open to utter some pronouncement. And it contained more of Garian than simply his looks. Arduously worked into that clay with complicated thaumaturgical rituals were Garian's hair and parings from his fingernails, his sweat, his blood, and his seed. All had been obtained by Sularia at the dark lord's command.

A huge kiln stood a short distance behind the stone platform, and a complicated series of wooden slides and levers designed to move the figure linked platform and kiln. Neither kiln nor slides were ever to be used, however. Albanus had allowed Stephano to construct them in order to allay the sculptor's suspicions before they arose.

Climbing onto the platform, Albanus began pushing the wooden apparatus off onto the floor. Unaccustomed as he was to even the smallest labor, yet he must needs do this. Stephano would have had to be chivied to it, his questions turned aside with carefully constructed lies, and Albanus had long since tired of allowing the sculptor to believe that his questions were worth answering, his vanities worth dignifying. Better to do the work himself.

Tossing the last lever from the platform, Albanus jumped to the floor, one hand out to steady himself against the kiln. With an oath he jerked it back from the kiln's rough surface. It was hot.

The door opened, and Stephano tottered in, green of face but much less under the sway of drink than he had been. "I want them all flogged," he muttered, scrubbing a hand across his mouth. "Do you know what your slaves did to me, with Varius giving the orders? They—"

"Fool!" Albanus thundered. "You fired the kiln! Have I not commanded you to do nothing here without my leave?"

"The figure is ready," Stephano protested. "It must be put in the kiln today, or it will crack rather than harden. Last night I—"

"Did you not hear my command that you were never to handle fire within this room? Think you I light these lamps with my own hands for the joy of doing a slave's work?"

"If the oils in that clay are so flammable," the sculptor muttered sullenly, "how can it stand being placed—"

"Be silent." The words were a soft hiss. Albanus' obsidian gaze clove Stephano's tongue to the roof of his mouth and rooted him to the spot as if it were a spike driven through him.

Disdainfully Albanus turned his back. Deftly he set out three small vials, a strip of parchment and a quill pen. Opening the first vial—it held a small quantity of Garian's blood, with the admixture of tinctures to keep it liquid—he dipped the pen and neatly wrote the King's name across the parchment. A sprinkling of powder from the second vial, and instantly the blood blackened and dried. The last container held Albanus' own blood, drawn only that morning. With that he wrote his own name in larger script, overlaying that of Garian. Again the powder dried the blood.

Next, murmuring incantations, Albanus folded the parchment strip in a precise pattern. Then he returned to the platform and placed the parchment into the open mouth of the clay figure.

Stephano, leaning now against the wall, giggled inanely. "I wondered why you wanted the mouth like that." At a look from Albanus he swallowed heavily and bit his tongue.

Producing chalks smuggled from Stygia, land of sorcerers far to the south, Albanus scribed an incomplete pentagram around the feet of the figure, star within pentagon within circle. Foul black candles went on the points where each broken shape touched the other two. Then, quickly, each candle was lit, the pentagram completed. He stepped back, arms spread wide, uttering the words of conjuring.

"Elonai me'roth sancti, Urd'vass teoheem. . . ."

The words of power rolled from his tongue, and the air seemed to thicken in silver shimmers. The flames of the unholy candles flared, sparking a seed of fear in the dark lord's mind. The flames. It could not happen again as last time. It could not. He banished the fear by main force. There could be no fear now, only power.

". . . arallain Sa'm'di com'iel mort'rass. . . ."

The flames grew, but as they grew the room dimmed, as if they took light rather than gave it. Higher they flared, driven by the force of the dark lord's chant, overtowering the clay figure. Slowly, as though bent by some impossible and unfelt wind, the silent flames bent inward until the points of fire met above. From that meeting a bolt, as of lightning, struck down to the head of the statue, bathing it in glow unending, surrounding it in a haloed fire of the purest white that sucked all heat from the air.

Frost misting his breath, Albanus forced his voice to a roar. *"By the Unholy Powers of Three, I conjure thee! By blood and sweat and seed, vilified and attainted, I conjure thee! Arise, walk and obey, for I, Albanus, conjure thee!"*

As the last syllable left his mouth the flames were gone, leaving no trace of the candles behind. The figure stood, but now it was dried and cracked.

Albanus rubbed his hands together, and put them beneath his arms for warmth. If only it had all gone correctly this time. He glanced at Stephano, shivering against a wall that glinted from the myriad ice droplets that had coalesced from the air. Terror made the sculptor's eyes bulge. There was no point in delaying further. The hawk-faced man drew a deep breath.

"I command you, Garian, awake!" A piece of clay dropped from one arm to shatter on the stone. Albanus frowned. "Garian, I command you awake!"

The entire figure trembled; then crumbling, powdering clay was spilling to the platform. And what the figure had moulded, stood there, breathing and alive. A perfect duplicate of Garian, without blemish or fault. The simulacrum brushed dust from its shoulder, then stopped, eyeing Albanus quizzically.

"Who are you?" it said.

"I am Albanus," the dark lord replied. "Know you who you are?"

"Of course. I am Garian, King of Nemedia."

Albanus' smile was purest evil. "To your knees, Garian," he said softly. Unperturbed, the replica sank to its knees. Despite himself Albanus laughed, and the commands poured out for the sheer joy of seeing the image of the King obey. "Face to the floor! Grovel! Now up! Run in place! Faster! Faster!" The duplicate King ran. And ran.

Tears rolled down Albanus' cheeks, but his laughter faded as his eye lit on Stephano. Slowly the sculptor pushed himself erect from his crouch. Uncertainty and fear chased each other across his face.

"Be still, Garian," Albanus commanded, not loosing Stephano's gaze from his own. The simulacrum ceased running and stood quietly, breathing easily.

Stephano swallowed hard. "My . . . my work is done. I'll go now." He turned toward the door, flinching to a halt at the whipcrack of Albanus' voice.

"Your gold, Stephano. Surely you've not forgotten that." From beneath his tunic Albanus produced a short, thick cylinder, tightly wrapped in leather. He hefted it on his palm. "Fifty gold marks."

Cupidity warred with fear on Stephano's countenance. He licked his lips hesitantly "The sum mentioned was a thousand."

"I am unclothed," the simulacrum said suddenly.

"Of course," Albanus said, seeming to answer

them both.

From the floor he picked up a length of filthy rag that Stephano had used while sculpting, and with it carefully scrubbed away part of the pentagram. Many things, he knew, could happen to one attempting to enter a closed pentagram charged with magicks, and each was more horrible than the last. Stepping up onto the platform, he handed the rag to the simulacrum, which wrapped the cloth about its waist.

"This is but a first payment, Stephano," Albanus went on. "The rest will come to you later." He thrust the leather-wrapped cylinder into the simulacrum's hand. "Give this to Stephano." Leaning closer, he added whispered words.

Stephano shifted uneasily as the image of the King stepped down from the platform.

"So many times," Albanus murmured, "have I been forced to endure the babble that spills from your mouth."

The sculptor's eyes narrowed, darting from Albanus to the approaching figure, and he broke for the door.

With inhuman speed the simulacrum hurled itself forward. Before Stephano had gone a single step it was on him, a hand with the strength of stone seizing his throat. A scream tore from him as obdurate fingers dug into the muscles on either side of his jaw, forcing his mouth open. Futilely Stephan clawed at the hand that held him; his fingers might as well have scraped at hardened leather. With that single hand, as if the sculptor were but a child, the replica forced him to his knees. Too late Stephano saw the cylinder descending toward his mouth, and understood Albanus' words. Desperately he clutched the approaching wrist, but he could as easily have slowed a catapult's arm. Remorseless, the construct forced the gold deeper, and yet deeper, into the sculptor's mouth.

Choking rasps came from Stephano's throat as the simulacrum of Garian dropped him. Eyes staring from his head, face empurpling, the sculptor clawed helplessly at his throat. His back arched in his struggles till naught but head and drumming heels touched the floor.

Albanus watched the death throes dispassionately, and when the last twitching foot had stilled, he said softly, "Nine hundred fifty more will go with you to your unmarked grave. What I promise, I give." His shoulders shook with silent mirth. When the spasm had passed, he turned briskly to the likeness of Garian, still standing impassively over the body. "As for you, there is much to learn and little time. Tonight. . . ."

riane sat despondently, staring at nothing. Around her the common room of the Thestis murmured with intrigue. No musicians played, and men and women whispered as they huddled together over their tables. Reaching a decision, Ariane got to her feet and made her way through the tables to Graecus.

"I must talk to you, Graecus," she said quietly. That deathly silence had contaminated her also.

"Later," the stocky sculptor muttered without looking at her. To the others at his table he went on in a low, insistent voice. "I tell you, it matters not if Taras is dead. I know where the weapons are stored. In half a day I—"

Ariane felt some of her old fire rekindle. "Graecus!" In that room of whispers the sharp word sounded like a shout. Everyone at the table stared at her. "Has it not occurred to you," she continued, "that perhaps we are being betrayed?"

"Conan," Graecus began, but she cut him off. "Not Conan."

"He killed Taras," a plump, pale-skinned brunette said. "You saw that yourself. And he's taken Garian's coin openly, now."

"Yes, Gallia," Ariane said patiently. "But if Conan had betrayed us, would not the Golden Leopards arrest us?" Silent stares answered her. "He has not betrayed us. Mayhap he spoke the truth about Taras. Perhaps there are no armed men waiting for us to lead the people into the streets. Perhaps we'll find we are no more than a stalking horse for some other's plan."

"By Erlik's Throne," Graecus grumbled, "you speak rubbish, Ariane."

"Perhaps I do," she sighed wearily, "but at least discuss it with me. Resolve my doubts, if you can. Do you truly have none at all?"

"Take your doubts back to your corner," Graecus told her. "While you sit doubting, we will pull Garian from his throne."

Gallia sniffed loudly. "What can you expect from one who spends so much time with that one-eyed ruffian?"

"Thank you, Gallia," Ariane said. She smiled for the first time since entering the room where Conan stood above Taras' body, and left the table to get her cloak. Graecus and the others stared at her as if she were mad.

Hordo was the answer to her problem, she

realized. Not as one to talk to, of course. An she mentioned her doubts to him, he would gruffly tell her that Conan betrayed no one. Then he would pinch her bottom and try to inveigle his way into her bed. He had done all of those things already. But he had visited her earlier that afternoon, and had told her that Stephano lived, and was at the palace of Lord Albanus. The sculptor had had a good mind and a facile tongue before his jealousy of Conan soured him. Either he would dispel her doubts, convincing her of the big Cimmerian's guilt, or, convinced himself he would return with her to the Thestis to help her convince the rest. She wrapped her cloak about her and hurried into the street.

When she reached the Street of Regrets she began to rue her decision to leave the Thestis. That street, always alive with flash and tawdry glitter, lay bare to the wind that rolled pitiful remnants across the paving stones. A juggler's parti-colored cap. A silken scarf, soiled and torn. In the distance a dog howled, the sound echoing down other empty streets. Shivering, though not from the wind, Ariane quickened her pace.

By the time she reached Albanus' palace, she was running, though nothing pursued her but emptiness. Panting, she fell against the gate, her small fist pounding on the iron-bound planks. "Let me in!"

A suspicious eye regarded her through a small opening in the gate, swiveling both ways to see if she was accompanied.

"Mitra's mercy, let me in!"

The bars rattled aside, and the guard opened

a crack barely wide enough for her to slip through.

Before she had taken a full step inside an arm seized her about the waist, swinging her into the air with crude laughter. She gasped as a hand squeezed her buttock roughly, and she looked down into a narrow face. The nose had the tip gone.

"A fine bit," he laughed. "Enough to keep us all warm, even in this wind." His half-score companions added their jocularity to his.

The mirth drained from his face as he felt the point of her short dagger prick him under the ear. "I am the Lady Ariane Pandarian," she hissed coldly. Mitra, how long had it been since she had used that name? "An Lord Albanus leaves anything of you, I've no doubt my father will tend to the rest."

His hands left her as though scalded; her feet thumped to the ground. "Your pardon, my lady," he stammered. The rest stared with mouths open. "All honor to you. I did not mean. . . ."

"I will find my own way," she announced haughtily, and swept away while he was still attempting to fit together an apology.

Arrogance, she decided as she made her way up the flagstone walk, was her only hope, arriving at a lord's palace without servants or guards. When one of the great carven doors was opened by a gray-bearded man with a chamberlain's seal on his tunic, her large hazel eyes were adamantine.

"I am the Lady Ariane Pandarian," she announced. "Show me to the sculptor, Stephano

Melliarus."

His jaw dropped, and he peered vaguely past
her down the walk as if seeking her retinue.
"Forgive me . . . my lady . . . but I . . . know no
man named Stephano."

Brusquely she pushed by him into the
columned entry-hall. "Show me to Lord
Albanus," she commanded. Inside she quivered.
Suppose Conan had been mistaken. What if
Stephano were not there? Yet the thought of re-
turning to those barren streets spurred her on.

The chamberlain's mouth worked, beard wag-
gling, then he said faintly, "Follow me, please,"
adding, "my lady," as an afterthought.

The room in which he left her, while going "to
inform Lord Albanus" of her presence, was
spacious. The tapestries were brightly colored;
flickering golden lamps cast a cheery glow after
the gloom of the streets. But the pleasant sur-
roundings did naught to stem her growing
apprehension. What if she was seeking one who
was not there, making a fool of herself before
this lord who was a stranger to her? Bit by bit,
her facade of arrogance melted. When Lord Albanus entered, the last vestiges of it were swept
away by his stern gaze.

"You seek a man called Stephano," the hard-
faced man said without preamble. "Why do you
think he is here?"

She found herself wanting to wring her hands
and instead clutched them tightly in her cloak,
but she could not stop the torrent of words and
worries. "I must talk to him. No one else will
talk with me, and Taras is dead, and Conan says
we are being betrayed, and. . . ." She managed a

deep, shuddering breath. "Forgive me, Lord Albanus. If Stephano is not here, I will go."

Albanus' dark eyes had widened as she spoke. Now he fumbled in a pouch at his belt, saying, "Wait. Have you ever seen the like of this?"

His fingers brought out a gemstone of almost fiery white; he muttered words she could not hear as he thrust it at her.

Despite herself, her eyes were drawn to the gem as iron to lodestone. Suddenly a pale beam sprang from the stone, bathing her face. Her breath came out in a grunt, as if she had been struck. Panic filled her. She must run. But all she could do was tremble, dancing helpless in that one spot as whiteness blotted out all her vision. Run, she screamed in the depths of her mind. Why, came the question. Panic dissolved. Will dissolved. The beam winked out, and she stood, breathing calmly, looking into the pale stone, now more fiery seeming than before.

"'Tis done," she heard Albanus murmur, "but how well?" In a louder voice he said, "Remove your garments, girl."

Some tiny corner of her being brought a flush to her cheek, but to the rest it seemed a reasonable command. Swiftly she dropped her cloak, undid the brooches that held her robes. They fell in a welter about her feet, and she stood, hands curled delicately on her rounded thighs, one knee slightly bent, waiting.

Albanus eyed her curved nudity and smiled mirthlessly. "If you obey that command so readily, you'll tell the truth an you die for it. Taras, girl. Is he in truth dead? How did he die?"

"Conan slew him," she replied calmly.

"Erlik take that accursed barbar!" the dark lord snarled. "No wonder Vegentius could not find Taras. And how am I to send orders...." His scowl lessened; he peered at her thoughtfully. "You are one of those foolish children who prate of rebellion at the Sign of Thestis, aren't you?"

Her answer was hesitant. "I am." His words seemed in some way wrong, yet the irritation was dimly felt and distant.

Albanus' fingers gripped her chin, lifting her head, and though they dug painfully into her cheeks she knew no urge to resist. Her large eyes met his obsidian gaze openly.

"When I wish the streets to fill with howling mobs," he said softly, "you will carry my words to the Thestis, saying exactly what I command and no more."

"I will," she said. Like the bite of a gnat, something called her to struggle, then faded.

He nodded. "Good. This Conan, now. What did he say to you of betrayal?"

"That Taras hired no armed men to aid us. That another used us for his own purposes."

"Did he name this other?" Albanus asked sharply.

She shook her head, feeling tired of talking, wanting to sleep.

"No matter," Albanus muttered. "I underestimated the barbar. He becomes more dangerous with every turn of the glass. Varius! A messenger to go to Commander Vegentius! Quickly, if you value your hide! Stand up straight, girl."

Ariane straightened obediently, and watched Albanus scribble a message on parchment. She wished only to sleep, but knew she could not until her master permitted. She accepted his will completely now; even the tiny pinpricks of resistance fled.

As the deep tone of a bronze gong sounded the first turn of the glass past full sundown, Conan uncoiled smoothly from his bed in the darkness of his room. Already he was prepared for his night's venture, in bare feet and tunic with a dagger at his belt. Sword and armor would hamper where he went.

On silent feet he moved to the window, climbed onto the stone lip, and twisted with catlike grace to find places for his fingers above. It was not a natural thing for men to look up, even when searching. Therefore the best way to go unobserved was to travel high. Scudding purple clouds crossed a gibbous moon, casting shadows that walked and danced. Conan became one with the shadows.

Even in that smooth-dressed stone, crevices and chinks were to be found by knowledgeable fingers and toes. Stone cornices and the rims of friezes made a pathway for him to the roof. With swift care he crossed its tiles, dropping on the far side to a rampart walk that bore no sentry, here in the heart of the Palace. Through an embrasure between man-high merlons he lowered himself to the roof of a colonnade three stories above the flagstoned courtyard below.

Within the Palace behind him an alarm bell abruptly began to toll, and he froze there in the shifting shadows. Shouts carried to him, though he could make out no word. He frowned. To such an alarm Vegentius would surely be summoned. And yet the hue and cry was not general, for no sudden lights or tramp of marching men disturbed the outer part of the Palace. Eventually it would subside, and Vegentius would of a certainty return to his quarters. A lupine smile split the Cimmerian's face. He would return to find one waiting to ask questions, and demand answers.

Swiftly Conan hurried on, running along the roof, scaling another wall at its end with ease, then along the length of it uncaring of the dark below him, or the stones that waited if foot should slip or grip fail. Halting, he lay flat, swiveled his legs and hips over the edge, and climbed down the short distance to the window of Vegentius' sleeping chamber.

Dagger sliding from its sheath, the big Cimmerian entered the room like silent death. Some few brass lamps were lit, casting dim illumination there and in the outer chamber, yet both were empty, as he had feared. Grimly he settled himself by the door of the inner room to wait.

Long was that vigil, yet he kept it with the silent, unmoving patience of a hunting beast. Even when he heard the door of the outer chamber open, only his hand on the dagger moved, firming its grip. But the tread was of a single man. Conan flattened himself against the wall by the door as the footsteps came closer.

A tall shape entered the room, golden-cloaked and wearing the red-crested helmet of the Golden Leopards' commander. Conan's empty fist struck against the back of the man's neck, and with a groan the other fell, rolling onto his back. The Cimmerian stared in amazement. It was not Vegentius.

And then a howling horde in golden cloaks poured through the outer chamber to fall on him. Roaring, Conan fought. His dagger found a throat, and was torn from his grasp as the dying man fell. Teeth splintered and jaws broke beneath his hammer blows. One man he neatly hurled screaming through the window by which he had entered. Yet by sheer weight of numbers did they force him down. He found himself on his back, three men holding each arm and leg, though many of them spat blood. Writhing, he strained every thew, but he could only shift them, not gain freedom.

Vegentius, helmetless and wearing a look of great satisfaction, appeared in the doorway. "You can see that I was right," he said to someone still in the other chamber. "He intended to slay me first, so that if your death were discovered before he could flee, my absence in command might aid his escape."

Wrapped tightly in a cloak, his bruise standing out against the paleness of his cheeks, Garian stepped into the room. He stood gazing down at Conan in horrified wonder. "Even when I heard the others I could hardly believe," he whispered. A shudder went through him. "A score of times has he had me at the point of his blade."

"But then he would have surely been known as your assassin," Vegentius said smoothly.

"Liar!" Conan spat at the massive soldier. "I came here to force you to admit your own foul treachery."

Vegentius' face darkened, and he put a hand to his sword, but Garian stopped him with a gesture. The King moved closer to address the Cimmerian.

"Hear me, Conan. Before dusk began to fall this day, Vegentius arrested those who conspired with you. A man called Graecus. A woman, Gallia. Some three or four others. Do you deny knowing them, or that they plotted against my throne?"

Conan's brain roiled. Was Ariane among those taken? Yet to ask, naming her, was to give her into their hands if they did not have her. "Foolish youths," he said. "They talk, and will talk till they are gray and toothless, harming no one. Yet there are those who would use them." He cut off with a grunt as Vegentius' boot caught him under the ribs.

Garian waved the soldier back and spoke on. "Vegentius put these you call harmless to the question, and within two turns of the glass he had broken them. He brought them before me, those who could still speak, and from their mouths I heard them admit they plotted my murder, and that you are he who was to wield the blade."

"I am no murderer!" Conan protested, but Garian continued as if he had not spoken.

"The alarm was given; you were sought. And found lying in wait, dagger in hand. Your actions convict you."

"His head will adorn a pike before dawn," Vegentius said.

"No," Garian said softly. "I trusted this man." He wiped his hands on the edge of his cloak, as if ritually. His eyes were cold on Conan's face. "Long has it been since the ancient penalty for plotting to slay he who wears the Dragon Crown was last invoked. Let it be invoked now." Drawing his cloak about him, he turned his face from the Cimmerian and strode from the chamber.

Vegentius stared after him, then down at Conan. Abruptly he laughed, throwing back his head. "The ancient penalty, barbar. Fitting. To the dungeons with him!"

One of those holding Conan shifted. The Cimmerian saw a descending sword hilt, then saw no more.

Albanus smiled to himself as his sedan chair was borne through the night, up the winding streets that led through the Temple District to the Royal Palace. So close now, he was, to his inevitable triumph. He savored each step the bearers took, carrying him nearer his goal.

Ahead two torchbearers strode, and twenty guards surrounded him, though the streets were as empty as a tomb millenia old. Those truly important to him marched on either side of his chair, heavily cloaked and hooded, the woman and the man-shape. So close.

As the procession approached the gate of the Palace, Albanus uttered a command. His sedan

chair was lowered to the ground. Even as the
hawk-faced man climbed out, Vegentius crossed
the drawbridge. Albanus looked at the guards
and raised an inquiring brow.

"As planned," the soldier said quietly. "All
men standing guard this night are loyal to me.
My best."

"Good," Albanus said. "And Conan?"

"In the dungeons. Garian shouted so about
invoking the ancient penalty that I could not kill
him out of hand. The alarm had wakened others
by then." His red-crested helmet bobbed as he
spat disgustedly. "But he can go to the same unmarked grave as Garian."

The hawk-faced lord laughed softly. "No,
Vegentius. I find the ancient ways a fitting end
for this barbarian."

"Better to kill him straight out," Vegentius
grumbled, but pursued it no further. Stooping,
he attempted to look under the hood of the man-
shape behind Albanus. "Does he truly look
like—"

"Let us go," Albanus said, and strode forward,
Ariane and the simulacrum at his heels. Vegentius could do naught but follow.

The dark lord hurried over the drawbridge
exultantly, and into the Palace. Often had his
feet trod these halls, yet now it was tread of
possessor, of conqueror. When a shadow moved
and resolved into Sularia, he stared at her with
imperious fury.

"Why are you here, woman? I commanded
you to remain in your apartments until I sent
for you."

Her gaze met his without flinching, and even

in the dim light the eager glow of her eyes was apparent. "I want to see him fall before you."

Albanus nodded slowly. There would be pleasure in that. "But make no sound," he warned. Shoulders back and head high, as a king in his own palace, he moved on.

Before the door to Garian's chambers four guards stood, stiffening at the party's approach.

Vegentius stepped forward. "He sleeps?" One of the four nodded. "Who else is within?"

He who had nodded spoke. "Only the serving girl, to bring him wine if he wakes."

"Slay her," Albanus said, and Vegentius started.

"You said you could make her remember nothing, Albanus. Questions may be asked if the girl disappears."

"The method can only be used on one person at a time," Albanus replied, fingers absently stroking the pouch that held the white gem. "Slay her."

Vegentius nodded to the guard who had spoken. The man slipped inside, returning in moments with a bloody blade to resume his post.

Albanus led the others in, sparing not a glance for the crumpled form of a woman lying across an overturned stool. The second room, Garian's sleeping chamber itself, was dim, the lamp wicks trimmed low. Garian lay on his bed amid rumpled blankets.

"Turn up the lamps, Sularia," Albanus commanded quietly. Not taking her eyes from the man in the bed, the blonde hastened to obey. To the two hooded figures, the lord said, "Remove your cloaks."

Vegentius gasped as the simulacrum obeyed. "'Tis Garian's very image!"

Sularia turned from a golden lamp, but her exclamation at the sight of the King's double was cut short as, with narrowing eyes, her gaze caught Ariane. "Who is she?" the blonde demanded.

Ariane looked straight ahead, unmoving, until another command was given. The simulacrum peered about him curiously.

On the bed, Garian suddenly sat bolt upright. Growing more amazed by the instant, his eye jumped from Albanus to Sularia to Vegentius. "What," he began, but the words died. Mouth open, he stared at the duplicate of himself. Unperturbed, the simulacrum gazed back inquisitively.

Albanus felt like laughing. "Garian," he said mockingly, "this is he who will sit on the Dragon Throne for the last days of your line. For your usurping lineage now ends."

"Guards!" Garian shouted. From beneath his pillows a dagger appeared in his hand, and he leaped from the bed. "Guards!"

"Take him," Albanus ordered the simulacrum, "as I told you." Growing more amazed by the instant, his eye jumped from Albanus to Sularia to Vegentius.

The duplicate moved forward, and Garian's dagger struck with a fighter's speed. To be caught easily by an inhumanly powerful grip on Garian's wrist. Astonishment was replaced on his face by pain as those fingers tightened. The dagger fell from nerveless fingers.

Before that blade clattered on the floor, the

simulacrum's other hand seized the true King by the throat, lifting him until his toes kicked frantically above a handspan of air. No sign of strain was on the construct's face as it watched that other like its own turn slowly purple. Garian's struggles weakened, then ceased. Casually the replica opened its hand and let the limp body fall.

Albanus hastened to bend over the King. Savage bruises empurpled his neck, and another darkened his cheek, though Albanus did not remember seeing the simulacrum strike. But the broad chest rose and fell, if faintly. Garian yet lived.

Vegentius, who had stood staring, sword half drawn, since the instant the duplicate moved, now slammed his blade home in its scabbard and cleared his throat. His eyes never left the simulacrum. "Should you not let him, it, kill him now?"

"I am King Garian," the creature said to Vegentius. The soldier muttered an oath.

"Be silent," Albanus commanded, straightening. "This," he prodded Garian's form with his foot, "will acknowledge my right to the throne before I let him die."

"But the danger," Vegentius protested. "He was to die now."

"Enough!" Albanus snapped. "Deliver him in chains to the dungeons beneath my palace. I'll hear no more on it."

Vegentius nodded reluctantly, and turned to go.

"And, Vegentius," the cruel-faced man added, "see that those who do this task are disposed of after. Fewer tongues to waggle loosely."

The big soldier stood rigidly in the door, then left without speaking. But he would do it, Albanus knew, even to his beloved Golden Leopards.

"Who is the woman?" Sularia asked again.

Albanus looked at her in amusement, wondering if there were room for two thoughts at once in that pretty head. All that had happened before her eyes, and it was Ariane that concerned her.

"Do not worry," he told her. "In the morning you will be proclaimed Lady Sularia. This," he touched Ariane's expressionless face, "is naught but a tool to build a path to the Dragon Throne. And tools are made to be discarded once used."

His gaze swung to Sularia, a reassuring smile on his face. Tools, he repeated to himself, are made to be discarded once used.

 onan awakened hanging spreadeagled in chains in the center of a dungeon. At least, he assumed it was the center. Two tall tripod lamps cast a yellow pool of light around him, but he could see no walls in any direction. The chains that held his wrists disappeared into the gloom above. Those holding his ankles were fastened to massive ringbolts set in the rough stone blocks of the floor. His tunic was gone; he wore naught but a breechclout.

Without real hope of escape he tensed every muscle, straining until sweat popped out on his forehead, beaded his shoulders and rolled down his broad chest. There was not slightest give in the chains. Nor in himself. He had been stretched to the point of joints cracking.

Cloth rustled in the darkness, and he heard a man's voice.

"He is awake, my lady." There was a pause. "Very good, my lady."

Two men moved into the light, burly, shaven headed and bare chested. One bore a burn across his hairless chest as if some victim had managed to put hand to the hot iron intended for his own pain. The other was as heavily pelted as an ape from the shoulders down, and wore a smile on his incongruously pleasant round face. Each man carried a coiled whip.

As they wordlessly took positions to either side of the Cimmerian, he strained his eyes to penetrate the darkness. Who was this 'lady'? Who?

The first whip hissed through the air to crack against his chest. As it was drawn back the other struck his thigh. Then the first was back, wrapping around an ankle. There was no pattern to the blows, no way to anticipate where the next would land, no way to steel the soul against pain like lines of acid eating into the flesh.

The muscles of Conan's jaws were knots with the effort of not yelling. He would not even open his mouth to suck in the lungfuls of air his great body demanded in its agony. To open his mouth would be to make some noise, however slight, and from there it would be but a step to a yell, another to a scream. The woman watching from the darkness wanted him to scream. He would make no sound.

The two men continued until Conan hung as limply as the chains would allow, head down on his massive chest. Sweat turned to fire the welts that covered him from ankles to shoulders. Here and there blood oozed.

From the darkness he heard the clink of coins, and the same man's voice. "Very generous, my lady. We'll be just outside, an you need us." Then silence until hinges squealed rustily, stopping with the crash of a stout door closing.

Conan lifted his head.

Slowly a woman walked into the circle of light and stood watching him. The woman veiled in gray.

"You!" he rasped. "Are you the one who has been trying to kill me, then? Or are you the one who uses those fools at the Thestis, the one who put me here with lies?"

"I did try to have you killed," she said softly. Conan's eyes narrowed. That voice was so familiar. But whose? "I should have known there were no men in Nemedia capable of slaying you. Where you hang, though, is your own doing, though I joy to see it. I joy, Conan of Cimmeria."

"Who are you?" he demanded.

Her hand went to her face, pushed back the veils. No disease-ravaged skin was revealed, but creamy ivory beauty. Tilted emerald eyes regarded him above high cheekbones. An auburn mane framed her face in soft waves.

"Karela," he breathed. Almost he wondered if he saw a vision from pain. The Red Hawk, fierce bandit of the plain of Zamora and the Turanian steppes, in Belverus, masquerading as a woman of the nobility. It seemed impossible.

That beautiful face was impassive as she gazed at him, her voice tightly controlled.

"Never again did I think to see you, Cimmerian. When I saw you that day in the Market District I thought I would die on the spot."

"And did you see Hordo?" he asked. "You must know he is here, still hoping to find you." He managed a wry smile. "Working with the smugglers you now command."

"So you have learned that much," she said wonderingly. "None but a fool ever accounted you stupid. Hordo surprised me almost as much as you did, turning up in Khorshemish while I was there. Still, I would not let him know who I am. He was the most faithful of my hounds, yet others were faithful, too, and even so remembered the gold on my head in Zamora and Turan. Think you I wear these veils for the pleasure of hiding?"

"It has been a long time, Karela," Conan said. "'Tis likely they've forgotten by now."

Her calm facade cracked. "The Red Hawk will never be forgotten!" Emerald eyes flaring, she faced him with fists on hips and feet apart. Almost he could see the jeweled tulwar at her hip as it had been.

"Now that you're no longer being the Lady Tiana," he said grimly, "why in Zandru's Nine Hells do you want me dead?"

"Why?" she screeched in furious astonishment. "Have you forgot so soon leaving me naked and chained, on my way to be sold to whatever man bid highest?"

"There was the matter of the oath you made me swear, Karela. Never to lift a hand to save—"

"Derketo blast you and your oaths, Cimmerian!"

"Besides which, I had five coppers in my pouch. Think you to have gone for so paltry a price?"

"You lie!" she spat. "I would not heel at your command, so you let me be sold!"

"I tell you—"

"Liar! Liar!"

Conan snarled wordlessly and clenched his teeth on any further explanation. He would not argue with her. Neither would he plead. That last he had never learned to do.

Pacing angrily, Karela hurled her words as if they were daggers, never looking at him directly. "I want you to know my humiliations, Cimmerian. Know them, and remember them, so the memory will be a blade to prick you constantly when you are in the mines, ever reminding you that when the King proclaims pardons for all who have served a certain time, I will be there to place gold in the proper hands so that one prisoner will be forgotten."

"I knew you would escape," Conan muttered. "As you obviously did."

Her emerald eyes squeezed shut for a moment, and when she opened them her tone was flat. "I was bought by a merchant named Haffiz, and placed in his zenana with two score other women. That very day did I escape. And that very day was I brought back and given the bastinado, the cane across the soles of my feet. I would not cry, but for ten days I could only hobble. The second time I was free for three days. On being returned, I was put to scrubbing pots in the kitchens."

Despite his position Conan chuckled. "A fool he was, to think to tame you so."

She turned to face him, and if her words were soft her eyes held murder. "The third time I was taken while still climbing the wall. I spat in Haffiz' face, told him to slay me, for he could never break me. Haffiz laughed. I thought I was a man, he said. I must be taught differently. Henceforth I was to be allowed no waking hour that I was not dressed as if about to be presented to a master's bed, in the sheerest silks and the finest fragrances, kohl on my eyelids and rouge on my lips and cheeks. I must learn to dance, to play instruments, to recite poetry. Failure in any of these, failure to be pleasing at all times, would be punished immediately. But, as I was like a young girl learning to be a woman, no punishment would I receive not suitable for a child. How he roared with laughter."

Conan threw back his head and roared as well. "A child!"

Raising a fist as if she wished it had strength to knock him senseless, Karela raged. "What do you know of it, fool? Having my buttocks turned up for the switch ten times a day. Spoons of ca'teen oil forced down my throat. A hundred more too shaming even to think on. Laugh, you barbar oaf! For a year was I forced to endure, and how I wish I could make you live a year in the mines for every day of it."

With an effort he managed to control his mirth. "I thought you would escape in half a year, perhaps less. But the Red Hawk turned to a thrush in a silver cage."

"Day and night was I watched," she protested. "And I did escape, with a sword in my hand."

"Because you tired of being sent to your bed

with no supper?" Chuckles reverberated in his massive chest.

"Derketo blast your eyes!" Karela howled. She raced forward to pound her small fists against his great chest. "Erlik take you, you Cimmerian bastard! You . . . you. . . ." Abruptly she sagged, clutching him to keep from falling. Her cheek was pressed against his chest; he was astounded to see a tear at the corner of her eye. "I loved you," she whispered. "I loved you."

The muscular Cimmerian shook his head in wonderment. Did she act like this when she loved him, he could not imagine anyone surviving her hate.

Pushing herself away, she stepped back from him, refusing to acknowledge the tears that trembled on her long lashes. "There is no fear in you," she whispered. "You are not trembling. Nor will you think, 'if she suffered so, what will she make me suffer?'"

"I have no blame for what happened to you, Karela," he said quietly.

She did not seem to hear. "But if you have no fear, still you are a man." A strange smile played about her lips.

Abruptly her fingers went to the brooches that held her robes; in an instant the gray silk lay in a pool about her slender ankles. Gracefully she stepped from the robes. She was as he remembered, full breasts and rounded thighs, long legs and a tiny waist. Karela was a sensual delight for the male eye.

Slowly, on her toes, she spun, arms raised, head turning to let her silken tresses caress now creamy shoulders, now satin breasts. With a gentle sway to her hips she walked to him, stopping only when her breasts touched him, just below the ribs as he hung in the chains. Touching her full lower lip with her tongue and looking up at him through her lashes, she began in a sultry tone.

"When you are taken into the mines only death can bring you to the surface again. You will live your life in dank, foul air and the dim light of guttering torches. There are women there, if you want to call them women. Their hands are as calloused as any man's." Her fingers stroked across his iron-hard chest. "Their hair and skin are filth encrusted, their stench foul; their kisses. . . ."

Her slender arms stretched up, her hands hooked behind his neck, and she pulled herself up until her face was level with his.

"They have no sweet kisses such as this," she whispered, and pressed her lips to his. He met her kiss savagely, until at last she broke free with a whimper. Her emerald gaze was tremulous, his the blue of windswept northern skies. "You will never have a kiss like that again," she said breathlessly.

Abruptly she dropped to the stone floor and backed away, biting her full lower lip. There was sudden uncertainty in her green eyes. "Now I will be the only woman in your mind for the rest of your life," she said. "The only woman for the rest of your life." And, snatching her robes from the floor, she ran into the darkness. After a time he heard the door squeak open and clash shut.

She had not changed, he thought. She was still the Red Hawk, fierce and hot-blooded as any bird of prey. But if she thought he would go meekly to the mines, or whatever the ancient penalty Garian had spoken of, then she was also as wrong-headed as she had ever been.

Conan eyed his chains, but did not again attempt to break them. Among the lessons taught by the treacherous snow-covered crags of the Cimmerian mountains was this: when action was not possible, struggle only brought death sooner; waiting, conserving strength, brought the chance of survival. The Cimmerian hung in his chains with the patience of a hunting beast waiting for its prey to come closer.

Breaking, the chains that held Conan's arms began to rattle down, lowering him to the stone floor. He could not suppress a groan as his position shifted; he had no idea how many hours he had hung there. The pool of light and the dark beyond were unchanging, giving no sign of time's passage.

His feet touched the floor, and knees long strained gave way. The full length of his massive body collapsed on the stone. Straining, he tried to get his arms under him, but the blood had long since drained from them. They could only twitch numbly.

The two men who had wielded the whips

hurried into the light and began removing the chains. His weakened struggles were useless as they manacled his hands behind him and linked his ankles with heavy iron chains. The man with the burn scar was as silent and expressionless as before, but hairy-chest, he with the oddly pleasant face, talked almost jovially.

"Almost did I think we'd let you hang another day, what with all the excitement of this one. Fasten that tighter," he added to the other. "He's dangerous, this one." The second man grunted and went on as he was, hammering a rivet into the iron band on Conan's left wrist.

"My men," the Cimmerian croaked. His throat felt dry as broken pottery shards.

"Oh, they were part of it," the round-faced man laughed deprecatingly. "Fought off the Golden Leopards sent to arrest them, they did, and disappeared. Might have been made much of, another time, but more has happened since dawn this day than since Garian took the throne. First the King banished all of his old councilors from the city on pain of death. Then he created the title High Councilor of Nemedia, with near the power of the King himself attached, and gave it to Lord Albanus, an evil-eyed man if ever I saw. And to top that, he named his leman a lady. Can you imagine that blonde doxy a lady? But all those fine nobles walk wide of her, for they say she may be Queen, next. Then there were the riots. Get the rest of it, Struto."

The silent man grunted again and lumbered away.

Conan worked his mouth for moisture. "Riots?" he managed.

The one-faced man nodded. "All over the city."

Looking about as if to see if anyone might overhear, he added in a whisper. "Shouting for Garian to abdicate, they were. Maybe that's why Garian got rid of the old councilors, hoping any change would satisfy them. Leastways, he didn't send the Golden Leopards out after them."

Ariane's people had finally moved, Conan thought. Perhaps they might even bring changes —indeed, it seemed as if they already had—but for better or for worse? He forced a question out, word by word. "Had—they—armed—men —with—them?"

"Thinking of your company again, eh? No, it's been naught but people of the streets, though a surprising number have swords and such, or so I hear. Struto! Move yourself!"

He with the burn scar returned, carrying a long pole that the two of them forced between Conan's arms and his back. Broad straps fastened about his thick upper arms held it in place. From a pouch at his belt, the round-faced one took a leather gag and shoved it between the Cimmerian's teeth, securing it behind his head.

"Time to take you before the King," he told Conan. "What they're going to do to you, likely you'd rather be in Lady Tiana's gentle care. Eh, Struto?" He shook with laughter; Struto stared impassively. "Well, barbarian, you have some small time to make peace with your gods. Let's go, Struto."

Grasping the ends of the pole, the two forced Conan to his feet. Half carrying, half pushing, they took him from the dungeon, up stairs of rough stone to the marble floors of the Palace. By the time they reached those ornate halls the Cimmerian had regained full use of his legs.

Pridefully he shook off the support of the two, taking what short steps the chains at his ankles allowed.

Round-face looked at him and laughed. "Anxious to get it over with, eh?"

They let him shuffle as best he could, but retained their grip on the pole. A grim smile touched his lips. Did he wish to, he could sweep both men off their feet using the very pole with which they thought to control him. But he would still be chained and in the heart of the Palace. Patience. He concentrated on flexing his arms in their bonds to get full feeling back.

The corridors through which they passed seemed empty. The slaves were there, as always, scurrying close to the walls. But the nobles, sleek and elegant in silks and velvets, were missing. The three men made their way alone down the center of the passages.

As they turned into a broad hall, its high arched ceiling supported by pilasters, another procession approached them from ahead. Graecus, Gallia and three others from the Thestis stumbled along under the eyes of two guards. All five were gagged and had their hands roped behind them. At the sight of Conan, Graecus' eyes widened, and Gallia tried to shy away from the big Cimmerian.

One of their guards called out to the two with Conan, "This lot for the mines."

"Better than what this one gets," the round-faced man laughed.

Joining in his mirth, the guards prodded their charges on. The bedraggled young rebels hurried past, seeming as fearful of Conan as of their captors.

The Cimmerian ignored them. He did not hold them to account for the lies they had told against him. Few men and fewer women could hold out under the attentions of an expert torturer, and Vegentius would have found another way to imprison him, if not through them.

Before them at the end of the hall great carven doors opened, swung wide by six golden-cloaked soldiers, and Conan passed into the throne room of Nemedia.

Double rows of slender fluted columns held a domed roof of alabaster aloft. Light from golden lamps dangling from the ceiling on silver chains glittered on polished marble walls. The floor was a vast mosaic depicting the entire history of Nemedia. Here was the explanation for the empty halls, for here the nobles had gathered in all their panoply, dark-eyed lords in robes of velvet with golden chains about their necks, sleek ladies coruscating with the gems that covered their silk-draped bodies. Through the center of them ran a broad path from the tall doors to the Dragon Throne. Its golden-horned head reared above the man seated there, and jeweled wings curved down to support his shoulders. On his head was the Dragon Crown.

Conan set his own pace down that path, though the two jailors tried to hurry him. He would not stumble in his chains for the amusement of this court. Before the throne he stood defiantly and stared into Garian's face. The men holding the pole tried to force him to his knees, but he remained erect. A murmur rose among the nobles. Rushing forward, guards beat at his back and legs with their spear butts until, despite all he could do, he was shoved to his knees.

Through it all, Garian's face had not changed expression. Now the man on the throne rose, pulling his robe of cloth-of-gold about him.

"This barbarian," he announced loudly, "we did take into our Palace, honoring him with our attention. But we found that we nursed treachery at our bosom. Most foully our trust was betrayed, and. . . ."

He droned on, but Conan's attention was caught by the man standing slightly behind the Dragon Throne, one hand resting on it possessively while he nodded at the King's words like a teacher approving a pupil. The Seal of Nemedia hung on a golden chain about his neck, which marked him as the High Councilor of Nemedia, Lord Albanus. But Conan knew that cruel face, seen in the dark meeting with Taras and Vegentius. Did madness reign in Nemedia, the Cimmerian wondered.

". . . So we pronounce the ancient penalty for his crime," the King intoned funereally.

That brought Conan's mind quickly back. There was on Garian's face none of the sadness he had shown when Conan was taken, only flat calm.

"When next the sun has dawned and risen to its zenith, let this would-be regicide be hurled to the wolves. Let the beast be torn by beasts."

As soon as the last word was spoken, Conan was pulled to his feet and hurried from the throne room. Not even the round-faced jailor spoke as the Cimmerian was returned to the dungeons, this time to a small cell, its stone floor strewn with filthy straw. The pole and the gag were removed, but not his chains. Another was added, linking that between his ankles to a ring set in the wall.

As soon as the two jailors were gone Conan began to explore his new prison. Lying full length on his belly, he could have reached the heavy wooden door were his hands not linked behind him, but there was nothing on which to get a grip even if his hands had been free. Nor did he truly believe he could break the stout iron hinges. The walls were rough stone, close set but with aged mortar crumbling. A man with tools might remove enough of them to escape. In a year or two. The rotting straw held nothing but a half-gnawed rat carcass. The Cimmerian could not help wondering whether the gnawing had been done by its fellows or by the last prisoner. Kicking it into a far corner, he hoped he would not long have to endure the smell.

No sooner had Conan settled himself with his back against the wall than a key rattled in the large iron lock, and the cell door creaked open. To his surprise Albanus entered, holding his black velvet robes carefully clear of the foul straw. Behind him the cloth-of-gold-clad form of the King stopped in the doorway. Garian's face turned this way and that, eyes curiously taking in the straw and the stone walls. He looked at Conan once, as if the big Cimmerian were just another fixture of the cell.

It was Albanus who spoke. "You know me, don't you?"

"You are Lord Albanus," Conan replied warily.

"You know me," the hawk-faced man said, as if confirming a suspicion. "I feared as much. 'Tis well I acted when I did."

Conan tensed. "You?" His eyes went to

Garian's face. Why would this man make such an admission before the King?

"Expect no help from him," Albanus laughed. "For a time, barbar, you were a worry to me, but it seems in the end you are no weapon of the gods after all. The wolves will put an end to you, and the only real damage you have done me is being repaired by the girl you sent seeking the sculptor. No, in the sum of it, you are naught but a minor nuisance."

"Ariane," Conan said sharply. "What have you done with her?"

The obsidian-eyed lord laughed cruelly. "Come, King Garian. Let us leave this place."

"What have you done to Ariane?" Conan shouted as Albanus left. The King paused to look at him; he stared into Garian's face with as close to pleading as he could come. "Tell me what he has done. . . ."

The words died on his lips even as the other turned to go. The door creaked shut. Stunned, Conan leaned back against the stone wall.

Since that first entrance into the throne room, he had felt some oddity in Garian but put it down to himself. No man sees things aright while hearing his own death sentence. But now he had noticed a small thing. There was no bruise on Garian's cheek. Garian was no man to cover such things with powder like a woman, and he had no court sorcerer to take away such blemishes with a quick spell and a burning candle. Nor had it had time to fade naturally. A small thing, yet it meant that he who had sat on the Dragon Throne and passed sentence on Conan was not Garian.

Mind whirling, the Cimmerian tried to make

some sense of it. Albanus plotted rebellion, yet now was councilor to a King who was not Garian. But it had been Garian in Vegentius' apartments only the night before. Of that Conan was certain. He smelled the stench of sorcery as clearly as he did the rotting straw on which he sat.

Patience, he reminded himself. He could do nothing chained in a cell. Much would depend on whether he was freed of those bonds before he was thrown to the wolves. Even among wolves a great deal could be done by a man with hands free and will unfettered. This, Conan resolved, Albanus would learn to his regret.

Sularia lay face down on a toweled bench while the skilled hands of a slave woman worked fragrant oils into her back. Lady Sularia, she thought, stretching luxuriantly. So wonderful it had been standing among the lords and ladies in the throne room, rather than being crowded with the other lemans along the back wall. If her acceptance had been from fear, the smiles and greetings given her sickly and shamefaced, it only added to the pleasure, for those who spoke respectfully now had oft spoken as if she were a slave. And this did not have to be the end. If she could move from the mistresses' wall to stand with the nobles, why not from there to stand beside Albanus? Queen Sularia.

Smiling at the thought, she turned her head on her folded arms and regarded her maid, a plump gray-haired woman who was the only one in the Palace Sularia trusted. Or rather, the one she distrusted least.

"Does she still wait, Latona?" Sularia asked.

The gray-haired maid nodded briskly. "For two turns of the glass now, mistress. No one would dare disobey your summons."

The blonde nodded self-satisfied agreement without lifting her head. "Bring her in, Latona. Then busy yourself with my hair."

"Yes, mistress," Latona cackled, and hurried out. When she returned she escorted the Lady Jelanna.

The willowy noblewoman looked askance at Latona as the serving woman began to labor over her mistress' hair, while Sularia smiled like a cat at a dish of cream. Only when receiving an inferior would servants be retained so. Some of the arrogance had gone from Jelanna with her wait.

Enough remained, however, for her to demand at last, "Why have you summoned me here, Sularia?" Sularia raised a questioning eyebrow. After a moment Jelanna amended, "Lady Sularia." Her mouth was twisted as if at a foul taste.

"You grew from a child in this Palace, did you not?" the blonde began in a pleasant tone.

Jelanna's reply was curt. "I did."

"Playing hide and seek through the corridors. Gamboling in the courtyards, splashing in the fountains. Your every wish met as soon as it was made."

"Did you ask me here to speak of childhood?" Jelanna asked.

"I did not," Sularia said sharply. "I summoned. Know you Enaro Ostorian?"

If the imperiously beautiful woman was surprised by the question, she did not show it.

"That repulsive little toad?" she sniffed. "I know of merchants, but I do not know them."

Sularia's feline smile returned. "He seeks a wife."

"Does he?"

"A young wife, of the nobility." Sularia saw the dart go home, and pressed to drive it deeper. "He thinks to marry the title he has not been able to buy. And of course he wants sons. Many sons. Garian," she added to the lie, "has asked me to suggest a suitable bride."

Jelanna licked her full lips uncertainly. "I wish, Lady Sularia," she said, a tremor in her voice, "to apologize if I have in any way offended you."

"Do you know the man Dario?" Sularia demanded. "The keeper of Garian's kennels?"

"No, my lady," Jelanna faltered.

"A foul man, I'm told, both in stenches and habits. The slave girls of the Palace hide from him, for his way with a woman is rough to the point of pain." Sularia paused, watching the horror grow on the imperious woman's face. "Think you, Jelanna, that one night with Dario is preferable to a lifetime with Ostorian?"

"You are mad," the slender woman managed. "I'll listen to no more. I go to my estates in the country, and if you were queen you could still choose which of Zandru's—"

"Four soldiers await without for you," Sularia said, riding over the other woman's words. "They will escort you to Dario, or to your wedding bed, and no place else."

The last shreds of haughtiness were washed from Jelanna's face by despair. "Please," she whispered. "I will grovel, an you wish it. Before the entire court on my knees will I beg your forgive—"

"Make your choice," Sularia purred, "else I will make it for you. Those soldiers can deliver you to Ostorian this day. With a note to let him know you think him a repulsive toad." her voice and face hardened. "Choose!"

Jelanna swayed as if she would fall. "I . . . I will go to Dario," she wept.

For a moment Sularia savored the words she had waited for, counting hours. Then she spoke them. "Go, bitch, to your kennel!" As Jelanna ran from the room, peals of Sularia's laughter rang against the walls. How wonderful was power.

hen next the door of his cell opened, Conan at first thought that Albanus had decided to have him slain where he lay chained. Two men with drawn crossbows slipped through the open door and took positions covering him, one to either side of the cell.

As the Cimmerian gathered himself to make what fight of it he could, the round-faced jailor appeared in the door and spoke.

"The sun stands high, barbarian. 'Tis time to take you to the wolf pit. An you try to fight when Struto and I remove your chains, these two will put quarrels in your legs, and you'll be dragged to the pit. Well?"

Conan made an effort to appear sullen and reluctant. "Take the chains," he growled, glow-
ering at the crossbowmen.

In spite of his words the two jailors kept clear
of the crossbowmen's line of fire as they broke
open his manacles with repeated blows of hammer on chisel. Did they think him a fool, he
wondered. He might well be able to take both
jailors and bowmen despite the way they were
placed, yet he could hear measured steps approaching the cell, the sound of a middling body
of men. Dying was not hard, but only a fool
chose to die for naught.

Rubbing his wrists, Conan rose smoothly to
his feet and let himself be herded from the cell.
In the hall waited a full score of the Golden
Leopards.

"Don't need so many," Struto said abruptly.

Conan blinked. He had thought the man without a tongue.

Struto's fellow jailor seemed only slightly less
surprised at hearing him speak. The round-
faced man stared before saying, "He near escaped from as many the night he was taken. You
know I don't like prisoners escaping. I asked for
twice as many. Move on, now. The King waits."

Half the soldiers went before him, and half
behind, the jailors walking on either side. The
crossbowmen brought up the rear, where they
could get a shot at him did he run, in whatever
direction. So they made their way up into the
Palace and through corridors once more bare of
nobles.

Conan strode in their midst as if they were an
honor guard and he on his way to his corona-
tion. There was no glimmer of escape in his

mind. At the wolf pit would most certainly be the imposter Garian and Albanus. Under the circumstances, a man could do worse than die killing those two.

Their way led through the parts of the Palace familiar to the Cimmerian, and beyond. Polished marble and alabaster gave way to plain dressed granite, then to stone as rough as that of the dungeons. Lamps of gold and silver were replaced by torches in iron sconces.

The wolf pit was an ancient penalty indeed, and had, in fact, not been imposed since the time of Bragorus, nine centuries earlier. Nor had any come to this portion of the Palace at all in several centuries, to judge by its appearance. The halls showed signs of hasty cleaning, here a torn cobweb hanging from the ceiling, there dust left heaped against the wall. Conan wondered why Albanus had gone to all this trouble after replacing Garian with the imposter. And then they entered the circular chamber of the pit.

Though of the same rough stone, it was yet as marvelously wrought as any of the great alabaster rooms in the Palace. Like half of a sphere, its walls rose to a towering height unsupported by column or buttress. Below, a broad walk spotted with huge tripod lamps twice as tall as a man was crowded with the nobility of Nemedia, laughing gaily as men and women at a circus, pressing close about the waist-high stone wall that encircled the great pit.

A path to that wall cleared at their entrance, and the soldiers escorted Conan to it. Not waiting to be told, the Cimmerian leaped to the top of the wall and stood surveying those who had

assembled to watch him die. Beneath his icy
blue gaze they slowly fell silent, as they sensed
that here was a man contemptuous of their titles
and lineages. They were peacocks; he was an
eagle.

Directly across the stone-floored pit from him
stood the imposter King, Albanus to one side in
robes of midnight blue, to the other Vegentius,
his face still showing bruises beneath his red-
crested helmet. Sularia was there as well, in
scarlet silk and rubies, and Conan wondered
why he had thought she would not attend.

Below the imposter was the man-high gate
through which the wolves would be let into the
pit. Conan saw no eager muzzles pressed between the bars of the gate, heard no hungry
whines and growls. A complicated system of
iron chains served to draw the gate aside. Perhaps he need not die.

Albanus touched the arm of the man wearing
the Dragon Crown, and he began to speak. "We
have gathered you—"

Conan's wild war cry rang from the rocky
dome; shouts and screams ran through the
nobles as, massive arms raised above his head,
the Cimmerian hurled himself into the pit. Soldiers forced their way through the nobles to the
wall; the crossbowmen took aim. About the
straw-strewn pit Conan strode with all the cocky
arrogance of youth that had never met defeat in
equal combat, and in few unequal. Albanus
motioned, and the guards moved back.

"Fools!" Conan taunted the assemblage. "You
who have not a man among you have come to see
a man die. Well, must I be talked to death by
that buffoon in the crown? Get on with it, unless

your livers have shriveled and you have no stomach for killing." Angry cries answered him.

Albanus whispered to the imposter, who in turn said, "As he is so eager to die, loose the wolves."

"Loose the wolves," someone else shouted, relaying the command. "Hurry!" The gate slid smoothly back.

Conan did not wait for the first wolf to emerge. Before the astonished eyes of the court the Cimmerian ran into the tunnel, roaring his battle cry. Behind, in the pit, yelling nobles dropped over the wall to seize and slay the escaping barbarian who had denied their manhood.

In the dark of the tunnel Conan found himself suddenly in the midst of the snarling wolfpack. Razor teeth ripped at him. He matched them snarl for snarl, his fists hammers that broke bones and knocked beasts the size of a man sprawling. Seizing a growling throat in his hands he dashed the wolf's brains out against the low stone roof.

In the hellish cauldron of that tunnel, the wolves knew the kindred ferocity of the young giant who faced them. As Conan fought his way deeper into their pack, they began to slip past toward the pit, seeking easier meat. The noble lords' angry yells turned to screams as bloody wolves raced among them to slay.

Ahead of him Conan saw a light.

"Accursed wolves," a voice snarled from that direction. "You're to kill some fool barbar, not each—"

The man who spoke faltered as he saw Conan coming toward him. He stood with the iron-barred gate at his end of the tunnel half open, a spear in his hand. Instead of stepping back and slamming the gate shut, he thrust at the Cimmerian.

Conan grasped the spear with both hands and easily wretched it from the other's grasp. Before the man could do more than gape the butt of his own spear smashed into his chest, hurling him back through the gate, Conan following close behind. The wolf-keeper scrambled to his feet, a curved blade the length of his forearm protruding from his fist, and lunged.

The spear reversed smoothly in the Cimmerian's big hands. He had not so much to thrust as to let the man run onto the point, spitting himself so that the whole blade of the spear stood out from his back. A cry of both pain and horrified disbelief wrenched from the wolf-keeper's throat.

"Your wolves will not kill this barbar," Conan growled, then realized that his words had been spoken to a dead man.

Letting spear and transfixed man fall, he closed the gate, thrust the heavy iron bar that fastened it into its brackets and shoved the latch pins home. It would take time to get that open from the other side, time for him to escape. Though, from the screams and snarls that yet echoed down the tunnel, it might be some while before the soldiers dealt with wolves and panicked nobles and reached that gate.

Little there was in that chamber to be of use to him. Crude rush torches guttered in rusty iron sconces on the walls, illuminating six large, iron-barred cages mounted on wheels. No weapons were in evidence excepting only the long, curved dagger, which Conan retrieved, and the spear. He left that lodged in the wolf-keeper's body; its length would make it a cumbersome weapon in the narrow confines of the old stone corridors. There was not even cloth to bind his gashes unless he tore from his own breechclout or from the filthy, and now blood-soaked, tunic on the corpse.

The wolf-keeper had, however, brought a clay jug of wine and a large spiced sausage on which to sup while his charges did their bloody work. On these Conan fell eagerly, ripping the sausage apart with his teeth and washing it down with long gulps of sour wine. He had had no food or drink since before his imprisonment. No doubt his jailors had deemed it a waste to feed one who was to die soon. Tossing the empty jug aside and popping the last bit of sausage into his mouth, the Cimmerian took one of the rush torches and set about finding his way out of the Palace.

It did not take him long to discover that those ancient corridors were a labyrinth, never straight, crossing and recrossing themselves and each other. He had no wonder in him that the secret passages beneath the Palace had been lost; it would be all men could do to keep track of these.

Suddenly, in crossing another pitch-dark hall, he realized that his footprints had mingled with others. Other fresh prints. He bent to examine them, and straightened with a curse. Both sets were his own. He had doubled back on himself, and could continue to do so until he starved.

Face grimly determined, he followed his own

prints until he came to a forking of the passage. The trail in the dust went left. He went right. A short time later he found himself again staring at his own backtrail, but this time he did not pause to curse. Hurrying on to the next turning, he again took the opposite way to that he had taken before. And the next time. And the next.

Now the passages seemed to slope downward, but Conan pressed on regardless, even when he found himself burning a way through halls choked with cobwebs that crisped drily at the touch of the flame. Turning back held no more assurance of escape than going forward, only a greater chance of encountering the Golden Leopards.

Coming to a fork, the Cimmerian turned automatically right—he had taken the left at the last—and stopped. Far ahead of him was a dim glow, but it was no opening to the outside. Bobbing slightly, it was coming closer.

Hurriedly he turned back, ducked into the other side of the fork. On silent feet he ran twenty paces and hurled the torch ahead of him as far as it would go. The flames flared, fanned by the wind of the torch's flight, then winked out, leaving him in blackness.

Conan crouched, facing the direction of the fork, curved dagger at the ready. If those who approached went on, he would be without light but alive. If not. . . .

Diffuse light reached the fork, brightening slowly, resolving into two torch-bearing figures, swords in their free hands. The Cimmerian almost laughed. Hordo and Karela, but the Karela he had known long ago. Gone were the

veils and gray robes of a Nemedian noblewomen, replaced by golden breastplates and a
narrow girdle of gold and emeralds, worn low
on her rounded hips, from which hung strips of
pale green silk. A Turanian cape of emerald
green encircled her shoulders.

"Hordo," Conan called, "had I known you
were coming I wouldn't have drunk all the
wine." Nonchalantly he strolled to meet them.

The two whirled, swords coming up, torches
raised. From the other fork men in jazeraint
hauberks crowded. Machaon, Narus, more
familiar faces from his Free-Company, pushed
into the light.

Hordo took in Conan's gashes, but did not
speak of them. "'Tis not like you," he said
gruffly, "to drink all the wine. Mayhap we could
find some more, if we look."

Karela threw the one-eyed man a murderous
look and shoved her torch into Machaon's hand.
With gentle fingers she touched Conan's
wounds, wincing at purpled flesh and dried
blood.

"I knew you would change your mind," Conan
said, reaching for her.

Her hand cracked across his face, and she
stepped back smoothly with blade half raised. "I
should throw you back to the wolves," she
hissed.

From somewhere in the darkness beyond the
armored men, a voice called unintelligibly.
Another answered, both fading as the speakers
moved further away.

"They hunt me," Conan said quietly. "An you
know a way out of here, I suggest we take it.

Else we must fight a few hundred Golden Leopards."

Muttering, Karela snatched back her torch and forced her way through the men of the Free-Company to disappear back up the other fork.

"She's the only one knows the way," Hordo said quickly. He hurried after her, and Conan followed. Machaon and the rest fell in behind, their booted feet grating in the dust of centuries.

"How did you get into the Palace?" Conan demanded of the one-eyed man as they half-trotted after the auburn-haired beauty. "And what made Karela decide to let you know who she was?"

"Mayhap I'd best begin at the beginning," Hordo puffed. "First thing that happened was, after you were arrested, a hundred Golden Leopards came for us, and—"

"I know about that," Conan said. "You got away. What then?"

"You heard about that, did you? I'm too old for this running, Cimmerian." Despite his heavy breathing, though, the bearded man kept pace easily. "I took the company to the Thestis. Hell-gate is near the safest past of Belverus these days. Everybody who lives there is up in the High Streets waving a sword and shouting revolution. And maybe breaking into some rich man's house now and again."

"What else did you expect?" Conan laughed grimly. "They're poor, and have riches within their reach. But about Karela."

Hordo shook his shaggy head. "She walked into the Thestis this very morn. No, she strode in, looking as if she was ready for her hounds to follow her against a caravan of gold. From what you said, you knew she was here already, eh?"

"Not until I was in the dungeon," Conan replied. "I will explain later."

Suddenly Karela stopped, stretching on tiptoe to reach a rusty iron sconce. She seemed to be trying to twist it.

"Looks like where we came in," Hordo muttered softly. "Looks like twenty places we passed, too." Emerald eyes flashed at him scornfully, and he subsided.

Just as Conan was about to step forward to aid her, the sconce turned with a sharp click. A shot distance away on the same wall was another sconce, which Karela treated the same way. It swiveled, clicked, and there was a heavier thunk from deep within the wall. With a grate of machinery long unused, a section of stone wall as high as a man and twice as wide receded jerkily to reveal a descending flight of crude brick stairs.

"If you two can stop chattering like old women for a moment," Karela said bitingly, "follow me. And take care. Some of the bricks are crumbling. It would pain me for you to break your neck, Cimmerian. I reserve that pleasure for myself." And she darted down the steps.

Hordo shrugged uncomfortably. "I told you, she's the only one knows the way."

Conan nodded. "Follow me," he told Machaon, "and pass the word to watch for crumbling steps." The grizzled sergeant began muttering over his shoulder to those behind.

Taking a deep breath Conan followed Karela

down the dark stairs, lit only by her torch, now only a glimmer far below. He did not actually believe that she would come just to lead him into a trap of her own devising rather than let him die at someone else's hands. But then, he did not entirely disbelieve it either.

At the bottom of the long stair, Karela waited impatiently. "Are they all in?" she demanded as soon as he entered the light of her torch. Without waiting for him to reply she called up the stair. "Is everyone clear of the entrance?"

There was some scraping of feet on stone, then a voice called back hoarsely, "We're clear, but I hear boots coming."

Calmly Karela placed both feet on one particular stone, which sank a finger's breadth beneath her weight. The grating of machinery sounded again.

"It's closing," the same man's voice shouted incredulously.

Karela's tilted eyes met Conan's. "Fools," she said, seeming to include all men, but most certainly him. With a quick, "Follow or stay, I care not," she started down a long tunnel, torchlight glinting off damp walls.

Even the air felt moldy, Conan thought as he set out after her.

"As I was saying," Hordo resumed, striding beside the Cimmerian, "she walked into the Thestis ready to take command. Wouldn't tell me where she'd been, or how she knew where I was. Threatened to put a scar down my other cheek if I did not stop asking questions."

His lone eye swiveled to Conan expectantly, but the big youth was watching Karela, wondering what was in her mind. Why had she come to rescue him? "And?" he said absently when he realized that Hordo had stopped talking.

The one-eyed man grunted sourly. "And nobody tells me anything," he grunted sourly. "She had a woman with her. You remember the Lady Jelanna? 'Twas her, but not so haughty this time. Bedraggled and haggard, she was, with bruises on her face and arms, and terrified to tears. 'She will not stop,' she kept moaning, 'not until I am broken.' And Karela kept soothing her and looking at the rest of us like it was us had done whatever had been done to this Jelanna."

"Crom," Conan muttered. "Do you have to be so long-winded? What does Jelanna have to do with anything?"

"Why, it was her told Karela how to find this passage. Lady Jelanna grew up in the Palace, it seems, playing hide-and-seek and such, as children do. Only sometimes they played in the old parts of the Palace, and she found three or four of the secret passages. She got out of the Palace by one herself. She was desperate to get out of the city, Cimmerian, so I told off two men to escort her to her estate in the country. Least I could do, and her showing us how to get in to you. I tell you true, I thought the next time I saw you we'd both be taking a pull at the Hellhorn."

"That still doesn't tell me why she would aid me," Conan said, with a jerk of his head at Karela to indicate which 'she' he meant.

Hardly were the words out of his mouth than the auburn-haired woman rounded on him. "The wolves were too good for you, you big Cimmerian oaf. If you are to be torn to pieces, I want to do it with my own hands. I want to hear you beg my forgiveness, you barbar bastard. I get first call at you, before that fool Garian."

Conan eyed her calmly, a slight smile on his lips. "Did you stop because you lost the way, Karela? I will take the lead, an you wish."

With a snarl she drew back her torch as if to strike him with it.

"There it is," Hordo shouted, pointing to a short flight of stairs, barely revealed by the light, that led up to the ceiling and stopped. Relief dripped from every word. "Come on, Cimmerian," he went on, herding Conan quickly past the furious-eyed woman. "We had trouble getting this back in place, in case anybody should take a look at the other side, but you and I should be able to lift it clear." In a fierce whisper he added, "Watch your tongue, man. She's been like a scalded cat ever since Machaon and those other fools told her they'd never heard of the Red Hawk."

Eyeing the fierce scowl with which Karela watched them, Conan managed to turn his laughter into a cough. "This other side," he said. "Where is it? If there's anyone there, will they be likely to fight?"

"Not a chance of it," Hordo laughed. "Now put your shoulder into it."

The stairs seemed to end in one large slab of stone. It was to this Hordo urged Conan to apply himself. When he did, the thick slab lifted. With Hordo's aid he slid it aside, then scrambled warily up. A heavy smell of incense filled the air. As the others followed with torches, Conan saw that he was in a windowless room filled with barrels and bales. Some of the bales were broken open to reveal incense sticks.

"A temple?" the Cimmerian asked in disbelief. "The passage comes out in the cellar of a temple?"

Hordo laughed and nodded. Motioning for silence, the one-eyed man climbed a wooden ladder fastened to one wall, and cautiously lifted a trapdoor. His head went up for a quick look, then he motioned the rest to follow and scrambled out himself.

Conan was quick to follow. He found himself in dim light from silver lamps, between a large rectangular block of marble and a towering, shadowed statue. With a start it came to him that he was between the altar stone and the idol of Erebus, a place where none but sanctified priests were allowed. But then, what was one death sentence more or less?

Quickly everyone found their way out of the cellar and, by way of narrow halls of pale marble, to a courtyard behind the temple. There two more of the Free-Company waited with the horses. And, Conan was glad to note, with hauberk, helm and scimitar for him. Hastily he armed himself properly.

"We can be beyond the city walls," Hordo said, swinging into his saddle, "before they think to look outside the Palace."

"We cannot leave yet," Conan said quietly. He settled his helm on his head and likewise mounted. "Ariane is in Albanus' hands."

"Yet another woman?" Karela said dangerously.

"She befriended Hordo and me," Conan said, "and as reward for it Albanus has her. I swore to see her safely out of this, and I will."

"You and your oaths," Karela muttered, but when he galloped out of the courtyard she was first of the company behind him.

Isolated plumes of smoke rose into the bright afternoon sky above Belverus, marking houses of the wealthy that had been visited by revolutionary mobs. The sound of those mobs could be heard from time to time, borne on the breeze. It was a wordless, hungering snarl.

Once in that gallop across the city Conan saw one of those howling packs, some three of four score ragged men and women pounding at the locked doors and barred windows of a house with axes, swords, rocks, their bare hands. In the same instant that he saw them, they became aware of the Free-Company. A growl rippled through them, a sound that seemed impossible to come from a human throat, and like rats pouring from a sewer they threw themselves toward the mounted men. In their eyes was a hatred of any who had more than they, even if it was only armor. Many of the weapons they waved were bloodied.

"The bows will drive them back," Hordo shouted.

Conan was not so sure. There was desperation in those faces. "Ride," he commanded.

Galloping on, they quickly left the mob behind, yet even as it was disappearing from sight its members kept pursuing, their howls heard long after they could no longer be seen.

On reaching Albanus' palace, Conan did not pause. "Every third man stay with the horses," he commanded. "Everybody else over the wall. Bring your bows. Not you," he added, as Karela maneuvered her horse close to the wall.

"You do not command me, Cimmerian," she spat back. "I go where I please."

"Erlik take all hardheaded women," Conan muttered, but he said no more to her.

Standing on his saddle and taking a care where he placed his hands among the pottery shards, he hoisted himself to the top of the wall. As if they had trained for such a thing Hordo, Karela and four and twenty of the others smoothly followed. Below, half a score of men ran from the gatehouse. They had only time to gape before arrows humming like hornets cut them down.

Conan dropped to the ground inside, his eyes blue ice, and ran past the bodies. He half heard the thuds of the others following, but he paid them no mind. Ariane filled his mind. His word had sent her to Albanus. Now his honor demanded he free her if it cost his own life.

With a single heave of his massive arm he threw back one of the tall doors of the palace. Before the crash of its striking the marble wall had finished reverberating in the columned hall, a helmeted man in the cloak of the Golden Leopards ran to face the young Cimmerian giant, sword in hand.

"Ariane," Conan shouted as he beat aside the soldier's attack. "Where are you, Ariane?" His blade half-severed the man's head; he kicked the falling body aside and hurried deeper into the palace. "Ariane!"

More Golden Leopards appeared now, and Conan threw himself at them in a frenzy, his wild battle cry ringing from the arched ceiling, his blade slashing and hacking as if possessed of a demon, or wielded by one. The soldiers fell back in confusion, leaving three of their number dead or dying, unsure of how to face this wildman of the barbarian northcountry. Then Hordo and the others were on them as well. The one-eyed man's fierce mien was matched by the ferocity of his attack. Karela danced among them, blade darting like a wasp, each time drawing back blooded.

Even as the last body fell, Conan was shouting to his men. "Spread out. Search every room, if need be. Find the girl called Ariane."

He himself strode through the halls like an avenging god. Servants and slaves took one look at the thundercloud of his face and fled. He let them go, seeking only one person. Then he saw another that interested him. The gray-bearded chamberlain tried to run, but Conan seized a fistful of the man's tunic and lifted him till only the other's toes touched the floor.

Conan's voice held the promise of death. "Where is the girl Ariane, chamberlain?"

"I . . . I know no girl—"

Conan's arm knotted, lifted the other clear of the floor. "The girl," he said softly.

Sweat beaded the chamberlain's face. "Lord Albanus," he gasped. "He took her to the Royal Palace."

With a groan the Cimmerian let the gray-bearded man drop. The chamberlain darted away; Conan let him go. The Palace. How could he get to her there? Could he return through the secret passage from the Temple of Erebus? He would spend the rest of his life wandering in the ancient labyrinth without ever finding his way into the newer Palace.

He heard footsteps behind him and turned to find Hordo bearing down on him, Machaon and Karela close behind.

"Machaon found someone in the dungeons," Hordo said quickly. "Not the girl. A man who looks like King Garian, and even claims he—"

"Show me," Conan said. Hope took life again within him.

The dungeons beneath Albanus' palace were much like any others, rough stone, heavy wooden doors on rusting hinges, a thick smell of stale urine and fear sweat. Still, when Conan looked into the cell to which Machaon led him, he smiled as if it were a fountained garden.

The ragged, dirty man chained to the wall stirred uncertainly. "Well, Conan," he said, "have you joined Albanus and Vegentius?"

"Derketo," Karela breathed. "He does look like Garian."

"He is Garian," Conan said. "That bruise on his cheek names him so."

Garian's chains clanked as he touched the bruise. He laughed shakily. "To be known by so little a thing."

"If this be Garian," Karela demanded, "then who sits on the Dragon Throne?"

"An imposter," Conan replied. "He has no bruise. Fetch me hammer and chisel. Quickly." Machaon disappeared to return in moments with the required items.

As Conan knelt to lay chisel to the first manacle at Garian's ankle, the King said, "You will be rewarded for this, barbarian. All that Albanus possesses will be yours when I regain the throne."

Conan did not speak. One mighty blow with the hammer split the riveted iron band open. He moved to the next.

"You must get me out of the city," Garian went on. "Once I reach the army, all will be well. I grew up in those camps. They will know me. I'll return at the head of ten thousand swords to tear Albanus from the Palace."

"And to start a civil war," Conan said. He freed the other ankle, again with a single blow. "The imposter looks much like you. Many will believe he is you, most especially since he speaks from the Dragon Throne. Perhaps even the army will not be as quick to believe as you think."

Hordo groaned. "No, Cimmerian. This is not our affair. Let us put the border behind us."

Neither Conan nor Garian paid him any mind. The King was silent until Conan had broken off the manacles from his wrists. Then he said quietly, "What do you suggest, Conan?"

"Re-enter the Palace," Conan said as though that were the easiest thing in the world. "Confront the imposter. Not all the Golden Leopards can be traitors. You can regain your throne without a sword being lifted outside the Palace walls." He did not think it politic to mention the mobs roaming the streets.

"A bold plan," Garian mused. "Yet most of the Golden Leopards are loyal to me. I overheard those who guarded me here talking. We will do it. I go to regain my throne, Cimmerian, but you have already gained my eternal gratitude." His regal manner was returning to him. He regarded his own filth with an amused smile. "But if I am to re-enter the Palace, I must wash and garb myself to look the King."

As Garian strode from the cell, shouting for hot water and clean robes, Conan frowned, wondering why the King's last words had been so disquieting. But there was no time to consider that now. There was Ariane to think of.

"Cimmerian," Karela said angrily, "if you think I will ride at your side back to the Palace, you are a bigger fool than I believe you. 'Tis a death-trap."

"I have not asked you to go," he replied. "Often enough you've told me you go where you will."

Her scowl said that was neither the answer she expected nor the one she wanted.

"Hordo," the Cimmerian went on, "bring the men in from the street. Let all know where we go. Let those who will not follow go. I'll have no man ride with me this day against his will."

Hordo nodded and left. Behind Conan Karela uttered an inarticulate oath. Conan ignored her, his mind already occupied with the problem of gaining entry to the Palace and, more important to him than regaining Garian's throne, getting Ariane free.

When Conan strode from the palace with Garian, now resplendent in the best scarlet velvet he could find to fit him, the Cimmerian was not surprised to find all eight and thirty of his men mounted and waiting, even those who bore wounds from the past hour's fighting. He knew he had chosen good men. He was surprised, though, to see Karela sitting her horse beside Hordo. Her green glare dared him to question her presence. He mounted without speaking. There were enough problems to be confronted that day without another argument with her.

"I am ready," Garian announced as he climbed into the saddle. He had a broadsword strapped on over his tunic.

"Let us ride," Conan commanded, and led the small band out of the palace grounds at a gallop.

The approach to the Palace, up the winding streets to the top of the hill and across the greensward to the drawbridge, was made at a slow walk. Garian rode slightly to the front of Conan. A King should lead his army, he had said, even when it was a small one. Conan agreed, hoping the sight of Garian would make the guards hesitate enough to let them get inside.

At the drawbridge they dismounted, and the guards there indeed stared open-mouthed as Garian strode up to them.

"Do you recognize me?" Garian demanded.

Both nodded, and one said, "You are the King. But how did you leave the Palace? There was no call for an honor guard."

Conan breathed a sigh of relief. They were not Vegentius' men. The guards eyed those behind the King, most especially Karela, but kept their main attention on Garian.

"Do you think the King does not know the secret ways beneath this hill?" Garian smiled as if the thought were laughable. As the two guards began to smile as well, though, his face became grim. "Are you loyal men? Loyal to your King?"

The two stiffened as one, and both recited the oath of the Golden Leopards as if to remind Garian of it. "My sword follows he who wears the Dragon Crown. My flesh is a shield for the Dragon Throne. As the King commands, I obey, to the death."

Garian nodded. "Then know that there is a plot against the Dragon Throne, and its perpetrators are Lord Albanus and Commander Vegentius."

Conan put his hand to his sword as the soldiers started, but they merely stared at the King.

"What are we to do?" one of them asked finally.

"Take those who are in the barbican," Garian told them, "leaving only two to lower the portcullis and guard the gate, and go with them to your barracks. Rouse all who are there. Let your cry be, 'Death to Albanus and Vegentius!' Any who will not shout that are enemies of the Dragon Throne, even if they wear the golden cloak."

"Death to Albanus and Vegentius," one guard said, and the other repeated it.

When they had disappeared into the barbican,

Garian sagged. "I did not think it would be this easy," he told Conan.

"It won't be," Conan assured him.

"I still think I should have told them of the imposter, Cimmerian."

Conan shook his head. "It would only confuse them. They'll find out after he's dead, if luck is with us." It mattered little to him when or how they found out, so long as there was enough confusion for his purposes. He eyed the door to the barbican. What took them so long?

Suddenly there was a cry from inside the stone gatehouse, cut abruptly short. One of those who had stood at the gate appeared in the door with a bloody blade in his fist. "There was one who would not say it," he said.

One by one those others who had been on guard slipped out, sword in hand. Each paused long enough to say to the King, "Death to Albanus and Vegentius," then trotted into the Palace.

"You see," Garian told Conan as they led the Free-Company through the gate. "It will be easy."

As the portcullis rattled down behind them, shouts rang out from the direction of the Golden Leopards' quarters, and the clash of swords. An alarm gong began to ring, then stopped with a suddenness that spoke of the death of him who had sounded it. The sounds of fighting spread.

"I want to find Albanus," Garian said. "And Vegentius."

Conan only nodded. He, too, wanted Albanus. Vegentius he would take if he came across him. He hurried on, the Free-Company deployed behind him. First he would try the throne room.

Abruptly two score golden-cloaked soldiers appeared ahead.

"For Garian!" Conan called, not slowing. "Death to Albanus and Vegentius!"

"Kill them!" came the reply. "For Vegentius!"

The two groups ran together roaring, swords swinging.

Conan ripped the throat from the first man he faced without even crossing swords, and then he was like a machine, blade rising and falling and rising again bloodier than before. The way was forward. He hacked his way through, like a peasant through a field of wheat, chopping and moving forward, leaving bloody human stubble behind.

And then he was clear of the melée. He did not pause to see how his companions fared against those who had survived his blade. The numbers were on the Free-Company's side, now, and he yet had to find Ariane. Of Garian he cared not one way or the other.

Straight to the throne room he ran. The guards that normally stood at the great carven doors were gone, drawn into the fighting that sounded now in every corridor. The door that usually was opened by three men, Conan pushed open unaided.

The great columned chamber stood empty, the Dragon Throne guarding it with a malignant glare.

The King's apartments, Conan thought. He set out still at a run, and those who faced him died. He no longer waited to call out the challenge. Any who wore the golden cloak and did not flee were the enemy. Few fled, and he regretted kill-

ing them only for the delay it caused him.
Ariane. They slowed him finding Ariane.

Karela stalked the Palace halls like a panther.
She was alone, now. After the first fight she had
searched among the bodies for Conan, uncertain
whether she wanted to find him or not. There
had not been long to look, for other soldiers
loyal to Vegentius had appeared, and the fighting that followed had carried all who still stood
away from that spot. She had seen Garian laying
about him, and Hordo desperately trying to
fight his way to her side. The one-eyed man had
been like death incarnate, yet she was glad he
had not been able to follow. There was that she
had to do of which her faithful hound would not
approve.

Suddenly there was a man before her, blood
from a scalp wound trickling down his too-hand-
some face. The sword in his hand was stained as
well, and from the way he moved he knew how
to use it.

"A wench with a sword," he laughed. "Best
you throw it down and run, else I might think
you intend to use it."

She recognized him then. "You run, Demetrio.
I have no wish to soil my blade with your
blood." She had no quarrel with him, but he
stood between her and where she wanted to go.

His laugh turned into a snarl. "Bitch!" He
lunged, expecting an easy kill.

With ease she beat aside his overconfident
attack and slashed him across the chest with her
riposte. Shaken, he leaped back. She followed,
never allowing him to set himself for the attack
again. Their blades flashed intricate silver pat-

terns in the air between them, ringing almost continually. He was good, she admitted, but she was better. He died with a look of incredulous horror on his face.

Stepping over his body she hurried on, until at last she came to the chambers she sought. Carefully she pushed the door open with her blade.

Sularia, in the blue velvet robes of a noblewoman, faced her, frowning. "Who are you?" she demanded. "Some lord's leman? Don't you know enough not to enter my apartments without permission? Well, as you're here, what word of the fighting?" Her eye fell on the bloody sword in Karela's hand, and she gasped.

"You sent a friend of mine to the lowest of Zandru's Hells," Karela said quietly. With measured paces she stepped into the room. The blonde backed away before her.

"Who are you? I know none who are friends of your sort. Leave my chambers immediately, or I'll have you flogged."

Karela laughed grimly. "Jelanna would not know your sort, either, but you know of her. As for me, I do not expect you to recognize the Lady Tiana without her veils."

"You're mad!" Sularia said, a quaver in her voice. Her back was almost to the wall.

Karela let her sword drop as she continued her advance. "I need no sword for you," she said softly. "A sword is for an equal."

From beneath her robes Sularia drew a dagger, its blade as wide as a man's finger and no more than twice as long. "Fool," she laughed. "If you truly are Tiana, I'll give you reason to wear your veils." And she lunged for Karela's eyes.

The auburn-haired woman moved nothing but a single hand, which darted to close over the hand that held the dagger. Sularia's blue eyes widened in disbelief as her lunge was stopped by a grip made steel by long hours with a sword. Karela knotted her other hand in those blonde tresses, tight enough to force the women to meet her hard emerald gaze. Slowly she twisted, forcing the dagger and the hand that held it alike to turn.

"Despite it all," she whispered to the blonde, "you might have lived had not you put your sluttish hands on him." With all her strength she drove the dagger home in Sularia's heart.

Letting the dead woman fall, Karela retrieved her sword and wiped the blade contemptuously on a wall hanging. There was still the Cimmerian.

Her mind whirling with a thousand thoughts of what she would do to him when she found him, she stalked from the room. Almost she had been ready to let him live, but Sularia had brought it all flooding back, all the thousand humiliations she had suffered because of him. That he had lain with such as Sularia was the worst humiliation of all, though when she questioned that strange thought her mind skittered away from answering.

Then, from a colonnaded gallery, she saw him in a courtyard below, lost in thought. No doubt he still wondered how to find this precious Ariane of his. Her beautiful face twisted in a savage snarl. From the corner of her eye she caught a movement below, and her breath suddenly would not come. Vegentius had entered the courtyard, and Conan had not moved.

Slowly, like a murderer in the night, the big soldier, as big as Conan, crept forward, ensan-
guined sword upraised. His red-crested helmet
and chain mail looked untouched, though that
bloody blade was proof he had seen fighting. At
any moment he would strike, and she would see
Conan die. Tears ran down her face. Tears of
joy, she told herself. It would give her much joy
to see the Cimmerian meet his death. Much joy.

"Conan!" she screamed. "Behind you!"

Conan listened to the approaching footsteps,
footsteps that grew less wary by the second. The
Cimmerian's hand already rested on his sword
hilt. He did not know who it was that crept
toward him, save that by his actions he was an
enemy. Whoever he was, a few steps more and
the surpriser would be the one surprised. Just
one step more.

"Conan!" a scream rang out. "Behind you!"

Cursing his lost advantage the Cimmerian
threw himself forward, tucking his shoulder
under as he hit the flagstones, drawing his
scimitar as he rolled to his feet. He found himself facing a very surprised Vegentius.

A quick glance upward showed him the source
of the shout, Karela, half hanging over the stone
rail of a gallery two stories above the courtyard.
He knew it had to be his imagination, yet in that
brief look he could have sworn that she was crying. It did not matter, in any case. He must concern himself with the man he faced.

Vegentius wore a grin as if what was to come
were the greatest wish of his life. "Long have I
wanted to face you with steel, barbar," he said.

His face yet bore the yellowing bruises of their last encounter.

"That is why you try to sneak up behind me?" Conan sneered.

"Die, barbar!" the big soldier thundered, launching a towering overhead blow with his sword.

Conan's blade rose to meet it with a clang, and immediately he moved from defense to offense. Almost without moving their feet the two men faced each other, blades ringing like hammer and anvil. But it was always Conan's blade that was the hammer, always he attacking, always Vegentius parrying, ever more desperately. It was time to end, the Cimmerian thought. With a mighty swing, he struck. Blood fountained from the headless trunk of the Commander of the Golden Leopards. As the body toppled, Conan was already turning to look for Karela. The gallery was empty.

Still, he could not suppress a complacent smile at the thought that she did not hate him as much as she pretended. Else why had she cried out?

He looked around as Hordo hurried into the courtyard.

"Vegentius?" the one-eyed man asked, looking at the headless body. "I saw Albanus," he went on when Conan nodded. "And Ariane and the imposter. But when I got to where I saw them, they were gone. I think they were headed for the old part of the Palace." He hesitated. "Have you seen Karela, Cimmerian? I can't find her, and I do not want to lose her again."

Conan pointed out the gallery where Karela

had stood. "Find her if you can, Hordo. I've another woman to seek."

Hordo nodded, and the two men parted in opposite directions.

Conan wished the bearded man luck, though he suspected Karela had disappeared once more. But his own concern was still Ariane. He could not imagine why Albanus would go into the ancient portion of the Palace, unless it was to escape by way of one of the secret passages. If Jelanna knew some of them, it seemed reasonable that the hawk-faced lord might also. Yet the Cimmerian did not think he could find even the one he had escaped through, lost as it was in that maze of pitch-dark corridors. There was only the wolf pit to hope for. And hoping against hope Conan ran.

He thanked every god he could think of that he encountered no Golden Leopards as he sped through the Palace, into the rough stone corridor he remembered so well. He could afford not the slightest delay if he was to reach the wolf pit before Albanus departed. If Albanus had gone to the wolf pit. If Ariane was still alive. He refused to admit any of those ifs. They would be there. They had to be.

Almost to the pit, he heard Albanus' voice reverberating from that domed ceiling. The Cimmerian allowed himself one brief sigh of relief before entering the chamber, his eyes like blue steel.

"With this I will destroy them," Albanus was saying, caressing a blue crystal sphere in his hands as he spoke. The imposter stood beside him, and Ariane, staring unnaturally ahead, but the hawk-faced man appeared to speak only to himself. "With this I will unleash such power—"

Sorcery, Conan thought, yet it was too late to stop his advance. Albanus' dark eyes were on him already, and annoyingly seemed to see him as an irritation rather than a danger.

"Kill him, Garian," the nobleman said, and turned his attention back to the blue sphere. Ariane did not move or change expression.

Did the man truly think he was Garian, Conan wondered as the duplicate advanced. He noticed the sword the other carried, then, the same serpentine blade that he had sold to Demetrio what seemed like so long ago. That it was a sorceled weapon he no longer had any doubt, and his belief was confirmed when the blade was raised. A hungry, metallic whine sounded, the same he had thought he imagined when facing Melius.

Still he set himself. Death came when it would. No man could flee his appointed time.

The false Garian's blade blazed into motion, and Conan swung to block it. The shock of that meeting of blades nearly tore the Cimmerian's sword from his grip. There had been no such strength in Melius' blows. That force came not from any sorcery, but from the man wielding the blade, yet Conan refused to believe that anything human could have so much strength. The hair on the back of his neck rose. Nothing human. Warily he backed away, wondering what it was he faced.

Cupping the blue crystal, ignoring the two who faced each other not twenty paces from him, Albanus began to chant. "*Af-far mearoth,*

Omini deas kaan. . . ."

Conan thought he felt a rumble from deep in the bowels of the earth, but he had no time to consider it. The creature with Garian's face stalked him, the wavy-bladed sword darting with preternatural speed. Conan no longer attempted to block it, only to deflect it, yet even the glancing blows he felt to his heels. Once the tip of that ensorceled blade opened a shallow gash in his cheek, sending a thin rivulet of blood trickling. The metallic whine sounded again, but louder, almost drowning out Albanus' chanting.

The creature swung again, a decapitating blow an it landed, but Conan leaped back. The blade smashed into the iron leg of one of the massive tripod lamps, shearing it in two. Slowly the lamp toppled, and Conan saw the first true expression on the creature's face. Terror, as it gazed at the fire in that falling lamp.

As if in mortal danger, the false Garian jumped back. Albanus' voice faltered, then resumed its incantation. The lamp crashed against the wall surrounding the pit, flaming oil pouring down into the pit. Dry straw crackled alight.

Conan risked a glance at the hawk-faced lord. Above Albanus' head something was forming. A darkness, a thickening of the air. The stones beneath the Cimmerian's feet shifted, and he thought he heard thunder.

There was no time for more than a glance, though, for the creature grasped one leg of the heavy lamp and heaved it into the now fire-filled pit as easily as a man might throw aside a stick of kindling. The ground trembled continuously now, the tremors growing stronger. From the corner of his eye Conan saw the dark amorphous shape above Albanus' head lift higher into the dome, grow more solid. The nobleman's chanting became louder, more insistent. The creature advanced on Conan.

"Run, Ariane!" the Cimmerian shouted, and steadied his feet against the now pitching floor. No man could flee his own death. "Run!"

She did not move, but the simulacrum continued its steady approach, sword lifting for a strike that would smash through the Cimmerian's blade and split the man in twain.

Desperately Conan leaped aside. The tremendous blow struck sparks from the floor where he had stood. In that instant, when the creature tottered off balance from the force of its own blow and the quaking of the earth, Conan struck. Every muscle from his heels up he put into that blow, blade slamming against the creature's side. It was like striking stone. Yet, added to the rest, it was enough, for just that one instant. The simulacrum fell.

Conan had seen the speed of the creature, and had no intention of giving it time to recover its feet. Before it struck the stone floor he had dropped his sword and seized the simulacrum by its swordbelt and its tunic. With a tremendous heave the massive Cimmerian lifted the creature into the air.

"Here's the fire you fear," he shouted, and hurled it over the wall.

As it fell, a scream ripped from its throat. The sword was hurled away as it twisted in an inhuman effort to find some salvation from the flames. As it struck the burning straw there was a whoosh, as of oil thrown on a fire, and flames engulfed the simulacrum, yet even as a statue of flame its horrible screams would not cease.

As Conan raised his eyes from the pit, they met those of Albanus. The dark lord's mouth struggled to form the words of his chant, but from his chest projected the blood-hungry sword that had been hurled with such inhuman strength. Beside him Ariane stirred. Sorcerous spells died with the sorcerer, and Albanus was dying.

Conan hurried to her side. As he took her hand, she looked at him dazedly. Albanus fought still to form words, but blood was filling his mouth.

As the Cimmerian turned to lead Ariane from the chamber, his gaze was drawn by what occupied the height of the dome. He had an impression of countless eyes, of tentacles without number. His own eyes refused to take it all in, his mind refused to accept what he saw. From whatever floated horribly above, a ray of light struck down, shattering the blue crystal. Albanus' eyes glazed in death as the fragments fell from his hand.

Thunder rumbled in the room, and Conan knew it for the laughter of a demon, or a god. The dark shape above gathered itself. Conan scooped up Ariane and ran, as that which was above smashed through the dome. Stones showered down, filling the wolf pit, and dust belched after him. Collapsing walls toppled still other walls. Spreading out in a wave of destruction from the wolf-pit, the ancient portions of the Palace crumbled in on themselves.

Conan was running on polished marble floors before he realized that that floor no longer tossed like a ship in a storm and rubble no longer pelted him. He stopped and looked back through the slowly clearing dust. The corridor behind him was filled from top to bottom with shattered debris, and he could see the sunset sky through a hole in a ceiling that had borne three stories above it. Yet, except for a few cracked walls, there seemed to be remarkably little destruction outside of the ancient parts of the Palace.

Ariane stirred in his arms, and he reluctantly set her down. She was a pleasant armful, even covered in dust and rock chips. Coughing, she stared around her. "Conan? Where did you come from? Is this the Royal Palace? What happened?"

"I'll explain later," the Cimmerian said. Or some of it, he thought with another look at the devastation behind them. "Let's find King Garian, Ariane. I've a reward coming."

Strolling down the hall of the palace that had once belonged to Albanus—and had for two days now, by degree of King Garian, belonged to him—Conan paused to heft an ivory statuette. Intricately carved, it was light and would fetch a good price in almost any city. He added it to the sack he carried and moved on.

He reached the columned entry hall just as Hordo and Ariane came through the front doors, now standing open. "About time you came back," the Cimmerian said. "What is it like out there?"

Hordo shrugged. "City Guards and what Golden Leopards are left are patrolling the streets against looters. Not that many are left. Seems they thought that earthquake was the judgment of the gods against them. Then, too, some claim to have seen a demon hovering over the Royal Palace at the height of the earth-quake." He gave an unconvincing laugh. "Strange what people see, is it not?"

"Strange indeed," Conan replied in what he hoped was a reassuring tone. Even if he managed to convince Hordo of what had occurred at the wolf pit, the one-eyed man would only moan about being too old for such any longer. "What about the Thestis?" he asked Ariane.

She sighed wearily, not looking at him. "The Thestis is done. Too many of us saw too much of what our fine talk leads to. Garian is releasing Graecus and the others from the mines, but I doubt we will be able to look any of the others in the face for a long time. I . . . I intend to leave Nemedia."

"Come with me to Ophir," Conan said.

"I go to Aquilonia with Hordo," she replied.

Conan stared. It was not that he objected to losing her to Hordo—well, a little, he admitted grudgingly, even to a friend—but after all, he had saved her life. What sort of gratitude was this?

She shifted defiantly under his gaze, and put an arm around the one-eyed man. "Hordo has a faithful heart, which is more than I can say for some other men. It may not be faithful to me, but it is still faithful. Besides, I told you long ago that I decide who shares my sleeping mat." Her voice held an exculpatory note; a tightness at her mouth said that she heard it, and refused to admit that she had anything to excuse.

Conan shook his head disgustedly. He remembered an ancient saying. Women and cats are never owned, they just visit for a time. At the moment he thought he would take the cat.

Then her destination, and Hordo's, penetrated. "Why Aquilonia?" Conan asked him.

The one-eyed man passed him a folded sheet of parchment and said, "I heard a rumor she went east. There's something in there for you, as well."

Conan opened the sheet and read.

Hordo, my most faithful hound,
 When you receive this I will be gone from Nemedia with all my goods and servants. Do not follow. I will not again be so pleased to find you on my trail. Yet I wish you well. Tell the Cimmerian I am not finished with him.

Karela

Below the signature, in red ink, was the outline of a hawk.

"But you follow anyway," Conan said, handing back the sheet.

"Of course," Hordo replied. Carefully he tucked the letter into his pouch. "But why this talk of going to Ophir now? Garian will make you a lord, next."

"I remembered that blind soothsayer in the Gored Ox," the Cimmerian said.

"That old fool? I told you to see one of my astrologers."

"But he was right," Conan said quietly. "A woman of sapphires and gold. Sularia. A woman of emeralds and ruby. Karela. They'd both have watched me die, for exactly the reasons he named. The rest was right, as well. And do you remember how he ended?"

"How?" Hordo asked.

"Save a throne, save a king, kill a king or die. Whatever comes, whatever is, mark well your time to fly. He also said to beware the gratitude of kings. I'm taking him to heart, if a little late."

The one-eyed man snorted, looking about him at the marble columns and alabaster walls. "I see little enough to beware of in this gratitude."

"Kings are absolute rulers," Conan told him, "and feeling grateful makes them feel less absolute. On that I'll wager. And the best way to get rid of that feeling is to get rid of the man to whom he must be grateful. Do you see now?"

"You sound like a philosopher," Hordo grumbled.

Conan threw back his head and laughed. "All the gods forbid."

"Captain," Machaon said, entering from the back, "the company is mounted, every man with a sack of loot at his saddle. Though I never heard of a man ordering his own palace looted before."

Conan met Hordo's gaze levelly. "Take whatever you want, old friend, but do not tarry overlong." He held out his hand, and the other grasped it, a custom they had picked up in the east.

"Fare you well, Conan of Cimmeria," Hordo said gruffly. "Take a pull at the Hellhorn for me, an you get there before me."

"Fare you well, Hordo of Zamora. And you the same, if you're first."

The Cimmerian did not look again at Ariane as he strode from the hall. She had made her choice.

Behind the palace the Free-Company waited, the score that survived, mounted and armed. Conan swung into his saddle.

A strange end, he thought, riding away from proffered riches in this fashion. And two women, either of whom he would have been pleased to have ride with him, but neither of whom wanted him. That was a strange thing for him in itself. Still, he reminded himself, there would be women aplenty in Ophir, and the rumors of trouble meant there would be blade-fee for a Free-Company.

"We ride for Ophir," he commanded, and galloped out of the gates at the head of his company. He did not look back.

CONAN

☐ 54260-6	CONAN THE CHAMPION	$3.50
☐ 54261-4		Canada $4.50
☐ 54228-2	CONAN THE DEFENDER	$2.95
☐ 54229-0		Canada $3.50
☐ 54238-X	CONAN THE DESTROYER	$2.95
☐ 54239-8		Canada $3.50
☐ 54258-4	CONAN THE FEARLESS	$2.95
☐ 54259-2		Canada $3.95
☐ 54225-8	CONAN THE INVINCIBLE	$2.95
☐ 54226-6		Canada $3.50
☐ 54236-3	CONAN THE MAGNIFICENT	$2.95
☐ 54237-1		Canada $3.50
☐ 54256-8	CONAN THE RAIDER	(Trade) $6.95
☐ 54257-6		Canada $8.95
☐ 54250-9	CONAN THE RENEGADE	$2.95
☐ 54251-7		Canada $3.50
☐ 54242-8	CONAN THE TRIUMPHANT	$2.95
☐ 54243-6		Canada $3.50
☐ 54231-2	CONAN THE UNCONQUERED	$2.95
☐ 54232-0		Canada $3.50
☐ 54252-5	CONAN THE VALOROUS	$2.95
☐ 54253-3		Canada $3.95
☐ 54246-0	CONAN THE VICTORIOUS	$2.95
☐ 54247-9		Canada $3.50

Buy them at your local bookstore or use this handy coupon:
Clip and mail this page with your order.

Publishers Book and Audio Mailing Service
P.O. Box 120159, Staten Island, NY 10312-0004

Please send me the book(s) I have checked above. I am enclosing $＿＿＿＿＿
(please add $1.25 for the first book, and $.25 for each additional book to
cover postage and handling. Send check or money order only — no CODs.)

Name ＿＿＿＿＿＿＿＿＿＿＿＿＿＿＿＿＿＿＿＿＿＿＿＿＿＿＿＿＿＿＿＿＿＿＿＿＿＿

Address ＿＿＿＿＿＿＿＿＿＿＿＿＿＿＿＿＿＿＿＿＿＿＿＿＿＿＿＿＿＿＿＿＿＿＿＿

City ＿＿＿＿＿＿＿＿＿＿＿＿＿＿＿＿＿＿State/Zip ＿＿＿＿＿＿＿＿＿＿＿＿＿

Please allow six weeks for delivery. Prices subject to change without notice.

For the millions of people who have read the books, enjoyed the comics and the magazines, and thrilled to the movies, there is now -

THE CONAN
FAN CLUB

S.Q. Productions Inc., a long time publisher of science fiction and fantasy related items and books is announcing the formation of an official Conan Fan Club. When you join, you'll receive the following: 6 full color photos from the Conan films, a finely detailed sew-on embroidered patch featuring the Conan logo, a full color membership card and bookmark, and a set of official Conan Fan Club stationary. Also included in the fan kit will be the first of 4 quarterly newsletters. **"The Hyborian Report"** will focus on many subjects of interest to the Conan fan, including interviews with Conan writers and film stars. And there'll be behind-the-scenes information about the latest Conan movies and related projects, as well as reports on other R.E. Howard characters like Solomon Kane, Red Sonja and King Kull. Fans will also be able to show off their talents on our annual costume and art contests. **"The Hyborian Report"** will be the one-stop information source for the very latest about Conan. Another aspect of the club that fans will find invaluable is the **Conan Merchandise Guide,** which will detail the hundreds of items that have been produced, both in America **and** Europe. And as a member of the club, you'll receive notices of **new** Conan products, many created just for the club! Portfolios, posters, art books, weapon replicas (cast from the **same** molds as those used for the movie weapons) and much, much more! And with your kit, you'll get coupons worth $9.00 towards the purchase of items offered for sale.

Above all, The Conan Fan Club is going to be listening to the fans, the people who have made this barbarian the most famous in the world. Their suggestions, ideas, and feedback is what will make the club really work. The annual membership is only **$10.00.** Make all checks and money orders payable to: **CONAN FAN CLUB**
PO Box 4569
Toms River, NJ 08754

Response to this offer will be tremendous, so please allow 10-12 weeks for delivery.

JACK L. CHALKER

THE BEST IN FANTASY

GORDON R. DICKSON

Buy them at your local bookstore or use this handy coupon:
Clip and mail this page with your order.

Publishers Book and Audio Mailing Service
P.O. Box 120159, Staten Island, NY 10312-0004

Please send me the book(s) I have checked above. I am enclosing $_____
(please add $1.25 for the first book, and $.25 for each additional book to
cover postage and handling. Send check or money order only — no CODs.)

Name _____

Address _____

City _____ State/Zip _____

Please allow six weeks for delivery. Prices subject to change without notice.

BEN BOVA

Buy them at your local bookstore or use this handy coupon:
Clip and mail this page with your order.

Publishers Book and Audio Mailing Service
P.O. Box 120159, Staten Island, NY 10312-0004

Please send me the book(s) I have checked above. I am enclosing $_____
(please add $1.25 for the first book, and $.25 for each additional book to
cover postage and handling. Send check or money order only — no CODs.)

Name _____

Address _____

City _____ State/Zip _____

Please allow six weeks for delivery. Prices subject to change without notice.

GREG BEAR

BESTSELLING BOOKS FROM TOR